ALPHA IN THE SHEETS

BOOK ONE OF THE AFTER HOURS SERIES

TAMSEN PARKER

For Cara, my fairy smut mother. Thanks for taking a chance on me.

CHAPTER 1

I'm sulking with my head in Rey's lap after a dinner of the finest sushi and sake San Diego has to offer.

"Why can't you like women?"

"Same reason you can't. I could give you a good hiding just the same."

A split-second of indecision later, I roll my eyes, wrench my mouth sideways, and sigh. "Don't bother."

"But you're so pretty when you pout, kitten." Rey runs his hands through my hair, kneading talented fingers into my scalp.

"I know." I shrug, purring under his attentions. "But what the hell good does that do me with you?"

"None. Absolutely none. But don't you fear. I'll find you what you crave yet, Scout's honor."

"Were you really a Boy Scout, Rey?" He's not exactly outdoorsy, although very handy with knots.

He scoffs, as I expected. "Have you seen those uniforms? Even six-year-old me was screaming, 'Oh, *hell*, no.'"

I laugh, imagining raven-haired mini-Rey spouting obscenities as his long-suffering mother tried to make him into a joiner: *A neckerchief? What the fuck are you thinking?*

1

Rey shakes his head. "But back to you. You're not giving me much time."

"It's what I've got. I'm not thrilled about it either, but it's now or not for two months. I don't expect miracles. He doesn't need to be perfect. Just…serviceable."

It's not like I'm looking for Prince Charming. I don't have the time, never mind the inclination, to be searching for *The One*. I just need Rey to find me someone who can dull the sharp edges, slake my thirst to be dominated. At least until the next time.

Rey's handsome copper face settles into pensiveness. It's when he looks like this I call him Professor Walter. *Oh, my beloved Reyes. You would've made a wonderful professor.* But what fun would that be? He's far more suited to his current profession. And I suppose he is a professor of sorts—just not the kind who'll ever get tenure anywhere except in the hearts and minds of his students. Or, as he'd say, clients.

He tries to keep it professional, but for Rey, everything is deeply personal. I've never known someone with such a strong calling. Helping people navigate the wide world of kink is his vocation, and his talent for absolute discretion means he's sought after by some incredibly rich, powerful, private people who want to learn without having to venture into the community to do it. They pay handsomely for his specific services.

I met Rey my freshman year at Princeton, when he was the chipper RA welcoming me to my dorm. He's been more or less mentor, more or less friend ever since. That was ten years ago, and I still remember every single word of our first encounter.

When he'd introduced himself, the too-firm grip of his hand had caught my attention in a way that made my lips part. I'd stuttered when I told him my name.

"I-India Burke. You can call me Indie. Everybody does."

He'd raised a wicked eyebrow, smirked, and hadn't let go of my hand. "That's not a very good reason to be called something, now is it? Because you've always been?"

"I 'spose not," I'd granted, flushing.

"That stops here, little one. So which is it—India or Indie?"

"India," I'd said with certainty and a smile.

His confidence was infectious, and I'd melted at his response: "Well done, little one. Welcome to Princeton, India Burke. The world is now your oyster."

There had been no surprise, only comfort, when he called me "little one"—a total lack of the embarrassment or intimidation I'd always felt around really good-looking men. That's what he was: a man, not a boy. With the way he talked, the way he carried himself, I barely believed he was twenty-two and not thirty-two. He was so sure, so certain. I could feel the poise leaking into my hand from his. Yes, that was my introduction to my beloved Rey, who has made all the difference.

I don't like to think about where I would've ended up without him. He showed me a world I might never had known existed and taught me how to move in it safely and with grace. He keeps me tethered to it with the thinnest of strings, letting me dip a toe in without drowning. I soothe myself by thinking I'll never have to do without. His thighs are lean and muscular under my head as he continues to work his hands over my skull. I sigh with pleasure, about to fall asleep.

"Vasili?"

I wrinkle my nose and open my eyes. "You know I don't like him. I can take a beating as well as anyone—"

"Better, for such a pretty little thing."

I tip my chin in thanks before going on. "But he hit me in the face, and you know how I feel about that."

"I do. I forgot—the fucker. I'm sorry. I won't ask you about him again."

"I forgive you. I know it's hard to keep track. Sometimes I forget." It's quite the long and growing list.

"What about Ethan? You liked him, right?"

"I did, but he's got a girl now and I don't want to share."

"Luke?"

"Meh."

"I think Strider would like to see you again."

"Find me someone who hasn't named himself after a Lord of the Rings character and we'll talk."

Rey snickers. He knows I find it hard to take that guy seriously, which ruins the effect. He might as well have called himself Frodo.

"Takeo?"

"Too fussy. He spends too much time tying me up and not enough time getting me off."

"You're awfully demanding for a submissive, did you know that?" he teases, tugging on my hair.

"Only for you," I promise, batting my eyelashes.

"I know. You're a good little pet otherwise. I rarely hear complaints."

I allow myself to preen under his praise. Damn straight he doesn't hear many complaints. However picky I may be now, I never let my displeasure show when I'm with them. I took that backhand from Vasili like a champ. I only sniffed, letting a single tear roll theatrically down my cheek even as I inwardly seethed that I had to work on Monday and fuck if I was going to answer questions about a black eye.

I probably should've safed out after that, but I was deep in the scene and hadn't wanted to stop. It had been far too long since my last play date, and I was desperate. Besides, the damage was already done. What would a safeword have accomplished except to interrupt the flow? If he'd done it again, I would've called it. Probably. Rey had chastised me afterward for letting it go and made me put it in all my contracts since.

"Let me make some calls, and I'll get back to you. Do you care where?"

"Anywhere but here." I close my eyes under his cossetting.

Rey stays as late as he can, catching the last shuttle back to

San Francisco despite my invitation to stay the night. I don't have a spare bedroom, but it's not unusual for him to sleep in my bed. He's even got drawers—plural—one in the closet and one in the bathroom.

"I've got an early meeting with a prospect, but I'll call you as soon as I've got something."

I wrap my arms tight around him one last time. "I need this."

"I know, little one. I won't let you down." He presses a kiss to the top of my head and hugs me back.

I let him go reluctantly, but I'll see him soon. Probably next week, to debrief about my weekend with DTBD—Dom to Be Determined. This has the same potential it always has: to be a fucking disastrous nightmare or ridiculously hot. It's usually somewhere in the middle. Although with the state I'm in? It would have to be pretty bad for me to score it worse than tepid. The internal spring that coils tight when I'm stressed or uneasy is wound to the breaking point. I need some relief.

I wave my last goodbye as Rey turns the corner and go get ready for bed. I've got an early morning myself, so I only bother with the barest of bedtime routines before I slide between my cool sheets and fall into a restless sleep.

The next morning, Adam kicks my ass.

I bitch as he urges me into another lunge. "Jesus, Adam, I haven't even had my fucking coffee."

"And now you're not going to need it, are you, princess?"

I give him my best withering glare, the one that makes my assistant quake and my underlings scatter. Adam doesn't blink.

"Come on, you cream puff. Let's get on with it. I haven't got all day," he barks. Bark is accurate. I'm sure lots of girls would fawn over Adam—even in San Diego, he sticks out as a consummate beach body—but to me, he's a friendly mutt. Maybe a golden retriever. Adorable, loyal, and nice to have around, but thoroughly unremarkable.

I roll my eyes and do his bidding for the next half hour before grabbing my bag to head to work. I've made it a habit not to shower at the gym. It might be more convenient, certainly less nasty than plopping myself onto a towel and driving in dripping with sweat, but my club doesn't have private showers and I don't feel like having people stare at me. Not that they would most of the time. I have a nice body, I work hard to keep it that way between my crazy work hours and piles of takeout, but it's nothing extraordinary in this SoCal hell hole. But on occasion, I would get some strange and possibly horrified looks. Do I feel like telling Susie Treadmill that, yes, those are stripes from a cane across my ass? No, I don't. So it's a towel slung over my leather upholstery and a sticky drive to my office where my private bathroom is waiting for me.

When I arrive at quarter to eight, Lucy is already at her desk. "Good morning, Ms. Burke."

It would be rude to respond to her chirping with, "Fuck off, Lucy," right? I wouldn't win Miss Congeniality on my best days, but for the past two weeks, I've been in an especially foul mood. It's been well over a month since my last hook-up, and I'm edgy as fuck. I settle for, "Coffee?"

"Of course, Ms. Burke. And Mr. Valentine asked for you to come to his office as soon as you got in." She takes in my current state, her brown eyes disapproving as always when I come straight from the gym. "But…"

"I'll be there in ten."

"Yes, Ms. Burke."

Her chipper efficiency makes me ill. Even her reddish hair is bobbing cheerfully. If only she were half as good as she sounds.

As she looks. She could play a secretary on *Mad Men*. Maybe she should.

I shower and dress, slipping into a grey sleeveless dress and my signature black Louboutins, praying Lucy will have my coffee ready when I walk out my door. But, as always…

"Lucy! Coffee?" I cannot face Jack without it, not when I'm walking into this blind. There are a dozen things he could want to talk to me about, but I'm betting on the LAHA project.

I'm a consultant to public sector agencies. All that waste and bureaucracy people complain about in government? They hire me to clean it up. I get paid to tell people what they're doing wrong and how to fix it—professional bitch, a job built for me. I've dealt with some high-profile projects, ranging from restructuring the Santa Monica mayor's office to administering the public process of a proposed freeway, but LAHA… This is huge.

LAHA is how we refer to the Los Angeles Housing Authority. It's currently in receivership, which is what happens when an agency is so broken they're not allowed to fix themselves and HUD hires a babysitter. In this case, my firm: Jack Valentine Associates. It's a huge coup for us—me especially since Jack's made me his number two on this. It's an enormous undertaking by definition, and while I understood the basic premise of public housing coming into this, the industry is a morass of regulations and the nitpickiest requirements I've ever seen.

I think we're out of our depth, but there's no way in hell Jack would ever admit defeat. Instead, he's been riding everyone twice as hard to make this work. That's meant ninety-hour weeks and piles of takeout. Not to mention an extra and extremely unpleasant new duty for me.

Jack hates press. Abhors how he looks in newspaper photos, detests how he comes across in sound bites, and loathes how red his face gets when someone asks him a hard question he doesn't immediately have an answer to. So now this falls on my shoulders. I'd come as close to begging as I ever have with him to please, please not make me do this. I'm no more thrilled about the idea of being in the public eye than he is, but he was insistent, so here I am—the new public face of JVA.

But I don't think we're talking about press conferences today. No, today we're talking about the report due to HUD on Thursday—or so he bellows at me as soon as I set foot in his office. This is one of the things Jack likes about me: my ability to be yelled at without blinking. It's how he communicates. If you listen hard enough between all the curses, he's telling you what he wants and how he wants it done. But if you're too busy bursting into tears, you're not going to catch that, are you?

I take a seat and scribble notes while he—salt-and-pepper hair already in disarray, blue eyes blazing—rages at top volume. He's taken his suit coat off, his tie's been flung over a standing lamp, and he's pacing while he shouts. It's a good thing Lucy got her shit together so I at least have a cup of coffee to down amidst his emphatic cursing. He's very creative with his insults. They can be almost Shakespearean.

"Shit-eating maggots have more sense than these people do. They wouldn't know which end was up if they were part of the human centipede."

I see we're going more contemporary today. And so it goes. On. And on. And on.

Three hours later, I collapse at my desk. At least when I check my personal cell, there's a text from Rey:

Call me.

This is promising. I take a well-deserved minute to do just that, resting my feet on my desk.

"Aloha, kitten."

"Hawaii?"

"If you don't mind the flight."

"I don't."

"Good. I'll have Matthew make the arrangements."

"You're the best. Give Matty a kiss for me."

"Will do. We'll talk later."

I press the end call button on my phone and tuck it back into my purse. That's one thing I don't have to worry about anymore. Seventy-two hours of debauchery and my clock will be reset. I'll be good to go for another month or so. I take a deep breath and close my eyes before I press the intercom button.

"Lucy."

"More coffee, Ms. Burke?"

"Please."

It's going to be a long day.

Twelve hours later, I'm on my way home and Jack's got a draft of the report on his desk. He'll hate it, but it's better to give him a product that needs a lot of work than to give him nothing at all. He's not difficult to manage once you understand him, but I think most of my predecessors—my many, *many* predecessors— were scared off before they had the chance.

Not me. I've got my sights set on running the place one day. Of course, I'll have to change the name. Jack Valentine Associates has a nice ring to it, but I think Burke Consulting Group sounds better. I'll get rid of the heavy wood and leather bank décor and go more airy and modern. But I've got a few years to plan my interior decorating. Jack's still got two kids in college from his second marriage. Or are they from his third? I can never keep track, although I know he's on wife number four. Candi—with an *i* that I bet the vacuous woman dots with a fucking heart. Thinking about her bottle-blonde head and unsubtle boob job make me cringe. There you have reasons number seventy-eight and seventy-nine why I'll never get married: becoming that or being left for that.

At any rate, I think I've got, at most, seven years before I'm in Jack's corner office. Which is reason number three: it's hard to sit behind that luxuriously big desk if you've got a husband and kids on the other end of your phone. I know people do it and do it well, but it can't be easy and it's not worth the bother to me. I didn't bust my ass at Princeton and Columbia to change diapers, oh no.

I spend the rest of my drive mentally redecorating Jack's office and selecting the color scheme for my business cards. By the time I've parked my car in the garage, stumbled into and out of the elevator, and made it down the endless hallway to my apartment, it's eleven thirty, and I debate whether or not to call Rey. After a minute of half-hearted agonizing while I kick off my shoes and hang my bag by the door, I dial. If he's busy, he'll let it go to voicemail, but it's rare he doesn't take my calls. Sometimes if he's in the middle of a training, but often even then.

"Kitten, I'm glad you called. I've been waiting on you."

"I hope not. I should've texted to say I'd be late. I'm sorry."

"No, no, I didn't mean it like that. I've been looking forward to talking, that's all. I think you're going to be very pleased."

"Hawaii's a good start. What else have you got for me?"

"Y'ever play with a Cris Ardmore?"

I pause for a second. "No. Would I know him by any other name?"

"Nope." I hear his smirk all the way from the Castro, and I know why. He knows it annoys me when people play with ridiculous fake names (e.g., Strider the Hobbit), which is pretty hypocritical but can't be helped. I have huge respect for anyone who plays with their real names. "He goes by Cris. No *h*."

My nose wrinkles.

"No *h*, huh?" The respect-o-meter has gone down. That's

almost as bad as Candi with an *i*. Why no *h*? I shouldn't be too harsh. His parents could be dingbats, and I shouldn't fault the guy for that. God knows I'd get scrapped from just about anything if having sane parents were a requirement.

"Give the guy a break, India."

"You know me too well. Tell me more about this Cris Ardmore."

"He's on the big island, been active in the scene for a long time there and on the West Coast. I asked around—no one's got a bad thing to say about the guy. Safe player, knows the rules, keeps his subs happy."

"Why haven't I run into him before?"

Rey pauses, and I wonder if his hesitation is from reluctance or because he's so damned delighted with himself he wants to make a royal pronouncement.

"He's monogamous with his subs, and he just ended a five-year contract."

Holy. Shit.

"I get to be the rebound fuck?" I squeal with delight.

"Yes, you do."

"You're the best! How did you pull this off?"

"I know a guy."

"You know *all* the guys." I hold my phone to my ear with my shoulder as I pour the last of a bottle of Malbec into a glass. "But seriously, you're amazing. What do you want? I'll do anything."

He laughs. "Why don't you wait until you get back to sell your soul to the devil?"

"You're hardly the devil. I'm about to sing you the fucking Hallelujah chorus."

"And you'd sound like an angel, but we don't have time. Matthew is putting together a dossier for you. In the meantime, anything specific you want to know about the illustrious Mr. Ardmore?"

"How old is he?"

"Thirty-nine."

Well within my range.

"Do I get a picture?"

"You do."

"Is his contract weird?"

"I don't have it yet. He has to write one."

That's not unusual. Most of the guys Rey finds for me don't keep contracts like this on hand.

"Was he surprised to get your call?"

"They always are."

I snort. I know.

"You're the best thing that ever happened to me, Reyes Llewellyn Walter. I could kiss you on the mouth."

"Monday night. We'll see if you still want to kiss me or if we've moved on to the punching phase. For now, go change into that sexy lingerie I know you wear when I'm not there and get some beauty sleep. Don't want to be all puffy for—"

"Cris Ardmore," I breathe, my mouth caressing his name. The more I say it, the more I like it. I don't even notice the missing *h* much anymore. Yes, Mr. Cris Ardmore sounds promising.

A good thing, too, because the rest of my week is a fucking misery. The report gets done well and on time, but not for the lack of everyone and their mother trying to fuck me over. Tuesday went a lot like this:

"Janis, I don't care who you have to screw to get those numbers. Hell, I don't care who *I* have to screw to get those numbers, but I need them by close of business, or we'll all be fucked and not in a nice way.

"Look, this is my job on the line, but it's your life. If this doesn't work out, they know it's not our fault and you're going to flat-out lose the units. They're going to take your funding away, Janis. Every penny. Is that how you want to go down in history?

"Every single motherfucking last housing authority is watching you and I would suggest not making any more of a hash out of this than you already have. Get me the goddamn vacancy numbers by the end of the day, or I'll make the call to Cooper myself."

I slam the receiver down and am surprised by a slow clap coming from my door.

"Well done, Ms. Burke. I didn't think you had it in you."

"You know I do, Jack. I just like to save it for special occasions, not wank off every day like you."

Thankfully, he laughs like I thought he would. I've caught him in a good mood. His hair's only slightly disheveled, and his tie's still on.

"What's up?" I ask, not bothering to take my feet off my desk.

Jack launches into concerns about some of the other projects we're working on. I take notes on things I need to take care of and issue assurances on what I've already dealt with. It's not the longest laundry list he's ever had for me, and everything should be taken care of by the time I leave.

He says on his way out, "You sure are earning that three-day weekend you talked me into."

"I always do."

"Yes, you do."

Though I technically only get two weeks of vacation per year, I've talked Jack into giving me three for all intents and purposes. He doesn't seem to care as long as it doesn't interfere with my projects. Not to mention he can see the difference when I get back. I'm more focused, more patient, work longer hours, and don't flinch no matter how harsh he is. All in all, well worth it for him.

I check my personal cell when he's gone, and there's another text from Rey:

LMK when you're home. I've got a messenger in a holding pattern.

Fun. This must be the dossier on Cris Ardmore. That will make for some interesting reading while I lounge in the tub with a glass of Pinot tonight. But first…

"Lucy!"

"Coffee?"

"Please."

This budget for the City of La Jolla is a certified disaster, and it needs to be dealt with before I can go home. I don't bother to start looking at the spreadsheets until Lucy delivers what may as well be manna from heaven. She might be incapable of anticipating my needs, but the woman makes a damn good cup of coffee. I take a sip and dive in, emerging seven hours later with my rank gym bag and my ubiquitous roller bag stuffed with my laptop, notes for tomorrow, and a draft of the LAHA report Jack will scream at me for the second he gets me on the phone.

I text Rey as soon as I get home, and ten minutes later, there's a hipster with gauged ears and too many tats at my door. I guess Rey really did have him in a holding pattern. I give him a bottle of water and a nice tip before I send him on his way, and then slip into my waiting tub and get some more info on Mr. Ardmore.

Name: Ardmore, Crispin Michael
 Aliases: Crispin Ardmore, Cris Ardmore, ▮▮▮▮▮▮▮▮▮▮
 DoB: 10/25/▮▮▮▮▮
 Sex: M
 SSN: ▮▮▮▮▮▮▮▮▮▮
 License #: ▮▮▮▮▮▮▮▮▮▮
 Marital Status: Single
 Address: ▮▮▮▮▮▮▮▮▮▮▮▮▮▮▮
 ▮▮▮▮▮▮▮▮▮▮▮▮▮▮▮
 Occupation: ▮▮▮▮▮▮▮▮▮▮▮▮

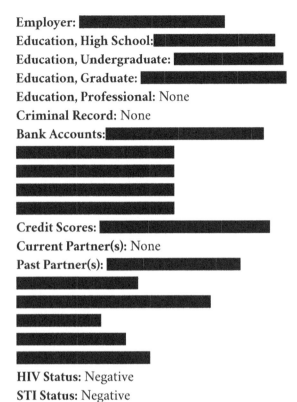

Employer: ▆▆▆▆▆▆▆▆▆▆▆▆
Education, High School: ▆▆▆▆▆▆▆▆▆▆▆▆▆
Education, Undergraduate: ▆▆▆▆▆▆▆▆
Education, Graduate: ▆▆▆▆▆▆▆▆▆▆▆
Education, Professional: None
Criminal Record: None
Bank Accounts: ▆▆▆▆▆▆▆▆▆▆▆▆
▆▆▆▆▆▆▆▆▆▆
▆▆▆▆▆▆▆▆▆
▆▆▆▆▆▆▆▆▆
▆▆▆▆▆▆▆▆▆
Credit Scores: ▆▆▆▆▆▆▆▆▆▆▆▆
Current Partner(s): None
Past Partner(s): ▆▆▆▆▆▆▆▆▆▆
▆▆▆▆▆▆▆
▆▆▆▆▆▆▆▆▆▆▆
▆▆▆▆▆
▆▆▆▆▆▆▆
▆▆▆▆▆▆▆▆
HIV Status: Negative
STI Status: Negative

A lot of it is redacted. Despite requiring the information, I don't want to see it. I do like proof that it's been collected, and I want Rey to have it as an insurance policy in case anything goes awry —or, really, to ensure nothing goes aslant in the first place. I rarely get refused, despite the invasive nature of the prerequisites I insist on, but maybe it's too strange an opportunity to pass up.

Imagine: You get a call out of the blue from a well-respected trainer you've almost certainly heard of, and if you haven't, someone you know has. He offers you a weekend of no-strings-attached play with a trained submissive provided you pass the screening process. She'll come to you, and should you choose to spend the weekend with her somewhere other than your home, all expenses will be taken care of. If it sounds pretty alluring, it's meant to.

I've never bothered to ask the men who say yes why they agree, and by definition, I don't have the opportunity to ask the ones who say no. There's no contact with refusals, and they don't get a second chance.

Everything here is in order, as I expected. Rey doesn't waste my time. And there's a perfectly reasonable explanation for the lack of *h* in Cris. *Crispin*. I like it. A lot. Not Christopher, not Christian—Crispin. I wonder giddily if he can recite the St. Crispin's Day speech from *Henry V*. I'd best get this out of my system before embarrassing myself by asking when we meet.

I'm also pleased by the undergraduate and graduate degrees. Not that I haven't played with some very fine men with a high school diploma or less—and a PhD by no means guarantees a guy knows his way around a woman's body—but Rey knows I'm slutty for postgraduate degrees. He must've been clapping his hands like a little girl at recess when he put this together. Or really, when he read it over after Matty put it together. I tease myself by flipping through a few more mostly-blacked-out pages consisting of some references Mr. Ardmore provided, along with a couple Rey sought out before he even talked to the guy.

I hold my breath before flipping to the last page where his picture awaits. When I get photos—and I don't always since I don't require it—they're usually full-body shots—although, mercifully, clothed. Believe it or not, Rey has to specify this. *Dude, we'll get there*. If it's not a head-to-toe, it's what looks like a professional headshot. But this… It's a candid of a man. Laughing.

What? Usually they do their best to look intimidating, intense. You know, *dominating*. But not this guy. You can't even see his whole face because he's turned to the side, and he's *laughing*. The corner of my mouth tugs up involuntarily.

What's your game, Cris Ardmore?

He's got a mop of curly dark hair, what some might call bushy eyebrows but I don't mind, and a layer of what I'm hoping is perma-stubble. His teeth are white, straight and sharp against his tanned skin, and he's got what I think are light blue eyes. Or maybe grey. The picture isn't taken from close enough to say for sure.

I don't know if he'd be considered conventionally attractive—there's something off there—but I won't kick him out of bed. If I have the chance. Sleeping arrangements can be sticky with what I do. I won't fret about that now.

I grab my phone from where it's resting next to my empty wine glass and text Rey, despite it being almost one in the morning:

Me likey.

My phone pings a minute later:

Thought you would. Now go the fuck to sleep.

I laugh, text back a kiss, and do as I'm told. I have an early morning tomorrow and don't even have Adam's puppy-dog face to look forward to.

Despite being wrecked and having had one—okay, three—glasses of wine, I have trouble falling asleep. I find myself wondering if I'll get to see Cris Ardmore laugh. I think I'd like to.

CHAPTER 2

*T*oday, I've got a press conference. The only nice thing about having to drag myself up to LA on the early shuttle is that Rey surprises me with a dinner reservation so he can hand-deliver the contract he received from Cris Ardmore.

It's good I have that to look forward to because the press conference is a total clusterfuck. Brad Lennox, that asshole from the *Times* (LA, not New York, thank god), is there, and he's done some homework, unlike most of the clowns who show up. While I'm impressed and I wouldn't mind discussing this over a stiff drink, he's making my client squirm and that's my job, so I field the rest of his questions. He backs off after realizing that he doesn't intimidate me and he's not going to badger me into spilling any newsworthy details.

That's why Jack tapped me for this: my ability to stay cool in the face of pretty much anything. It's a useful skill, but I still wish Jack didn't make me do press. I value my privacy too damn much. Though there aren't usually pictures and the stories are generally buried somewhere no one except industry wonks and old people with nothing better to do will see it, it's still my name in the paper. It's unnerving, but there's no way I'm explaining why to

Jack. Besides, I don't want to cash in my favors for an assignment I'm good at.

After the inquisition is over, I spend the rest of the day at LAHA's main offices. I check in and stroke Janis's ego after she managed to do her fucking job and get me the data I asked for. It's a long day but not as unpleasant as it could've been, especially when the town car pulls up out front to collect me at seven thirty.

The driver gets out and opens the door before I can make it all the way down the steps. He takes my roller bag and stows it in the trunk as I sink into the backseat. I wait until he's closed the door before I slide under Rey's waiting arm.

"You look great. Chanel, very nice."

"Thanks. It's a good thing these people wouldn't know Chanel if it bit them in the ass. Jack would have my head for *that* making the papers. As it is, I had to leave my shoes at home."

"I know." He soothes me with a squeeze of my shoulder. "But I'm taking you someplace nice, and I'mma show you a good time."

And he does. The restaurant is Latin-flavored, with a line out the door and a filled-to-crushing bar, but clearly Rey knows someone. We get shown in right away and to a private dining room on the third floor, no less. Almost the second we're seated, a server comes in with cocktails we didn't have to order. Goddamn it's good to be Rey's friend sometimes.

As I sip at my paloma, we chat about the day's events, but by the time the sea bass ceviche arrives, I'm ready to get down to business.

"You have something for me?"

"Of course." Rey takes a folded manila envelope from the inside of his jacket and hands it to me as I curl my fingers in a greedy, come-hither gesture. The envelope's not thick, a good start, and when I open it and slide out the neatly clipped pages,

I'm relieved to see a respectable font. I'd almost called it off once when I got a contract in Comic Sans.

"Comic Sans?" Rey's a fucking mind reader.

"How'd you know?"

"That always makes you smile."

"I need to start being less predictable. You'll get bored with me, and then where will I be?"

"You couldn't be boring if you tried, India. Now get reading before your soup gets cold."

I'm almost immediately peeved. The term of the contract is from one in the afternoon on Friday until six in the evening on Sunday. Going home Sunday night is fine, but what the hell? Why so late on Friday?

"Could Matty not get me an earlier flight?"

"Just read, kitten."

I frown, but do as he asks, hoping it'll get better.

Parties: Ms. Kit Bailey-Isles (the submissive), Mr. Crispin Michael Ardmore (the Dominant), and Mr. Reyes Llewellyn Walter (the Broker)

Provisions: The following provisions will be in effect during the term of the contract as stated above.

1. The Dominant accepts full responsibility for the care and well-being of the submissive.
2. The Dominant will provide a safe, clean and private environment in which the submissive is expected to fulfill her obligations outlined in this contract.

3. The submissive agrees to obey the Dominant without hesitation in all things except as outlined in the Hard and Soft Limits below.

4. The submissive agrees to be disciplined should she fail to meet any of the expectations or requirements of the Dominant at any time.

5. The Dominant will provide the submissive with any training or materials required to fulfill her obligations.

6. The submissive may not look at or touch the Dominant without his express permission.

7. The submissive will not touch or pleasure herself, nor orgasm, without the express permission of the Dominant.

8. Either the submissive or the Dominant may employ at any time the following safewords: *Yellow* to indicate she/he is nearing her/his tolerance for the current activity; and *Red* to indicate she/he has reached her/his limit and the activity must cease immediately.

9. The submissive will address the Dominant as "Sir" at all times unless directed otherwise.

10. The Dominant may address the submissive as he sees fit, but will at no time refer to her as "baby" or "sweetheart."

11. Anything that occurs during the term of the contract will be treated as strictly confidential by the Dominant. The submissive may only discuss the events of the term with the Broker of this contract.

Hard Limits:

1. No activities shall be undertaken that will result in

permanent marks or injury to either the submissive or the Dominant.

2. No activities shall be undertaken which are likely to result in the necessity of professional medical intervention or treatment for either the submissive or the Dominant. Should the submissive require first aid or the care of a medical professional, the Dominant shall follow the procedures provided by the Broker.
3. No acts involving blood.
4. No acts involving animals.
5. No acts involving electrical current or fire.
6. No acts involving knives, needles, scissors, or any other cutting or puncture instruments.
7. No acts involving breath control.
8. No acts which are likely to result in marks to the face or neck liable to last beyond the term of the contract.
9. No one outside of the Dominant and the submissive may participate or be present either in person or virtually during any portion of this contract.
10. The Dominant may only contact the submissive at any point in time outside of this contract through the Broker.
11. The Dominant will not attempt to obtain personal information about the submissive by any means prior to, during, or following the execution of the contract.
12. The submissive may not be photographed at any time.

Soft Limits:

1. Sex Acts: The submissive consents to participate in any of the following activities with the Dominant:
2. Vaginal sex

3. Anal sex
4. Cunnilingus
5. Fellatio
6. Masturbation
7. Vaginal Fisting

1. Sex Toys: The submissive consents to the use of any of the following implements by the Dominant:
2. Vibrators
3. Dildos
4. Butt plugs
5. Ben Wa balls
6. Anal beads
7. Wartenberg wheel

1. Discipline: The submissive consents to receive any of the following forms of discipline from the Dominant:
2. Spanking
3. Paddling
4. Flogging
5. Whipping
6. Caning
7. Hot wax
8. Nipple clips/clamps
9. Riding crop

1. Pain: The submissive consents to experiencing a

moderate amount of pain at the hands of the Dominant.

1. Bondage Methods: The submissive consents to any of the following methods of bondage by the Dominant:
2. Leather cuffs
3. Rope
4. Fabric ties
5. Spreader bars
6. Blindfolds
7. Gags
8. Ear plugs/headphones

1. Bondage Positions: The submissive consents to be restrained in any of the following manners:
2. Wrist to wrist; in front, behind back, behind neck or overhead.
3. Wrist to elbow
4. Wrist to knee
5. Wrist to ankle
6. Elbow to elbow
7. Elbow to knee
8. Bound to furniture/fixtures

Other Requirements:

1. The Dominant and the submissive each currently complete an STI screening every three months, and the

submissive maintains an IUD. Should the submissive or the Dominant engage in intercourse with another partner following the most recent preceding test, they are required to disclose this information prior to engaging in sexual contact with one another. Either party may request additional birth control and/or disease prevention measures at any time.

2. The Dominant and the submissive agree to comply with all safety-related protocols provided by the Broker. Should any of the protocols or above provisions be violated, this contract is subject to immediate termination.

3. The above contract will be completed and signed upon the satisfactory conclusion of a conversation between Ms. Bailey-Isles and Mr. Ardmore upon Ms. Bailey-Isles' arrival. Should either party elect not to complete the contract at that time, accommodations elsewhere on the island will be provided for Ms. Bailey-Isles at the expense of Mr. Ardmore. Upon completion of the contract, all provisions contained herein will immediately go into effect.

Conclusion: The Dominant and the submissive both agree they are entering into this contract consensually and with full knowledge and understanding of its contents and the risks inherent in the activities they agree to undertake. By signing, they certify they have the honest intention to fulfill the requirements and responsibilities listed above and will do so to the best of their respective abilities at all times within the specified timeframe.

Standard date and signature lines for Mr. Ardmore, myself, and

Rey tie the whole thing up at the end. I flip back to the beginning and lay the document on the table, tapping a nail on the first page. "Did you edit this at all?"

Rey tsks at me. "You know I don't touch them. Do you think Comic Sans would've made it through unscathed if I did?"

Of course it wouldn't have. But as with the photographs, these guys tend to use contracts as an opportunity to convey exactly how much of a badass Dom they are. They capitalize every damn thing. Not just Dominant and Sir—those I can live with. It's the He, Him, His—and to hell with grammar—that rankle. I recognize and respect the convention, but it still bugs the living crap out of me. Maybe it irritates Cris Ardmore, too. If so, this particular idiosyncrasy makes me like him even more, but it also throws me. This man…

I shake it off and reread the whole thing, making sure I didn't miss anything, but I haven't. It's not bad. Concise, neat, orderly. No hearts and flowers. It includes all the provisions I require, and there's nothing that's patently offensive to me. In fact, aside from a few minor details, I'm ready to sign off. Except for one thing.

"He wants to talk to me?"

"It appears he does."

"Why?" I hate the incredulous whine in my voice, but come on.

"I don't know, little one. You are a terrible conversationalist. Dull as a pile of bricks. I tried to talk him out of it, but he wouldn't listen."

"You know what I mean."

I've never had anyone make a stipulation like this before. He wants to *talk* to me? That's usually pretty far down on the list of what the men I play with want to do. There's always a few words exchanged when I first meet someone, but I'm already in character because the contracts have been signed. I don't blink when I introduce myself as Kit because I *am* Kit. Mr. Ardmore, however, has been very specific that we're to have our conversation prior to the contract going into effect. His acuity makes me uncomfortable.

"I do," says Rey. "I can't say I wasn't surprised, but perhaps our friend Mr. Ardmore is feeling skittish. It's not every day something like this falls in your lap. Maybe he wants to make sure you're doing this of your own free will."

"It's not like you're getting paid." Rey's never been paid for anything where I've been concerned, not even my extensive training. And not from the lack of an offer on my part.

"Although I bet I could make a pretty penny off of you."

"I'm sure you could."

Truth be told, I *should* be paying Rey for this. I know how well compensated he is by his clients, even for introductions not nearly as involved and convoluted as this. I can't imagine the time and energy this takes. Good thing Matty's such a peach.

"You could cancel if it bothers you. But from what I know about this guy, I'm inclined to think it's for chivalrous reasons. You may want to give him the benefit of the doubt. Not to mention I don't think I'd be able to find you someone else. This deal was a bit of an eleventh-hour miracle."

"I know. What am I even supposed to say to the guy?"

"I'm sure he'll tell you."

"No, he won't. He won't be my Dom yet, Rey!"

He's trying hard not to laugh. No doubt if he gave in, his Sazerac would go all over the crisp white linens covering our table. Out his mouth or out his nose is anyone's guess. Rey is an enthusiastic laugher, and more than one article of my clothing has fallen victim to his friendly fire.

"And what precisely is so funny about this?"

Rey swallows and tries valiantly to contain his grin. "You do understand that, for most people, *talking* would not be the alarming part of this contract."

"Yes."

27

"Even for people like us, this shouldn't be such an issue. What are you afraid of?"

He's hit the nail on the head. I'm afraid. I can stand being rejected as a submissive; that's like an actress not getting a callback. *We're going in a different direction. I like knife play, you don't, que sera, sera.* That makes sense to me. But being rejected for being myself is a lot harder to take, and I avoid it at all costs. It's one of the many reasons I do what I do.

"What if he doesn't like me?" I can't meet Rey's eyes.

"Then he's a fucking moron, and it's better you find out before he fucks you."

"True."

"But he doesn't seem like an idiot to me, and while my track record's not perfect, it's pretty damn good. So what do you say?"

I pause for a millisecond, but like I told Rey, I need this. Badly. "Can we go over these soft limits?"

"Ixnay on the Wartenberg wheel and the hot wax?"

"Got it in one."

CHAPTER 3

"*M*s. Burke?... Ms. Burke?"

Goddammit. Can the woman not give me an ounce of peace? I'm in the fucking shower for god's sake.

"Yes, Lucy?" I shout above the spray, feeling ridiculous.

"Mr. Valentine buzzed and said he wants to see you five minutes ago," she offers nervously.

"Tell him unless he'd like to see me naked and wet he can wait five more."

"Y-yes, Ms. Burke."

I can't decide whether to laugh—I would give up one of my quarterly bonuses to watch her say that verbatim to Jack—or berate myself. That was mean. While I don't feel guilty about giving Lucy a hard time when she's earned it, this is not one of those times. I'm a grouch because this damn report needs to be picture-perfect by five o'clock East Coast time and because I'm on edge about this weekend.

I'd woken to a text from Rey:

Changes to contract all approved. You're good to go. Call me tonight.

That was a relief, but I find my mind drawn back to Cris Ardmore again and again. What is it about this guy? I've had varying degrees of Dom-crushes on these men before we meet, but no matter how hot the picture or tantalizing the contract, I've never been so damn distracted. I scrub my fingers over my scalp, humming to myself, and then rinse the suds from my hair, along with thoughts of this diverting man. Down the drain you go, Mr. Ardmore. For now.

I turn the spray all the way to cold and force myself to stand under it for a full minute. I'm going to need all my wits about me to get out of here alive at the end of the day, and this will be a good wake-up call.

Not as good as the pounding of a heavy fist at my door, though. That is *not* Lucy.

"India!"

"And a good morning to you, Jack." A few seconds short of a minute, but I turn off the water.

"I didn't give you an office with an en suite so you could be Bathtime Barbie."

I open the door as I finish tucking the towel around myself and look up at him. He's a lot taller when I haven't got my heels on.

"I know. It was to up the likelihood for delightful moments of sexual harassment like this one."

"Jesus, India. Put some goddamn clothes on!"

I roll my eyes as I slam the door in his beet-red face. "Will do."

When I walk into his office three minutes later, fully clothed as requested in a bright yellow sheath dress with a wide black belt, he's mellowed some. He looks me up and down. "I preferred the towel."

"Sleaze bag."

He cocks his head in consideration before shrugging and starting in on his tirade about the latest draft of the report. It's a short rant, and I feel good about being able to get this in on time.

I saw earlier that Janis sent me more of the numbers I need. Hopefully, it's the last of them. Otherwise, we're going to have another delightful phone call.

When Jack's through with me, I haul ass back to my office and busy myself filling in the blanks, only to look up and see it's heading on one o'clock. Shit. I have an hour. I need an hour and a half for this to be spit-polished and sparkling, so I pick up my phone.

"Cooper," snaps a rude voice.

"Constance, my love."

"Hello, India." Her snarl turns into a purr in an abrupt about-face. "I thought I wouldn't be hearing from you for another fifty-nine… Oh, wait, make that fifty-eight minutes."

"Would it ruin your day if I had this in your inbox at five thirty?"

"No. I'm about to leave, and I'm not going to look at it until tomorrow, anyway. Take all night if you want it."

"I don't. I want this off my desk as much as you do. It'll be there by five thirty."

"Can I call you if there are problems? I prefer dealing with you."

"Monday. I'll be in early—ten your time."

"Another lost weekend?"

"Here's hoping." The thought of Cris Ardmore slips into my mind. "But, hey, do me a solid? At least keep up appearances. Call Janis first and give her a hard time. I'll tell her to let me handle you if you get too rough with her, and then we can catch up."

"You're a crafty bitch, Burke. I like it. Now stop flapping your very well-paid gums and finish my damn report. You're billing us for this, aren't you?"

"By the word," I chirp, and she laughs her throaty laugh.

"Have a good weekend."

"You, too. Tell Glory I say hi. We'll talk Monday."

I hang up in a much better mood. Cooper happens to be our

HUD liaison on the LAHA receivership, and everyone involved is terrified of her. Her name—*Cooper*—strikes fear in the heart of the most seasoned housing administrator. I really think they believe that's her only name. She even made the IT department at HUD, against policy, change her email address to just cooper@hud.gov. She's a self-described big, black butch, and she can clear a room like no one else I know.

Cooper also happens to be the alter ego of the sweetest girl I knew at Princeton—Constance Cooper from Asheville, North Carolina—and she adores me. I've had the pleasure of eating her mother's fried chicken and okra more than once, but nobody needs to know that. I'll let them think I'm a fucking unicorn.

I remember the night I met Cooper almost as clearly as I remember meeting Rey. That late September evening had been a night of a lot of firsts. My first play party, held at an opulent home halfway between Princeton and Manhattan, which proved to be a little different from the keg parties that were going down back on campus. It was the first time I felt the comfort of a collar around my neck. It had bound me to Rey in a way I'd never been attached to anyone before. The leather buckled snug around my throat made me feel secure—like part of Rey would never leave me, he'd always be thinking of me, because I belonged to him. I was his responsibility. That's what the closed silver lock hanging heavy at my throat said to everyone else in the crowd, too.

Perhaps most importantly, that was the night I met Hunter. He was the host of the party and the owner of the impressive house. Older and so handsome, he'd made my mouth water. Not to mention he'd played the white knight—or maybe a black one—by rescuing me from an uncomfortable encounter with a disrespectful Dom who'd laid hands on me in a way I didn't care for.

Hunter had apologized for the guy's behavior and promised no one there would've actually let something bad befall me. "You'd never come back."

"What makes you so sure I'll come back now?"

He'd leaned back and smiled, a small, knowing smile. That's when I knew I was in trouble. There was something about him...

"Won't you?" He'd cocked an arched brow, and my whole self had clenched around a part of my body I was becoming increasingly familiar with.

"Yes, sir."

His hand had tightened around my arm. Unlike when the other Dom had crushed me, the pressure felt good. I'd been surprised but hadn't protested when his other hand snaked around my waist and he'd pulled me flush against him. He'd slid his hand over my shoulder, up my neck, and into my hair where he'd tugged it back until I looked at him.

"There's a good girl."

I was a lost cause. I would've done—eventually *did* do—anything to hear him say that again.

The thought of Hunter—a brief stab of bleakness like a knife between my ribs—snaps me back to attention. No time to fall down that particular rabbit hole. I've got shit to do.

I scramble to get the report finished and into Cooper's inbox at 5:29 p.m. EST. When it's sent, I'm unsurprised there's a knock at my door.

"Come in." I extend the invitation, though I know who it is. He's already opening the door, and he's got a bottle and two highball glasses in his hands.

"Well done, Ms. Burke," Jack booms, setting the glasses on my desk next to my red soles. He opens the bottle with a flourish and pours us both a generous amount. I don't bother to ask what it is. I know. It's bourbon and a really good bourbon, at that.

"To you, India, and your silver tongue. I don't know what your secret with Cooper is, but I'm glad you're on my side." He raises an arm in a toast and offers me his glass to clink.

"Giving-me-a-better-parking-spot glad?" Bourbon time is a good time to ask favors. Partly because he only drinks it when he's pleased, but also because I know he's already had one in his office before he gets to mine.

Jack drops into one of the chairs across from my desk, takes a long draught, and looks thoughtful. "Why not? Lucy!"

"Yes, sir?"

Poor Lucy. She's terrified of Jack. She's never mastered the whole not-crying-when-he-yells thing.

"Tell Jerome Ms. Burke will be parking in 1702 from now on."

"Yes, sir," Lucy squeaks before skittering out of my office.

I'm taken aback. That's the spot right next to Jack's, and it's reserved for the current Mrs. Valentine. Not that she visits often, but when she does, god forbid she should have to walk more than a couple yards to the front door.

"And what is Candi going to say about that?"

"Probably much the same as she said last night when I told her I wanted a divorce. It sounded an awful lot like 'Go to hell, you spineless motherfucking bastard.'"

Shit.

"I'm sorry, Jack." I don't want to talk about this, but I should observe the bare minimum of social niceties, right?

"We were never a good match. More?" Jack's already pouring another measure into his glass.

"No, thanks."

I'm still sipping at the first ration, and I'm only having the one. I have a few things to take care of before I leave for the day —for the weekend!

"You know any nice girls you could set me up with? Or nice women? Either one, I'm not picky. So long as she has two thoughts in her head to keep each other warm at night," he muses, sounding maudlin.

Must get Jack out of my office before this turns into a sob-fest.

"I don't know anyone nice. I spend too much time with you."

"You were a bitch when you got here, Burke. Don't try to blame me."

"That's one of the reasons you like me so much. I'm the only kind of girl who can put up with you."

"Too bad you're way more valuable to me sitting behind that desk than bent over it."

Whoa. What the fuck? Jack frequently says inappropriate things to me, and I don't care. I can give as good as I get—witness Towelgate—but this has a different flavor. I've never thought Jack had any lascivious interest in me and I sure as hell don't have any in him, but what he said and the way he said it… It gives me the creeps.

"And don't you forget it." Though my face stays light and teasing, there's an edge to my tone that he catches, coloring.

"Never. You'll have everything on my desk before you go?"

"Consider it done."

I push my chair away from my desk to put my feet back on the floor. Jack takes this as the cue to leave it is, raising his glass to me on the way out. "Excellent. See you Monday."

It's ten thirty when I deposit documents for three projects on Jack's long-abandoned desk. There are already digital copies in his inbox. I've set up my out-of-office message on my voicemail and email and left my Blackberry on my desk in plain view. When I take time off, I take it *off*.

I turn up my music loud on my way home and sing at the top of my lungs. I need to pack, but it shouldn't be difficult. Mr. Ardmore hasn't specified wardrobe or grooming requirements. Thank god, too, because I didn't have time to go shopping or get a wax. I hum my way up to my apartment and take up my phone and a glass of wine as soon as I'm inside. Rey picks up after the first ring. He's been waiting for me.

"Please tell me you're done for the day."

"Yes, I just set foot in the door."

"Packing?"

"Starting now." I drag my weekend bag out from my closet and start to select clothes for the trip on the off-chance I'll need them.

"Are you excited?"

"Yeah. More than usual. There's something about this guy. I can't get him out of my head."

"I think you're going to like this one." Rey's tone is a sing-song tease, sounding like my BFF helping me get ready for a big first date. Which I suppose he is.

"I hope so."

We chat while I get my things together. As we're signing off, Rey sneaks in a final reminder. "Remember, when you get there, you're not his sub yet. He wants to talk to *you*. So give the man what he wants for an hour, and then you can play."

"All right, all right." I roll my eyes, although I'm thankful for the advice. Cris Ardmore's demands for conversation throw me.

"Matthew will meet you when you land in Kona. Be good, be careful."

"I always am."

CHAPTER 4

*T*he flight is long, which I'm not usually in favor of, but I need the sleep. When the pilot announces our descent into Kona, I'm awake and feeling rested. It's happening. In a few hours, I will meet the man who's occupied my thoughts more than I'd like to admit for the past... Has it only been sixty or so hours? It seems like so much longer.

I touch up my makeup, not wanting to waste the time once we've landed. When I'm done, I settle back, starting to get into character—but I can't. Not until we've had our little chat. I have to be India Burke for a little while longer. Although he'll still think of me as Kit Bailey-Isles, and that'll be disconcerting. Damn Cris Ardmore and his need for *conversation*. This is far more trouble than I usually go to. He'd best make it worth my while.

When we filter off the plane, Matty is waiting, and I give him a hug.

"Aloha, kitten." Matty was born on St. John and didn't leave the Virgin Islands until college. He's got the most beautiful latte complexion and lovely accent to show for it. Tall and wiry, his dark hair is clipped short, and he's wearing a white linen button-down over pressed khakis. He doesn't look like he spent the same six hours as I did on a plane.

"Aloha, Matty." I greet him with a kiss and take his hand. People often comment on what a handsome couple we are, which is hilarious. We are affectionate with each other and move with the easy synchronicity of people who've been together for a long and happy time, so it's easy to forgive and we don't correct them. The truth is far too complicated for your average bear. Matty is Rey's sub, although they more regularly play with other people. He runs the administrative side of Rey's business and, oh right, acts as my sometime babysitter/escort/bodyguard.

While Matty picks up our rental car, I find a bathroom to change in and slip into an orange, white and navy tunic dress. I frown at my reflection. My hair's made it through the flight relatively intact, black curls loose and glossy, and though my gaze catches on it, no one else will pay attention to the slight rise at the bridge of my nose. The only person who's ever had a problem with that was my mother. Not even Hunter had said anything about it, and he'd had something to say about every square centimeter of me. My mom started dragging me to plastic surgeons when I was twelve, all of whom had been professional enough to turn us away.

So, no, it's not my "imperfect" nose that's bothering me. It's my eyes. They're more conspicuous than usual. Most people don't notice they're two different colors because the difference is subtle—one green, one hazel—but not today. Through some trick of lighting or maybe the contrast with what I'm wearing, I'm practically emerald on one side and chestnut on the other. My sister used to tell me it was the mark of the devil.

When I get outside, Matty's leaning against a black 4x4 Jeep. It's spotless and new, but a far cry from the luxury car we usually have.

I cock my head in question.

"Our friend lives off the beaten path."

A smile creeps over my face, and I bite my lip in anticipation. Matty laughs and raises a dark eyebrow as he holds open my door.

"Rey said you were looking forward to this, but I had no idea. You have got it bad." He hands me up before slipping into the driver's side. The beast roars to life. "Can't say I blame you. He is...appealing."

I gape at him as he pulls into traffic. Matty rarely expresses an opinion about the men I'm going to see, unless he doesn't like the look of them. Then he'll try to warn me off, which I should really take more seriously. He was right about Vasili. But this is the first one he's had anything complimentary to say about, and he knows far more about this guy than I do, having put together the dossier. Perhaps I should take this seriously as well. *Cris Ardmore, you've put a spell on us all.*

Matty wasn't kidding when he said the man lived off the beaten path. I'm glad we have the Jeep, with the heavy-duty grab bars and four-wheel drive, when we're careening over dirt and rock paths that narrowly accommodate the vehicle's width. I bounce in my seat as we drive over a copious number of ruts, and I have to keep pushing my hair back from my face as it whips around in the breeze. We're surrounded by jungle, and it smells of dirt and living things instead of sunbaked concrete and car exhaust. I feel like I'm on wild safari ride at an amusement park—it's fun.

By the time we arrive at what I assume is Mr. Ardmore's home, my nerves have been shaken loose and I'm pink with delight. Matty is less enthused, probably because he'll have to drive the path at least three more times before he can fly home to his nifty little Audi coupe and the comparatively smooth hills of San Francisco.

We pull up a few yards away from what appears to be the

largest of several raised, wood-and-glass huts joined by covered walkways. My eyes wander over the structure, but only for a second because there he is, ambling down the steps. Seeing Cris Ardmore in person sends a thrill through me. He's about six feet tall, powerfully built without being bulky, and moving with no apparent hurry in our direction. His wardrobe consists of a faded blue cotton button-down, open at the collar and rolled up at the sleeves; clean but worn khaki shorts; and a pair of flip-flops. *Flip-flops? Someone's feeling sure of himself.*

He opens my door and offers me a hand. I can see the reason he looked a little off in his photograph: his nose has clearly been broken, probably more than once. He doesn't seem like a brawler and a record for assault would've shown up in his dossier, so I'm intrigued instead of concerned. His dark curls are shot through with stray strands of grey, and his eyes are…curious. No wonder I couldn't tell if they were blue or grey in his picture. I still can't say for sure, and he's looking right at me. They're the color of the sky when you know a storm is gathering but you don't rush inside because you know you've still got a while before it starts to pour.

He's still got the stubble, as I'd hoped, and I have to consciously refrain from running my fingers over it. Lines are etched around his mouth from smiling, and I hope again I'll get to see him laugh. He is, as Matty said, appealing.

He looks me over from head to toe. Not in a vulgar way, but with decided interest. I've got him at a disadvantage. Rey tells them what I look like, but they don't get to see a picture beforehand. Rarely do they seem disappointed, though, and this is no exception.

"Ms. Bailey-Isles, I presume?"

He has a nice voice. Not the warm, languid caramel of Matty's, but a pleasant, deep tenor that could turn sharp or sweet on a dime. Very nice, indeed.

"Were you expecting anyone else?" I deadpan.

He blinks, surprised, but recovers with a lopsided smile. "I believe that would be contrary to the letter of our agreement."

"Touché, Mr. Ardmore. And Ms. Isles will do." I place my hand in his and return his smile. His hand is large and smooth and warm. There's nothing worse than a man with clammy, sweaty palms or frigid fingers when you know they're going to be all over you—possibly in you—in a few hours. Or minutes, as the case may be. But, no, Cris Ardmore is checking all my boxes.

He helps me out of the 4x4 and releases me. I'm disappointed and annoyed now that I need to talk to him before those hands will be anywhere else. *If* they'll be anywhere else.

He comes around the car and extends a hand to Matty. "Mr. St. James."

"Mr. Ardmore."

"Mr. St. James will wait here while we talk." I take charge, placing a slight emphasis on the word *talk*.

"Sure." He looks relieved. I don't blame him. What *is* the protocol for dealing with the man who's escorted your potential rent-a-sub to your doorstep? I don't think Miss Manners ever wrote a column on that. "Ms. Isles, shall we?"

I'm pleased when he lays a hand at the small of my back. He *is* going to touch me. Excellent. His fingers are warm through the fabric of my dress, and his touch is sure as he leads me in the direction from which he came.

"There's lunch in the house if you'd like. Or if food isn't… appealing, right now…"

I try to contain my smile.

"Do you think I'm squeamish, Mr. Ardmore?" I glance up at him, the lightest mocking in my tone. "That I have a weak stomach? That you're going to offend my delicate sensibilities?"

For god's sake, we've brokered an agreement that includes the word *dildos*. I'm hardly a shrinking violet.

He colors under tanned skin and stutters, "No, I..."

Oh, he's adorable. This is freaking *adorable*. I could have some fun with him and make him squirm, but I like him. I'll throw him a line.

"If it helps, Mr. Walter and I discussed the contract over ceviche."

His brow wrinkles for a second before he laughs. *Oh, my.* Something liquefies in my stomach. No one's laugh has ever done that to me before. It's better than I imagined.

"You know, that does help. Ceviche, huh?"

"Sea bass. It was delicious."

"Okay, Ms. Isles, lunch it is. It's no ceviche, but I hope it'll meet with your approval."

Cris Ardmore shows me into the largest hut, and when I enter, I freeze. It's bigger than I thought it would be and beautiful, all warm wood and light. There's a long dining table set with ten chairs, a seating area with off-white couches and benches scattered with bright throw pillows, and a shiny kitchen against one wall with some kind of stone countertops. That would be a pleasure to cook in, unlike the barely serviceable Formica nightmare in my apartment.

There are also some bookshelves (filled with *books* and not dusty knickknacks, I note with satisfaction) and solitary chairs with ottomans in corners supplied with small side tables and lamps—places made for reading. There are doors recessed off the walls that must lead to the other huts and probably a bathroom. I could look around forever, but to be honest, I'd rather peruse the shelves, find something familiar, and curl up in one of the chairs.

I realize he's staring at me, and I'm embarrassed.

"I'm sorry, I'm being rude. You have a lovely home."

There's the slightest shrug of his broad shoulders before he responds. "It's my parents' house."

What?

I must look some shade of horrified because he volunteers, "They don't live here. It's just me. They built this place a long time ago, thinking they'd retire here, but my father's health isn't good. They live in Kona, much closer to civilization. I've lived here since I finished school. Added a couple things, redone the place. I've thought about leaving, having them sell—"

"No, don't!"

He looks surprised by my outburst. I am. Why the hell do I care?

"You shouldn't. It's a beautiful spot, and…"

"You haven't seen the best part. I'll show you after lunch."

After lunch, huh? We both realize what he's said and regard each other shyly. *Really? Ceviche, people—there's no room for shyness here.*

"Come, eat. You must be hungry." He takes my hand and leads me to one end of the large dining table. The places are set, simple but pretty. There's even a bowl with white and yellow plumeria floating in water. Whoa. I'm being wooed. Courted. Flowers. Lunch. It's like a date. I haven't been on a date in…

He pulls out my chair and gestures for me to sit. When I have, he wanders off toward the kitchen, and I take a sip from the glass of water at my place. I feel…nervous. I don't get nervous. This guy is throwing me off my game.

He comes back with two plates and sets one in front of me. It's filled with blackened fish, wild rice, and grilled vegetables. I wait for him to take his seat before laying my napkin in my lap and starting to eat. Holy shit, this is good. Cris Ardmore knows his way around a kitchen.

"So, Mr. Ardmore, you wanted to speak with me?"

"I did."

"And what did you want to speak with me about?"

"I don't know." His brow creases. "I guess I wanted to make sure…"

"I wasn't some sort of sex slave? I'm not being coerced? That's very gallant, but entirely unnecessary, I assure you." I take another bite of fish, hoping I appear cooler than I feel.

"I can see that. You'll have to forgive me. This isn't the way I usually do things."

"It's not the way most people do things. But, it's the only way *I* do things."

He looks surprised but covers it with a joke. "So you're the world's foremost expert on this type of arrangement?"

"Possibly. You're starting out with the best. I'll ruin you for anyone else."

"I think you might."

He mutters this under his breath, and I'm not sure if he intended me to hear him. We sit in silence for a minute, but I'm getting antsy. *Let's move this along, shall we?* "Is there anything else you wanted to ask me?"

"Lots of things, but I don't think I'm allowed."

"Probably not."

I enjoy a few more bites of my food, trying to play it cool, even though I've rarely felt less so. Is this what he expected? Is this what he wants? How can I tell? This is maddening. I stab another piece of perfectly cooked zucchini and shove it in my mouth before I let on exactly how discomfited I am. I'm swallowing when he leans back in his chair and takes up his glass of water.

"This… This is, by far, the strangest date I've ever been on."

"Is that what this is? A date?"

"What did you think it was?"

"Well, I don't know about you, but I was under the impression that I had signed up for a weekend full of very hot, very kinky sex."

This causes Cris Ardmore to have a narrow miss with a spit-take. Instead, he covers his mouth with the back of his hand and coughs into his arm. He really is the cutest. How has he managed to do this for so long and still be such a prude?

"I'm sorry. I told you I'm not shy."

"Ceviche?" he croaks.

"Indeed, Mr. Ardmore."

"I think if we're going to fuck, you can call me Cris."

That's more like it.

"All right then, Cris. You can call me Kit. For now."

We finish our lunch over a series of verbal parries and thrusts, and when we're through, I set down my knife and fork and lay my napkin on the table. "Thank you for lunch. It more than met with my approval."

"You're welcome. I'm glad you enjoyed it."

We look at each other for a beat, daring the other person to make the first move, but I'm impatient and clearly don't play coy.

"So have I passed muster?"

He looks unhappy. "This was never about you passing muster. I won't have you thinking that."

Ah, my first glimpse of the Dominant I've been promised. I like. He leans back in his chair and studies me.

"I like to think of myself as a fundamentally responsible person. I wanted to know from *you*, not the submissive you, that this was something you wanted. I don't coerce women. I don't force them. I never have, and I won't start now. But you clearly have more than your fair share of wits about you and a very clear understanding of what's going to happen here, so my requirements have been satisfied."

His words make me feel startled and raw. Cris Ardmore's understanding—or, at least, suspicion—of the extent to which my submissive self is discrete from the rest of me is perturbing. Will this man never stop throwing me for a loop?

I cover the best way I know how. "All of your requirements?"

"We'll have to wait until we sign those contracts to find out, won't we?" A change has come over him. He's committed to this. He doesn't want to be polite and charming anymore. He wants to fuck me over this table, and I'm totally on board.

I pull the three copies of the contract that Rey has already signed out of my bag along with two pens and hand the stack to him. He initials the bottom of each page, as well as by the more unique requirements I insist upon, and signs at the end. When he's finished with the first one, he hands it to me.

"I'll need to bring these out to Mr. St. James when they've been completed and collect my things."

"Of course. I'll take you."

I smile at him, one last free and flirty smile. I've enjoyed talking to him, however awkward parts of our conversation might've been, and I feel a pang of what might be regret that we'll be playing roles from now on. At least I got to see him laugh. I could live off that for weeks.

I initial and sign. It's done. 1:05 p.m., and I am officially Cris Ardmore's submissive.

Cris pushes his chair back from the table and stands, taking the contracts from me. He somehow looks taller.

"Come," he commands, holding out a hand. Something deep inside me constricts at the word coming out of his mouth, and I can think of nothing I'd like to do more for this man. If we hadn't signed the contracts yet, my reply would be a saucy "yes, please." But we have, so my training kicks in and I rise from my seat, putting my hand in his.

Matty is waiting where we left him, and his face doesn't betray anything as we approach. Cris hands him the contracts, and Matty flips through each copy. Satisfied all the *t*'s have been crossed and the *i*'s dotted, he hands one to me, one to Cris, and keeps the last.

"Would you mind if I have a word with Ms. Isles, Mr. Ardmore?"

"Please." Cris relinquishes his grip on my hand and steps back ten paces, not taking his eyes off me.

"All set?"

"Yes, thank you."

"You'll text me?"

"I will."

"It's your pick this time."

"Fish."

It's a safety precaution Matty and I use, although it's really more of a game at this point. I text Matty at least once every four hours with a code we agree on beforehand. Matty tends to like geography: countries that begin with *C*, state capitals, etc. I'm more inclined to the eclectic: car makes, James Bond movies, presidents. While the guys I'm with are aware I need to text Matty, they don't know the code. So if Matty got an "*I'm okay :)*" he'd know I wasn't and call in the cavalry. It's never happened, but it's a cute little failsafe.

"Fish it is. Have fun."

"I plan to."

He smiles at me, shakes his head, and lays one of his elegant, long-fingered hands on top of my head. "I'll see you Sunday. You'll call if you need me."

"Promise."

He nods in satisfaction, removes his hand, and settles his face into what I call his "don't fuck with me" glare before motioning to Cris to collect me and my small weekend bag. They shake hands before Matty climbs into the Jeep, and I watch him reverse and head down the overgrown path.

Cris is standing beside me. I'm more aware of him than I have been before, and I can feel what I refer to as my sub-sense tingling. He leans down, his lips an inch away from my ear.

"Let the games begin, pet."

CHAPTER 5

*S*o it's to be *pet?* I can live with that. It's better than the *bitch* or *slut* I sometimes get. *Kitten* I like, and though it's a bit sickly sweet, I have a special fondness for *precious*. As long as they steer clear of *baby* or *sweetheart* as they've been told, I don't care. I stand up straighter, and his hand comes to the small of my back.

He urges me back where we came from without a word and, when we've entered the main hut, steers me toward one of the recessed doors.

"This leads to my room. You shouldn't need to go in there, but if for some reason you need me and can't find me anywhere else, you'll knock before you come in." He leads me to the next door. "This goes to the studio. It's locked most of the time. Don't forget where this is—you'll be expected in there later."

I note where I'm at, finding landmarks to remind me which of the plain wood doors this is. "Yes, sir."

He points out a few more as bathrooms, closets, and a pantry before showing me to the last door. It leads to a covered walkway, elevated like the huts and made of the same wood. It connects the main house to another, smaller building, and he opens the door to reveal a bedroom.

There's a queen-sized, framed-four-poster bed with an upholstered bench at its foot where Cris deposits my bag. A beautiful, orange and white Hawaiian quilt hangs on the wall behind it. The linens are white and look soft and freshly washed. On either side is a small bedside table and a plush chair. There are a couple of doors on the opposite wall—leading to what I imagine are a closet and a bathroom—with a dresser in-between. The far side is taken up by sliding glass doors that lead out to a balcony. Between them is a desk with bookshelves overhead. It's a simple room. Not the most luxurious accommodations I've had by far, but pretty and comfortable. I like it here.

"This is where you'll stay when you're not with me. You're welcome to anything in here. I expect you to make yourself comfortable. You'll let me know if you need anything. You can have a little while to get settled, and you'll meet me in the studio in twenty minutes. There's a robe in the closet for you to wear around the house unless I say otherwise."

"Yes, sir." I'm starting to settle into my part.

Eighteen minutes later, I'm standing outside the door that leads to Cris's studio, which I assume is a pleasant euphemism for dungeon. While I don't care for beating around the bush, I like this. It's easy to make kink sound tawdry and juvenile, but *studio* implies effort, beauty, discipline, and care. I'm barefoot and wearing only the short, orange silk robe that was in the closet. I've left my hair down, although there's a tie in my pocket. I take a deep breath and open the door to a walkway. At the end, I open another door and find myself in a room a little larger than mine.

I was right. It's a dungeon, but not like any I've ever seen. They're usually in an attic or basement and either painted in dark

49

colors with glinting metal and forbidding black leather everywhere or bland, contractor-beige with easy-to-clean surfaces.
Not this one. It's the same warm wood as the other huts, but
there aren't any sliding glass doors, only windows running along
the entire perimeter just below the ceiling. It's a nice effect—
natural light filtering in without compromising the room's
privacy. The default St. Andrew's cross is prettier than most. It's
anchored in one corner and has brown leather straps hanging at
regular intervals and, for good measure, chains affixed to each
corner. There's a bed, too—another framed-four-poster big
enough that a person might be tethered to the four corners
without leaving any limb unsupported.

There's no gallery wall, but an oversized and solid chest of
drawers where toys and restraints must be kept. A large table
with anchor points along the sides stands in one corner, and in
another, a fair-sized leather couch and a matching ottoman.
There's also a door I'm guessing leads to a bathroom. If so, it's a
nice touch. Most of the rooms I've played in don't have one.

We're getting close to the twenty-minute mark. Keeping time
in my head is a skill I have a special talent for. He hasn't given me
any instructions for what to do when I get here, so I stand by the
door with my hands clasped behind my back and my eyes cast
down.

My heart quickens when I hear footsteps coming down the
walkway. It sounds like Mr. Ardmore is also barefoot. No flip-
flops now. The door opens, and he enters, closing it behind him.

"I like punctual, pet. Nicely done."

I glow under his casual praise. He walks around me, and I see
his feet and his legs up to his thighs. He's got nice feet—I've seen
my fair share of men's feet, I would know. And he's wearing
jeans, which I like. I didn't expect the full-on, leather getup from
him, but I've been surprised before.

He grips my arm above my elbow and steers me toward the
center of the room, turning me to face the table and standing in

front of me. Taking my chin between his thumb and forefinger, he tips my head up. "Look at me."

I like what I see on the way up. An open and worn plaid shirt reveals a toned but not bodybuilder-quality torso and a smattering of dark chest hair. A small medal on a leather thong hangs around his neck, though I don't have enough time on my brief glance to tell what it is. Under damp curls, his blue-grey eyes are intense on mine. He's looking for something, but I'm not sure what he thinks he's going to find.

"Are your eyes different colors?"

"Yes, sir."

He pauses for a moment, still staring, and my heart stutters. "Fitting, I think. And lovely."

"Thank you, sir."

That's not the standard reaction I get when people notice, but Cris has done nothing but surprise me since before I even met him. *Fitting. And lovely.*

He lets go of my chin and traces my jaw with his fingers before running them down my neck, over my sternum, and between my breasts to where the robe is tied at my waist. He tugs at the sash. It comes undone, and the robe parts. He runs his fingers up the same path they traveled before, but this time he stops at my collarbone and slides one side of my robe over my shoulder before repeating the motion on the other side. I release my hands long enough for the pretty orange silk to puddle at my feet.

My breath is coming faster, but I'm practiced at keeping myself under control. It's possible he doesn't notice. He takes a step back and surveys me, drinking in every inch.

"Turn around."

I do as I'm told, keeping my hands clasped, and I feel him studying the contours of my body.

"Do you have any injuries I should know about?"

"No, sir."

TAMSEN PARKER

"Allergies?"

"No, sir."

"Anything I need to be careful of?"

"Only what was in the contract, sir."

I'm startled and can't suppress a brief shudder when he traces the T-shaped scar on my lower back. He drops his hand immediately. "Tell me your safewords."

"Yellow for caution and red for stop."

He gathers up my hair, running his fingers from my scalp to the tips, and plaits it before twisting it into a knot and fastening it up off my neck with a clip. After he's through, he proceeds to run his hands over every inch of me. His touch is confident but gentle. I'm being examined, inspected, but also learned, studied, memorized. He's familiarizing himself with my body.

His hands glide over my hipbones, over my stomach, and up my ribcage to my breasts. He cups them, hefting them in his palms and running his thumbs over my nipples. When they harden under his touch, there's an appreciative noise low in his throat. He squeezes my breasts lightly before continuing his tour, over my chest, up my neck, before cupping my face.

"Mr. Walter was very complimentary when he described you, but he managed to sell you short. Neither he nor Mr. St. James told me you were perfect."

Perfect! Before I can say, "Thank you, sir," he leans in and presses a kiss to my mouth. His lips are warm and full, moving surely but not aggressively over mine. I'm aching to run my hands through his hair and pull him into me, but he hasn't given me permission to touch him. So I surrender to his attentions, parting my lips in invitation.

He accepts my offering and slips his tongue into my mouth while sliding one hand into my hair and the other to my back to pull me closer. My knees get weak and something deep in my belly constricts—from a kiss. There's a better-than-even chance that the men I'm with never kiss me. I don't miss it when they don't, but I don't think I've ever been kissed like this before. It's…perfect.

When Cris pulls away, I'm left wanting, my eyes closed and my lips parted. Only my training stops me from pushing myself into him and begging for more. I'm mollified when he gathers up my wrists and presses them into the small of my back.

"You're delicious."

He leans in for another kiss, this one short and chaste, and I'm left wanting again. He takes his hand from my hair and leads me toward the closed door. It's a bathroom, bigger than I thought it would be, with the same windows running the length of the ceiling. The entire thing is tiled—grey stone on the floor and rich green glass on the walls—and there's a shower with a hand-held sprayer on the far side. On this end, there's a large stone sink and freestanding stone tub to one side and a toilet in a corner with a small screen folded beside it. Next to that are wood shelves sunken into the wall, stacked with fluffy white towels and various supplies: bars of soap; bottles of shampoo, conditioner, lotion and oils; a fine shaving kit with a strop hanging on the wall. The baskets that slide into the bottom shelf leave me curious.

He leads me into the shower before releasing my wrists. "Hands at shoulder height against the wall."

I step close to the tile, careful to only touch the surface with fingers and palms. He covers my hands with his and slides them farther out to the sides. I inhale as he steps closer and his body presses into my back. His clothes are soft, worn, his bare torso is hard against my skin. I want to push against him, but I don't. Not until he grasps my hipbones and pulls me into him.

"Head back." At his soft invitation, I turn my head and lay my cheek against his chest, closing my eyes and dropping my shoulders. "That's right, you can let go now."

With his encouragement, I let my body loosen further and lean into him more.

"That's a good girl." He grips my shoulders and neck in his large, warm hands and starts to massage me. It feels incredible, and I allow myself a small moan to let him know.

"You like that?"

"Yes, sir."

"There's no need to be wound so tight here. I'm going to look after you." He nuzzles behind my ear, and the coil that carries so much tension in my core lets go a little. It usually takes a collar being fastened around my throat, but Cris is working some strange and delicious magic I don't totally understand. "You need this so badly, don't you?"

The spring snaps back, and I hesitate before giving in, my voice a choked whisper.

"Yes, sir."

"Oh, pet. It's okay, hush," he soothes, redoubling his efforts at my shoulders. "Don't worry. I'm not going to spill your secret, I promise. No one but me will know how sweet you are, how supple. I don't like to share. I'm going to keep you all to myself."

His assurances let me relax again, and I settle into his attentions. I'm disappointed when he pulls away, even though I'd slip through the drain in the center of the floor if I were any more relaxed.

"Let's get you cleaned up." There's a gentle tug at my earlobe, and I straighten up as he withdraws, trying to blink myself back to reality. I catch sight of him taking his shirt off out of the corner of my eye and want to turn my head to get a better view, but I don't. I do get a nice glimpse of finely muscled arm when he reaches past me to take the sprayer in hand and flicks on the water. He points the stream away from me, and I hear the interruption in the flow as he runs his hand through to check the temperature. When he turns it on my skin, it's pleasantly hot.

"Too hot?"

"No, sir."

He wets me down thoroughly before turning the water off,

unwrapping a fresh bar of soap, and running it over my skin. It smells of verbena, and again I get to enjoy his hands covering every inch of me. He's thorough, taking far more time than necessary. When he's satisfied, he turns the water back on and rinses me just as meticulously before replacing the sprayer. It's nice to be clean after such a long flight. He dries me off, and I still have my palms against the wall as he pulls his shirt on, leaving it unbuttoned and rolling up the sleeves.

"Better?" He's standing behind me once again with his hands on my hips.

"Yes, sir."

He grasps my wrists and tugs them down to the small of my back where he takes them in one hand. "Then let's get started."

He leads me back to the main room and over to the table. Patting the short end, he says "Up you go," and releases me.

I press up onto the table, leaving my legs and feet dangling over the side. He unclips my hair and runs his fingers through it until it's flowing down my back.

"I'll be right back." He touches my arm on his way past, and I watch him walk over to the chest of drawers and slide one open and shut. When he comes back, he's got a pair of leather cuffs in his hand. They're brown and well-used, so they'll be comfortable and won't chafe.

"Hands."

I offer them to him, palms up, and he fastens the cuffs on my wrists smoothly. Yes, he's well-practiced. When he's finished, he grips my hipbones and scoots me back on the smooth table.

"Knees into your chest."

I'm not sure what his game is, but I do as I'm asked. Still sitting, I bend my knees until my thighs are pressed against my torso and my feet are flat on the table. He comes to my side, wraps an arm around my waist, and cradles the back of my head in his other hand. "Back you go."

Having the bare skin of his chest and forearms on mine is the most heavenly feeling. He's warm and in good shape, more like from honest physical labor than spending hours in a gym. I like it, very much. I sink into his grasp, and he lays me back on the table. I'm pliant already, comfortable following his gentle instructions. Sometimes it takes me a while to acclimate to a Dom's style, but this is easy. He slides my cuffed wrists over my head and clips them to an anchor point I can't see. When he's done, he takes a step back.

"Very nice."

I have to agree. He has a very nice body I'm getting to admire more closely. I still haven't been able to discern what the medal around his neck is, though.

He traces a path from my tethered wrists down to my shoulders and my ribcage before cupping my breasts, stroking his thumbs over my nipples again until they peak under his touch. I arch my back, pushing them into his hands.

"You like to be touched?"

"Yes, sir."

He starts to knead at me. Gently at first, then harder, the sweet attentions of earlier left behind. I press my feet into the table.

"You're a responsive little thing, aren't you? You can close your eyes, kitten."

Kitten! This just keeps getting better. I mewl to let him know I liked it and take advantage of his invitation. Thank god. Not that I don't enjoy looking at him—on the contrary—but having my eyes closed makes it easier to behave and increases the intensity of the sensations. A win-win.

He works me over, and as he hasn't demanded I be quiet or still, I give him cues when he's done something I particularly enjoy: a groan here, a squirm there. He's a fast learner, and it's not long before I'm writhing under his attentions, careful to keep my feet flat on the table. He's got me pretty riled up when he starts to hush me. I'm not surprised but only a little disappointed. Of course it's not going be this easy. What fun would that be?

I calm under his gentling and open my eyes. He's smiling down at me, a knowing, predatory smile. "You're such a treat to watch. Beautiful. And this is only the beginning."

I can't help the moan that escapes at his promise, and he shakes his head. "This time you'll be quiet."

"Yes, sir," I squeak, and I'm rewarded by a hard squeeze to my breasts. This is going to be good. He starts in on me again, picking up the intensity, and I'm glad he's only asked me to be quiet and not still, too, because he's driving me insane. His fingers dig into me as he squeezes. It's only just not painful—precisely how I like it. His fingers grasp my nipples, and he pinches and rolls them before tugging hard. My gasp is followed by a slap to the side of my breast.

"I said quiet." His voice is sharp, and he doesn't pause in his torments.

"Yes, sir."

Fuck am I in trouble, and he knows it. My breathless response gave me away. He teases me before tugging sharply again. While I don't gasp, I can't help the strangled grunt he's forced out of me. My disobedience results in another slap, this time to my other breast, and a warning.

"I said no noise. If you make another sound, it will mean punishment and not the little reminders you've been getting. Is that clear?"

"Yes, sir." I don't know whether to hope for this or not. First punishments are telling, and I can't say I'm not curious about what this might mean for Cris. I've been caned for less, although I suspect that's not his style. Not yet at any rate.

He torments me for another few minutes, driving me wild with his talented and sure hands. He's going to go for it again, so I steel myself and manage to stay quiet. But he's a stubborn and wily son of a bitch, and he does it again, more sharply, yielding a squeal. This isn't idle threats and disappointment. He *wants* to punish me. I get another slap to my right breast, followed quickly by one to my left, harder this time.

His hands are on either side of my ribcage, and he leans over me, his mouth brushing by my ear. "It's such a shame you're so badly behaved. I was starting to enjoy myself."

I whimper in response and get a hand at my throat.

"And how should we punish you, pet?" He poses his question idly, as if he has all time in the world to compose a dissertation on the topic. "So many ways to pink up your pretty pale skin and help you learn to do as you're told."

CHAPTER 6

"You'd almost think you weren't enjoying yourself. Were you not?"

"I was, sir." It's all I can do to not thrust my hips at him in invitation, so yes, I was enjoying myself.

"I'd like to see for myself. Drop your knees."

I let my knees fall until they nearly touch the table, leaving me open and exposed. He reaches under the table for god knows what, but when he stands up, he's got two rolled towels. He places them under my knees so I can relax and my legs won't cramp. This is not Cris's first rodeo.

He steps to the far end of the table, and my mouth goes dry. He wants me. It's written all over his face. *The feeling is mutual, Cris.* I do my best to not squirm as he studies me because I'm aching for his hands. After what seems like forever and a day, he places the heel of one hand onto my mound and presses, spreading his fingers over my low belly. Fuck that feels good. He's such a tease, but his torture doesn't last long. A finger from his other hand slips inside of me. I press my head back into the table but don't make a sound.

"You weren't lying. You were enjoying yourself."

His finger is entering and retreating at a pace designed to be tempting, not satisfying. I'm trying to temper my reaction to him, knowing I'm not going to get any satisfaction yet. He's making it challenging at best, especially when two fingers enter me. I sigh in pleasure, and I'm distracted enough that I'm startled when he starts to talk again.

"While I'd like to forgo your punishment altogether and go straight to fucking you, I don't want to spoil you. I'm curious. How do you think you should be punished?"

"However you'd like, sir." That's obvious. But instead of the, "Very good, pet," I'm expecting, I get a light slap between my widely spread legs that makes me jump. The contact with my clit isn't unwelcome and I've been spanked this way before, but it's a surprise.

"Don't be trite with me. I don't like it. You might've gotten away with that with someone else, but I expect a real answer. And you'll stay still, otherwise I'll restrain your legs as well. Do you need to be strapped down or can you behave for me?"

"I'll behave, sir."

"That's right. You're my good girl, aren't you?"

"Yes, sir, I'm your good girl." I whimper as he slips his fingers in and out of me in that maddening rhythm, and I clench around him.

"Don't even think about it. You'll be sorry. Now, let's talk about your punishment."

Oh my god. Is he going to make me talk about punishment while he's still doing this? I'm going to expire. And by expire, I mean come. Hard. Without permission. *Fuck.*

"I think caning's a little harsh for a first offense. Would you agree?"

"Yes, sir."

"Ditto for whipping."

"Yes, sir."

"And the crop seems a little fussy. I'd like to work you over with that nice and slow, and I don't want to waste time right now."

"Yes, sir."

He's making me crazy. With every option he dismisses, a picture runs through my head of him doing exactly that. For the love of all that is holy, this man is absolutely maddening, and I want him. Badly.

"I'd love to flog you, make you pink up from head to toe, but that I want to savor," he muses, dragging a groan from me at the thought—I bet Cris is handy with a flogger—and I'm greeted by another slap between my thighs. "Quiet. I'm trying to concentrate."

I tug at my wrists. *Me, too, Cris, me, too.* At least he doesn't threaten me. It was more of a passing reminder.

"Paddling?"

My back arches at the suggestion. There's very little in this world as satisfying as smooth wood or a plane of leather making diffuse contact with my ass over and over again. If it's measured and not too, too hard, I could be paddled for hours. God, I love a good paddling.

"You'd like that?"

I want to say no. Not because I'm embarrassed, but because I think he'll do something else if he thinks I'll enjoy it too much. But I don't want to be punished for lying. *That* I could see him caning me for.

"Yes, sir."

"Better than a spanking?"

"Yes, sir."

There's too much variability in hand spanking, too much inconsistency. I like the predictability of the paddle. Plus, it's challenging for Doms to hit me as hard as I like to be hit with a bare hand. Yes, paddling is preferable to spanking, and I wonder what he's going to do with this information.

He nods thoughtfully, stroking in and out of me. I have to

admire the man's concentration. This is multitasking at its finest. I do wonder what's taking him so long. He's not indecisive, and he's already narrowed the options. The only thing I can think of is that he's playing the long game, like a chess player planning out his next half-dozen moves. I like the idea of Cris meditating on all the things he'd like to do to me in the future while driving me crazy in the present.

"I think you've had enough. Don't want you earning another punishment already. Knees together, legs down."

He withdraws his hands, and I close my legs and slide my feet over the wood until the edge of the table is at the back of my knees as he untethers me. He leaves the cuffs on my wrists and slides one hand under my back and another under the base of my skull to help me sit up. I find myself chest-to-bare-chest with him. Appealing is not going to cut it. I find Cris Ardmore...delectable.

The nearly irresistible urge to kiss him overwhelms me. I want his lips on mine, his tongue in my mouth, my hands in his hair. I want him to hold me tight against him and not let go.

This is disturbing.

I'm not unaccustomed to urges, oh no, but the urge to kiss... This is new. India Kittredge Burke doesn't want to *kiss*. Children kiss, vanilla lovers kiss, people who don't know any better *kiss*. I like to fuck. I like to be hit. I like to have unspeakable things done to me. What the hell?

Cris tips his head, and his brows pinch in curiosity. "Go ahead. You can touch me."

I don't hesitate. I grip his biceps before sliding my hands over his shoulders, his neck, and into his curly, dark hair, knotting my fingers into fists and pulling his face to mine. And when I kiss him... Yes, this is what I was after. He pulls me into him by my hair, and it's as delicious as I imagined it to be. It's possible I've underestimated kissing, but I don't think that's it. It's that I've never been kissed like this.

We kiss for a while, and I don't get bored. Every taste of him is delicious, every touch inflaming, setting off sparks in my core. I could do this forever. I'm so consumed by him that when he pulls away, I realize I've barely been breathing. That's what this lightheadedness is from, right? Right?

"You like to be kissed?" Suspicion colors his voice.

"Only by you, sir."

I expect a pinch or a slap or a tug at my hair for being pat, even though I'm not—not this time—but he seems to understand. He slides me off the table and leads me over to the couch, sitting in the center and pulling me next to him.

"Over my lap."

I turn and drape myself over his legs, one below my breasts, the other at the juncture of my hips and thighs. I fold my arms to rest my head on and settle. He's stroking my back and my ass, and I start to purr. This is familiar, and the pleasure I take in it isn't uncomfortable. Not like the kissing. Jesus.

"Tell me why you're going to get a spanking."

"For not being quiet like I was told, sir."

"Is that good behavior?"

"No, sir."

"Do you deserve to be punished?"

"Yes, sir."

"Every time you make noise without permission, this is what's going to happen. Remember that."

"Yes, sir," I confirm, and I'm barely able to keep still. He's going to make an example of me, and I can't wait.

"You don't need to be quiet, but can you keep still for this?"

"Yes, sir."

I'm disappointed, not surprised, when the first blow lands. *That's it?* But when he gets no response, the next one is harder. And again. He works up steadily, but then he stops, a warm hand resting on my low back and his voice quiet in my ear.

"Are you okay, Kit?"

I'm startled he's used my name, but other than that, I'm fine. I nod.

"Are you sure?"

Oh, no. This happened once before. Rey took a chance, and the guy I ended up with was reluctant to hit me. I wanted to take him over my knee and show him how it's done, and I so rarely get the urge to top. Ugh. And everything had been going so well. While I wouldn't normally offer anything other than a "yes, sir," I hate the idea that things are about to go downhill. Cris doesn't seem prissy, just cautious.

"It would be...difficult for you to hit me too hard. Sir."

There's a pause, and I wonder if he's disturbed by this. Lots of guys are, but not most Doms. As long as everyone's signed on the dotted line, we're usually good to go. Hardcore sadists aren't really my bag, but a little further along the spectrum you find my sweet spot: Dominants who like to tell me what to do and have enough of a sadistic streak to enjoy administering a good beating. I'm hoping Cris is located somewhere in the latter category.

When he strikes again, he forces a sound out of me: a small grunt. Now we're talking. It's followed by one that's still harder and another. He's thorough, not skimping on time, effort, or force until he reaches a plateau I'm okay with—measured, consistent, nearly hard enough. Good coverage, too, though there's a spot he returns to over and over, hitting forcefully and frequently enough I'm guessing he'll leave a mark. Means to leave a mark. It's not a paddling, which I've got my fingers crossed he's saving for later, but it's satisfying.

He starts to pause between strokes, rubbing me, and I know we're nearing the end. I give Cris a B+ on spanking.

"Nicely handled. I like my pets to be able to take a solid spanking. I'm pleased with you. Now spread your legs."

A thrill runs through me, splitting the warm glow of his praise. I know what he's going to find. He's going to be even more pleased with me. I'm rewarded with a noise low in his throat as he slips two fingers inside me.

"You're a dream come true." I push my hips back to meet him.

"That's right, you've been a good girl. You deserve a reward. Go on, I want to see you come."

I thrust back, his hand a solid backstop, his thigh providing a counterpoint of pressure as I rock. It only takes a couple minutes before I'm panting.

"That's right, give it up. Show me what a good girl you are and come for me."

His words are my undoing, and I come hard around his fingers. I moan wordlessly and continue my motions—erratic, in time with the aftershocks running through me—until I've wrung every last bit out of my orgasm. I'm left breathing heavily, collapsed over his lap with his fingers still inside me. Oh, that was good. For a first time especially? So good.

CHAPTER 7

J'm draped across Cris's lap in a state of pleasant oblivion. His thighs are thick, warm, and muscular under my torso. I'm so very comfortable. Especially when he withdraws his fingers and starts to stroke my stinging ass, occasionally tweaking his favorite spot. I'm going to be bruised. Not your typical souvenir from a Hawaiian getaway, but one I'll enjoy.

"And you like the paddle better?" His tone is light with amusement.

"Yes, sir," I confirm with a modest nod.

"I'm a lucky man." He runs his hand over my cheeks, which are likely a ripe shade of watermelon, and admires the canvas of my body he's colored. He strokes me in silence for a few more minutes as my eyes close and my breath evens out. I might take a catnap.

"I think you'd better let Mr. St. James know you're okay before you fall asleep."

"Yes, sir." He's right. It's been several hours since Matty's left, and I owe him a text. I start to push up, but I'm met with resistance between my shoulder blades.

"You don't need to get up. I'll get your phone if you don't mind me in your room. You can rest. I'm not finished with you, not by a long shot."

That rouses me a bit, but not enough to refuse his offer. "Please, sir. It's on the desk. Thank you."

He lifts my hips to slide out from under my legs, and takes his shirt off, draping it over the arm of the couch. I'd like to take the worn fabric between my fingers and hold onto it until he gets back, but I won't. Instead, I watch him walk away. His back is beautiful, smooth muscles rolling under tanned skin as he heads toward the door. I'll have to remember to have that under my fingertips the next time we kiss instead of putting my hands in his hair. I drowse on the couch while he's gone, daydreaming of all the places I'd like to touch him.

He can't just be getting my phone. He's gone for almost twenty minutes before the door opens. Cris sets a wooden bowl on the ottoman in front of me before going into the bathroom and returning with two glasses of water.

"Sit up."

I tuck my legs up and sit to one side of the couch. He hands me my phone, warm from his pocket, and nudges the ottoman closer. I text Matty:

Sea bass.

And just as quickly as it sends, I delete the record, laying the phone next to the bowl. Cris sits close to me and hands me a glass I sip.

"More?"

"No, thank you, sir."

He takes my glass, sets it down with his, and beckons. "In my lap."

I climb onto him and nestle in, laying my head on his shoulder and a hand on his bare, flat stomach. I wait for him to

67

scold me for touching, but he doesn't, so I rest my hand more heavily.

"I brought you a treat."

"Another one?" My sass is rewarded with a light slap to my behind. I smile, pleased. He doesn't mind a little banter.

"Open your mouth."

I'm greeted by a familiar but somehow strange taste. It's like pineapple but not. It's smoothly sweet, not acidic. Almost like pineapple candy, but the texture is exactly like the fruit. It's delicious.

"Do you like it?"

"Yes, sir. Very much."

"It's white pineapple. You can't get it outside the islands." He offers me another morsel, and I take it, letting my mouth surround his fingers more than necessary. I could eat it all day, unlike the few bites I can tolerate of whatever it is you can get on the mainland. He continues to feed me and I get less subtle with my attentions to his fingers. My efforts aren't going unnoticed or unappreciated, judging by the growing pressure at my hip. I hope he's not uncomfortable, but he doesn't say anything, just scoops the occasional bit into his own mouth until he offers me a piece I don't accept.

"Finished?"

"Yes, sir. Thank you."

He pops it into his mouth and holds out his fingers. I suck off the sweet juice, continuing even after there's no taste of pineapple left.

"I see you're ready for round two."

I suck harder in response, and a low noise issues from his throat. He pushes the ottoman away, puts his feet flat on the floor, and presses my hip. Adjusting to straddle him, I take his hand in mine.

"Don't stop sucking."

Two can multitask, Cris, and I'm a professional. Well, not a *professional* professional, but I could be. I sink into a straddle, my knees tucked up astride his thighs, still laving his fingers.

"You'll get me off, pet. You know how."

Yes, I do. I finish up on his fingers, aiming to leave him wanting, and lick, kiss, and nip my way up his arm. His skin is such a nice color, interrupted by the occasional pale scar. Did he get these the same way he broke his nose? I don't have long to linger. I've reached his neck and make my way to his ear, running my tongue along the edge before sinking my teeth lightly into his lobe.

I get a grunt I can't read, and I'm paralyzed until he says, "You and your kitten tongue. You're so sweet."

His clarification lets me go about my business with confidence. I work my way down his chest and make out that the disc on the leather thong around his neck is a silver St. Michael's medal. St. Michael, patron saint of so many—soldiers, the sick and the dying, grocers of all things. Why does Cris wear it? It was possibly just a gift, his middle name is Michael.

I scold myself for letting my mind wander. I should be concentrating on what I'm doing. I've been the recipient of his full attentions, and he deserves the same. So I savor the taste of his skin on my tongue, the feel of him under my hands, his skin and the generous trail of dark hair that leads down his chest and into his jeans.

I climb down between his knees, making sure to rub my breasts against him as I go. My hands and mouth go to the waistband of his worn jeans, and I undo the button and slide down the zipper. My mouth waters when I realize he doesn't have anything on under them. I tug at his waistband, and he raises his hips. When I've freed him and slipped his jeans completely off, I take a second to survey him. Yes, Cris is a beautiful man.

Every bit of him is well-formed, and I mean every bit. He's large, both long and thick, big enough to make me feel full, genuinely penetrated. The nest of curls that surrounds him echoes the ones on his head, but coarse instead of soft. His legs are well-muscled, with still more scars that show pale against his browned skin and dark hair. He's nice to look at, but I won't take any longer.

Instead, I crawl close and lick cautiously. I'm relieved but not surprised that he tastes clean. He showered while I was settling in. I start my attentions in earnest, licking him from base to tip, finishing with a swirl around the head before taking him into my mouth—not much at first, teasing my way down until I have most of him. I don't have much of a gag reflex, but this is about as much as I can do. I work at him and feel smug when his hands fist desperately in my hair when I start to use my hands, too. Yes, I'm damn good at giving head.

I don't want this over too fast, I want to give him his prover-bial money's worth, show him I like him, but not make him feel like I'm being coy or cruel. It's several minutes before I intensify my efforts, and he responds with a buck of his hips, fucking my mouth. I follow his cues, letting him thrust into me and set the pace that's going to take him to the edge.

"I'm going to come."

He doesn't release my hair but tugs me close to be at the back of my throat. I swallow his release and stroke him with my tongue, finishing him, not letting him go until I'm sure he's done. I stay on my knees and lay my head on his thigh, waiting for my next instructions. He pets me idly for a few minutes before he tugs at my hair. "In my lap."

I climb up, rest against him, and savor his arms coming around me. Sometimes I chafe against being held. It feels too familiar, too intimate, but I like when Cris does it. The man can get away with murder. Kissing, holding—what's next? Making love? *Ugh, Burke, you are losing it.*

"Nicely done, pet. You're a pleasure."

"Thank you, sir."

I'm pleased by his praise. He's not effusive, but sincere. I like that Cris is taking his time. It makes me feel relaxed, cared for, willing. Ethan had been this way, too. And Jorah. Not like Krishna. Talk about insatiable. He'd had me more ways than I could count with barely a breather in between. Not that I'd minded, but sitting down had been challenging for three days after I got back. Cyrus was a different story. Most of them warm me up before getting into the heavy stuff, but not him. He was harsh from the second I'd arrived and not in a way I'd cared for. I'd nearly cried as Matty cuddled me on the plane ride back from Helena.

But the hesitant ones... They're just as bad. Worse, in some ways. It feels like a waste of my time. With a name like Ivan, I'd been expecting better. But he'd never even gotten around to fucking me and my orgasms—the two I'd managed by virtue of the voices in my head rather than what he was actually doing to me—had been underwhelming. Terrible, indeed. No matter how the rest of this goes, Cris has made it into my top ten. If he keeps it up, he'll slide into the top five. And if he's holding back, as I suspect he is, he may medal. We'll see what else the weekend holds.

Cris retrieves a dinner of ratatouille that I devour, the eggplant satisfying the desire for something substantial without the weight of meat. I suspect there will be more play before we go to sleep tonight, and I don't want to gorge myself on this pleasure of the flesh if others await me. When we've sated our appetites for food, Cris leans back against the couch and knits his hands over his stomach. His partially clothed body tempts me even in repose.

I ought to be exhausted. Somewhere deep down, I am. Even light play can be tiring after so much travel and a big time change. It's not just the physical exertion, either. For however much I enjoy my lost weekends, it's not easy to give myself over entirely to someone I've never met before.

It's not so much a trust issue. If something ever happened to me, the perpetrator would either be blackballed from the kink community and/or wind up in the back of a police cruiser before my flight touched down. Rey would make sure of it. He carries an awfully big stick. Some of it's simply the unease that comes from being a guest anywhere. If the Dom is any good, that feeling doesn't last long because my place is rapidly made clear. Cris is incredibly attentive, and any time uncertainty starts to creep in, he's been ready with instructions or assurances to keep it at bay.

"Are you finished?"

"With dinner?"

He smirks at my sass. "Yes, pet, with dinner."

Ah, *pet*. While we were eating, our conversation had drifted into something not exclusively Dom/sub. We're weaving this intricate pattern of threads that need to be tied to keep the tapestry of our game steady, and so far, we haven't let any slip through our fingers. It's the same delighted giddiness you get when you sit down to a chessboard or walk onto the tennis court and realize your opponent is a good match. That spark of interest, anticipation, because this is going to be fun.

"Yes, sir. Thank you."

"Then you'll help me clear, get cleaned up, and meet me back here in twenty minutes."

"Yes, sir."

He pushes off the couch and takes up our plates. I grab our empty glasses and follow him down the walkway to the main house, waiting a few paces away while he puts our dishes in the sink. When we pass by each other, he snags me by the hip, tips up my chin with the knuckle of his forefinger, and stares at me for a few seconds. I want to look away because of how his intense gaze makes me feel, but I can't. Won't.

"I'm looking forward to it."

Like a drop of food coloring in water, the pleasure falls hard in my core and billows out, dissipating through my body until it touches my toes. "Me, too. Sir."

He smiles, sliding a hand into my hair and tugging slightly. "Good."

It hits again. That goddamn desperation for his mouth, for his tongue to part my lips and tangle with mine. A *kiss*. I have got to get a grip. I tighten my fingers around the glasses so I don't drop them, give in to my craving, and claw at him. He releases me, and my knuckles turn white gripping glass while I wait for his footsteps to recede. *I will not turn around, I will not turn around.*

Eighteen minutes later finds me pushing open the door to the studio. When I step inside, Cris is waiting. Wordlessly, he steers me to the center of the room and removes my robe. Like earlier, he examines me with his hands and his gaze. He studies my skin where he applied restraints, looking for marks, but the only ones he'll find are the light bruises on my behind I'm certain he left on purpose.

Still, the fact that he's taking the time to check so thoroughly what effect his ministrations have had on me before he goes any further warms me in a way I've become unfamiliar with outside of when I'm under Rey's care. Cris's level of conscientiousness is unparalleled.

"Are you sore?" He runs a palm over the pale blue break of vessels blooming on one side of my ass.

"A little, sir."

"Too sore?"

"No, sir." That level of marking is child's play. I'd be disappointed if that satisfied him. He squeezes the palmful of flesh, and I inhale as the pressure evokes the earlier spanking. When he steps behind me and begins to knead my cheeks in earnest, focusing on that same damn spot, my lips part and my eyes close.

"You've been an awfully good girl for me, kitten. Perhaps too well-behaved for your own good."

Oh? I like where this is heading.

"I could toy with you, spin you in circles until you screw up, but I get the feeling that could take a while. And why go to all that trouble when all I want to do is put a little color on your ass and then fuck you until you don't know what day it is?"

A small noise of hunger is forced from my throat, and my fingers clench in craving. *Yes.* Screw the reasons, the rationale. Lay your hands on me. Mark my skin before you sink inside me and make me forget everything.

"Would that bother you, pet, if I took a paddle to you just because I felt like it and you're mine to do with as I please?"

He's stepped in close behind me, and the hardness of his erection presses through his jeans against the newly sensitized flesh of my ass. His hands wander to grip my hipbones, and he pulls me back against him hard. The minor impact forces the air from my chest and I'm left breathless, sucking in a lungful of air before I can say, "No, sir."

Hunter used to have at me whenever he felt like it, earned or no. At first, it piqued the part of me that demands fairness, but once I gave in, I enjoyed it and could appreciate the logic. I don't require justification anymore, an excuse to be punished. Punish me for being alive; for being in front of you; for knowing that, at some point, I earned the abuse you're going to ply my flesh with. But most of all, do it because it pleases you to color my skin, to hear my whimpers or cries. Know that when you sink your fingers inside me, my body will confirm I've enjoyed it, too.

Cris grasps my arm above the elbow and steers me to the cross, pressing my abdomen into the wood. The cool surface is a mild shock that dulls as the wood absorbs my body heat, and I quickly sink back into that easy pliancy he inspires as he affixes cuffs to my wrists and ankles. When my arms have been stretched high and the cuffs attached to chains dangling from the frame, I wrap my fingers around the cool metal links, enjoying the heft of them. He urges my feet apart enough that it doesn't feel natural, and I'm immediately conscious of how badly I'd like him inside of me.

When I'm firmly tethered, he stands close, touching me everywhere except where I want him to the most. He finally cradles my breasts and squeezes but quickly withdraws. Though I shouldn't, I tense and wait for the first blow to fall. But all I get is the gentle pressure of his hand on my lower back and a tut.

"Relax, pet. You know better."

I do. Being trained out of that particular impulse had been unpleasant, and it's a mark of how long it's been since I've been with someone this good that I've sunk into such a bad habit. I take a deep breath, let loose, and that's when he hits me, warming me up with a hand spanking. The intensity is automatically higher because of the bruises, and he works up slowly until he's got my behind glowing hot with the impacts.

There's a pause and his hand is at my lower back again, warning me, and then, a second later, there's the welcome feel of what I'd guess is a leather-covered wood paddle. He's not reluctant now. No, he's forced a sound and keeps it up until my ass is throbbing and hot, my whole bottom half swollen with want. He's hit me hard and long enough to have me squirming, genuinely dreading the next strike, without drawing tears. Damn near perfect.

When I think I can't take it anymore, the paddle clatters to the floor, and Cris's hands are cool on my heated behind, fingering the marks he's made.

"The way you color is textbook. I couldn't dream a more perfect shade of red."

It's not as if I can control it, but his compliment pleases me. It's not the kind of praise I get every day. Then he grips my hips and thrusts hard against me, making me mewl. "That's what you've done to me. That's what's going to be inside of you. Would you like that?"

"Yes, sir." *More than anything.*

The sound of clothing being removed and dropped to the floor makes me smile. Soon he's behind me, letting out the chains attached to my wrists and ankles to give them more play. When he's satisfied, he drags my hips back a few paces until the bonds are taut again and angles them to give him access. I think he's going to fuck me and I'm primed for him, but he drops to his knees and suddenly his tongue is lapping hot at the apex of my thighs, toying with and teasing my clit, his fingers digging into my hips.

The sensations drag moans from me, and with each one, he pinches or tweaks one of the marks he's made. I'm seconds from coming when he stops and kisses the base of my spine and those two indentations above the rise of my ass. He trails kisses and nips up my back, then grabs my hips hard and eases into me.

He takes his time, pressing slowly but steadily, and when he's fully seated, I sigh. He fits inside me like I was built to hold him— snug with enough of a stretch to make me feel full, possessed, but not split open or violated.

His forehead drops to my shoulder, and his arm circles my ribcage. It's thick and warm, a band of protection holding me close and tight as his breath drifts hot and fast across my skin. "God, do you feel good."

He pulls out, only to thrust inside me again. I cry out, the raw sound mirroring the violence of the air being forced out of me, but he doesn't stop. *Don't stop.* I close my eyes, focusing on how good he feels inside of me, on being soft and receptive to let him take me over. He reaches a hand around to provide a surface for me to rock my clit against, and soon, I'm ready. So ready my mouth's gone dry from panting.

"Come on, pet. Come for me."

My body's been holding out for his permission, but now it takes advantage, pulsing around him. The sensation urges his own ground-out release, his thrusts becoming uneven as he buries choked sounds of pleasure where he's sunk his teeth into the curve of my neck and shoulder.

His chest heaves against my back until our breathing evens out, and then he withdraws, quickly untethering me from the cross and turning me around to hold me close. I lay my head against his chest, enjoying the solid beat of his heart. I hold up a hand, hesitant, before he says, "Go on, kitten. Touch all you like."

I wrap my arms around him, my forearms on either side of his spine, my hands covering his shoulder blades. His skin is smooth under my greedy fingertips and covered with the barest sheen of sweat.

He lays a cheek on the top of my head and pulls me tight against him, but somehow it's not enough contact. I want to be surrounded by him and his clean smell and the heat that's keeping me warm now that I'm coming down. He squeezes me before letting go, and I can't help the whimper that escapes as he takes a step back. *Please don't go.*

But he takes me up in his arms and carries me to the bed where we lie down together, limbs tangling until I'm nearly close enough. He strokes my hair and my back and tells me sweet things until I feel pieced together instead of blown apart.

He leans back to brush some stray strands from my face and smiles, slow and lazy, a smile I can't help but return. Then he leans in for a kiss, and I melt.

"Not bad, right?"

I laugh and shake my head. "No, sir."

"Think we can do better?" The way his eyebrow kicks up makes me want to bite it, but I purse my lips instead.

"I'd be willing to give it a shot. Sir."

CHAPTER 8

*W*hen I wake, I don't open my eyes right away. I've slept well, and I feel rested. The bed is comfortable, the soft sheets light on my skin. I left the door to the balcony open last night, liking the distant sound of the waves and the smell of the air. It's at once the salty tang of the ocean and the lushness of the surrounding greenery. I allow myself a smile, remembering last night, wondering what's to come today. With a sigh and stretch, I roll onto my side and nuzzle into the pillow.

When I reluctantly raise my lids, it's to see the stormy blue eyes of Cris Ardmore staring back at me from the chair against the wall. I blink once before I remember myself and look down.

"Good morning, pet."

"Good morning, sir."

He sounds amused, although I can't see his face to say for sure.

"Sleep well?"

"Yes, sir. Very well, thank you."

"I could tell." His tone is light, but my eyes widen. *What the fuck time is it?* "It's almost eleven."

Shit.

"I'm so sorry, sir."

"Not to worry. If I'd wanted you earlier, I would've woken you."

He didn't want me? He doesn't like me. I've disappointed him. Tears are rising, but they're easy to stow. I thought last night was pretty great, but apparently I was the only one. Will he want me to leave now? I could change my flight…or maybe I'll stay with Matty and we could go sightseeing. It wouldn't be the first time.

"Look at me," he commands, interrupting my contingency planning.

When I do, he's looking at me sternly.

"I know what you're thinking. Don't. I'm not messing with you, and I'm not angry. I told you to sleep, and you did. As far as I'm concerned, you've done as you were told and that pleases me. If I'd wanted you up at seven, I would've told you so. I don't play games.

"You must've been exhausted. If I'd known how much, I would've put you to bed earlier. I'm glad you've rested, but it's time to get up. You have half an hour to be dressed and ready and in the main house. Wear what you like. You'll make lunch."

"Yes, sir." I feel at once relieved and off-balance. I believe he's not unhappy with me, but his assertion that he doesn't play games is disconcerting. What is this if not a game? Perhaps the philosophical musings are best left for later. For now, it's enough he still wants me.

He ducks his chin, satisfied, and pushes out of the chair. He's wearing a T-shirt that looks like it used to be blue, some worn khaki shorts, and he's barefoot. Pure deliciousness. Except for Hunter, I've never had this much of a visceral attraction to someone so immediately…and look where *that* got me. Heartbroken, disowned by my family, and banished to the other side of the continent. If he's a fraction as dangerous as Hunter, Cris Ardmore could prove hazardous to my health indeed.

I'm waiting for him to go before I move a muscle, but his eyes meet mine and I don't look away. He takes a few deliberate steps toward me and plants his hand on my neck. I hold my breath and stay stock-still, not even blinking.

"Breathe."

I inhale sharply at his command, not breaking eye contact, and he smiles his crooked smile. "Good girl. I'll see you in half an hour."

With a gentle tug at my earlobe that sends desire coursing through me, he leaves. When I'm sure he's gone, I grab my phone and text Matty:

Carp.

Check-in complete, I roll out of bed and head into the en suite. It's nicely done, which I didn't get to appreciate last night, spent as I was. I eye the wooden bathtub covetously, hoping I'll get to make use of it before I go. For now, a shower will do.

It's the most amazing thing I've ever seen in a bathroom, and I've been in some nice bathrooms. But this—this is incredible.

It's enclosed in glass and sits in a corner that juts out into space, affording an unobstructed view of the tropical flora that surrounds the house and somehow managing to feel private despite being entirely exposed. They must've used mitered glass at the far seam. Call me insane, but that is one of my biggest architectural turn-ons. Do other people have those?

I switch on the water and step under the stream, pausing to run my finger over the far seam. *Whose idea was this?*

I shake my head. *Don't ask those questions, India.* Questions lead to answers, and answers lead to intimacy. *You're here for a quick fuck. Don't make it into more than that. You'll only be sorry.*

I pad down the walkway in a camisole and skirt, still barefoot, taking a cue from the man himself. When I come into the main house, Cris is lounging on one of the sofas reading a paperback. And what does Cris Ardmore read, pray tell? He's not close enough for me to see the cover, and I've already been given my instructions so I don't have the opportunity to go look.

In the kitchen, I send a silent thanks to Rey for teaching me how to cook. When I arrived at Princeton, I literally did not know how to boil water. Play the cello, put in a respectable match on the tennis court, pull an appropriate literary quotation from thin air, or speak fluent Mandarin, sure. But cook? My parents had been so busy making sure I was accomplished they'd forgotten to make me competent.

I find several nice pieces of fish and heaps of fresh fruits and vegetables, so I set to making a salad with poached salmon. Even in the unfamiliar kitchen, the accustomed feel of the food and the knives in my hands is relaxing, and in half an hour, I have a respectable meal on the table.

I kneel in front of Cris, note he's reading *Blindness* by José Saramago—one of my favorites—and wait for him to acknowledge me. He only makes me wait a minute.

"Yes, pet?"

"Lunch is ready, sir."

"Let's eat then. You must be hungry. You may look at me while we eat."

"Yes, sir."

He surprises me by taking my hand and waiting for me to stand before tugging me toward the table. Surprises me even more by pulling out a chair and gesturing for me to sit. He slides the chair in as I do. Such manners, still.

"Thank you, sir."

He takes his own seat and begins to eat. He's taken a few bites before he realizes I haven't started and looks faintly alarmed. "You may start."

"Yes, sir."

He raises his eyebrows and shakes his head. "You don't need my permission to eat."

"Yes, sir." I pick up my knife and fork and start to eat less delicately than I'd like, but he's right. I'm starving. I'm aware of him watching me, but I pretend not to be.

"Are you finding your accommodations acceptable?"

"Yes, sir. My room is very nice, thank you."

"What's your favorite part?"

Caught off-guard, I smile. "The mitered glass in the shower."

His crooked grin spreads over his face as he cocks his head. "You noticed that?"

"Yes, sir."

"You can drop the 'sir' while we're eating. I'd like to have a conversation with you."

With his stern tone and severe expression, it's all I can do to bite back the "yes, sir" that's rising in my throat. "Okay."

"Are you an architect?"

The glare he gets in return would blind a lesser man.

"Sorry, I forgot." Consternation has an adorable effect on him, making him look much younger than he is.

I let it sink in for a few seconds. I hate playing the stonewalling game all weekend. For the first time in a long time, I had the urge to answer, so I make a counter-offer. "I noticed you were reading *Blindness*. Are you enjoying it?"

His face relaxes but then he looks suspicious. "I am. Have you read it?"

"I have. More than once. Saramago is a personal favorite."

The corner of his mouth tugs up. "Something personal we're allowed to talk about?"

"Yes." I offer him a smile before making an innocuous observation about Saramago's unique style of prose. I don't want to embarrass him, but he responds readily with a more sophisticated observation of his own. *Two can play at this game.* I up the ante until our conversation wouldn't seem out of place at one of my lit seminars at Princeton. Well, well, Cris Ardmore is more than literate. Another pleasant and dangerous surprise.

It's five o'clock on Sunday, and Cris has returned me to my room to shower and pack. I'm disappointed we won't be showering together. I don't want to waste a minute of our time, but he's being courteous and I appreciate it. I've been left a disreputable-looking mess and had to get cleaned up in the car on the way to the airport more than once. Luckily Matty keeps a spare set of clothes and some baby wipes handy.

It occurs to me as I'm soaping up and gazing dreamily at the mitered seam that Cris never showed me the best part of the house. Or maybe he did and didn't identify it as such? The porch where we had dinner last night is awfully nice. That could've been it.

I feel sated and well-used. This has been an excellent use of my time. I'll be good to go for the office early tomorrow morning, hopefully starting with a call from Constance. That'll be an easy hour on the phone and a nice way to slip back into real life.

I'm sad to leave this beautiful bathroom. I don't like to speculate about whether or not I'll see a man again, but this time I can't help myself. I'd like to see Cris again, and I got the distinct impression he'd like to see me again, too. I search my mental calendar for when that might be possible, and I'm annoyed it won't be for two months. Maybe if I…

No, India, don't. Just don't.

I slip back into the dress and sandals I wore for the drive here and take one last turn to make sure I haven't forgotten anything. I'm finished with fifteen minutes to spare, so I pick up my bag and head to the main house. Cris is sitting on one of the couches with a book, and I set my bag by the front door before kneeling in front of him. He's moved on to *All the Names*, and I fight to keep a smile off my face. Maybe next time we'll get to have another book discussion.

Next time? Oh, stop.

"Are you ready to go home, pet?"

I hesitate the barest bit. "Yes, sir."

I'm not ready to go home. To be honest, I'd like to stay. Indefinitely. What the fuck has come over me? Surgical strikes are my style, not getting mired in land wars. Get in, get your kink on to clear your head, and get the hell out.

"Would you mind if we called this a little early?"

What? Does he have something *better* to do? How rude. Maybe I don't want to see this guy again after all. But like a good little sub, I won't be contrary. "No, sir."

He gets up from the couch and offers me a hand. I hope Matty's already waiting outside. How humiliating would it be to have to sit on his steps or stand in the drive waiting for my ride to pull up? I'd be like the kid whose parents forgot to pick her up from daycare. But instead of showing me to the front door, he tugs me toward the other side of the room and opens a door that leads to a set of steps.

"I wanted to show you something. We didn't get the chance after lunch on Friday."

Whoa. I have to slam on the brakes and put myself in reverse. He's done this on purpose—ending our contract. He didn't want to show this to his pet, his submissive. He wanted to show it to Kit Bailey-Isles, the girl who discusses sex toys over raw fish soup.

"A second date so soon?"

"What can I say? I don't play hard to get." He smirks and leads me down the steps, keeping ahold of my hand. How cute.

When we get to the bottom, there's a path that leads off into the jungle and I wonder where he's taking me. I don't have to wonder long because the trees and vines and greenery thin, the soil under my feet turns sandy, and I see the ocean. My face splits into a delighted grin. I knew we weren't far from the water—you rarely are in Hawaii—but I had no idea.

We're in a tiny cove of mostly rocks, but with a narrow strip of sand that leads to the water. There are two yellow kayaks tied up on the beach, and a giant white hammock held up by two trees. It couldn't be more picture perfect.

"This is yours?"

"Yeah. Couldn't build the house down here because the ground's not stable enough, but it's not far."

"It's beautiful, Cris. Thank you for bringing me."

"My pleasure."

We stand there for a while, not saying anything, only looking out at the waves and the sky, clasping hands.

The spell is broken when Cris checks his watch. "I'd better get you back. I doubt Mr. St. James takes kindly to you being late."

I laugh. It's true. Matty has overcome his island heritage and is extremely punctual. Almost Scandinavian-ly so. Not to mention, he starts to worry if I'm not on time returning from my little adventures. With reluctance, I let Cris tow me back to the house. He puts my bag over his shoulder and, curiously, picks up a wooden box from the kitchen counter before he shows me out to the drive where Matty is waiting.

Matty holds out a hand for my bag. Cris passes it off and then turns back to me, looking uncertain.

"Could we have a minute, Mr. St. James?"

This is not standard operating procedure, and I silently beg Matty to be cool. But I needn't have worried—Matty's a professional. He ducks a nod, a smile only I notice on his face as he climbs into the 4x4.

"Would it be weird for me to say thank you for this weekend?"

One of Cris's eyes squints. He doesn't want to offend me. So freaking cute.

"Do you mean would it make me feel like a hooker? Only if you tried to give me a tip."

I've made Cris laugh again. I'll enjoy that feeling in my belly on my flight back.

"Well, then, thank you. That was better than I could've hoped for."

Damn right it was, Mr. Ardmore. "Likewise."

"Can I see you again?"

"Call Mr. Walter."

He looks disappointed. I hope he's not discouraged. He takes a step toward me and holds out the wooden box.

"This is for you. I hope you have a safe trip back to wherever you're headed."

I take it. A present? That's a first. "Thank you."

Is this it? I think he might turn and go back to his house, but instead, he grips my hair at the nape of my neck and kisses my cheek. For some reason I can't explain, I blush. I don't remember the last time I blushed. India "Ceviche" Burke does not blush. But here I am, the color of a ripe summer rose.

He doesn't seem to think it's odd as he leads me to the car and hands me up. "Goodbye, Kit."

"Bye, Cris."

Then my door is closed and he's walking away. I have to busy myself tugging at my seatbelt to not fling myself after him. I keep it together long enough for Matty to start the Jeep and roll off down the path, back toward where I came from a little over two days ago. I'm feeling flustered, and Matty can tell. He doesn't launch into his usual interrogation right away. Only after a few minutes does he try to pry some information out of me.

"What'd he give you?"

Oh, right, my little wood box. It's sitting, unopened, in my lap. I lift the lid, and my mouth drops open. It's a bento box filled with a few rice balls, a piece of veggie frittata, edamame, sliced mango, and a pair of chopsticks.

"Dinner. He made me dinner, Matty."

"Oh, you're in trouble, girl."

"You have no idea."

CHAPTER 9

"*I*'m concerned about these vacancy numbers, India."

Shit. Yes, I know the vacancy numbers are an issue, but instead of losing my cool, I take another sip of my coffee. "I know. We're working on it. Jack's been riding Janis, but she's being more dimwitted than usual and keeps making excuses. They've gotten rent collections up and they're nearly caught up on filings, so some of the fires are being put out."

"That's all well and good, but if these vacancies aren't down by next quarter's report, we're going to need to have a serious talk. All of us."

"I'll lease them up myself. What would make you happy?"

"Nothing less than ninety-three percent occupancy, but I'd kiss you if you could get me ninety-six."

"Ninety-seven it is. Hope you warned Glory, I'll be coming to collect."

She laughs, and we wrap up with a few small changes she'd like made. I promise to have the revised report to her by the end of the day. Not a bad start to my first day back. Next stop, Jack's office.

I knock on his glass door but don't wait for a response before coming in. "Would you mind if I went up to LA on Friday? We need to put the fear of god in Janis about these vacancy numbers because fear of Cooper doesn't seem to be cutting it."

"Go." He doesn't look up from his desktop. "But you better get your bitch face back on because that dreamy look you've had on all morning isn't going to cut it."

"Don't worry, Jack. I'm sure four days of the vitriol that spews out of your ugly maw will wipe it right off."

Note to self: stop thinking about Cris. Apparently even Jack has noticed, and I doubt Jack would notice if I shaved my head.

"You'll only have two. I'm going to Chicago on Wednesday."

"Client?"

"Possibly."

Fuck. I can't go to Chicago.

"Two should be plenty. If we get Chicago, give it to Leo. His kids are there."

Jack loosens his tie in response. That's never good. I should get out of here before the shit hits the fan. When I get back to my desk, I check my personal cell for the ten thousandth time since leaving Cris's house and find a text from Rey:

Call me.

Even though my stomach has dissolved into butterflies and I want nothing more than to call this second, I don't. Instead, I use it as motivation to slog through some numbers for Provo. A few hours later, I dial my reward.

"You must have been a very good girl."

"He called?"

"Yes. Last night. He'd like to see you again. As soon as possible."

It's all I can do to keep from squealing.

"Oh."

"That's cute, India. Really." Rey chuckles, and I picture his eyes rolling from five hundred miles down the California coast. "I'll see you tonight."

~

I happily bust my ass for the rest of the day, writing up a grant for Alameda County and sending the revised report to Cooper. I drop copies of everything on Jack's desk and hustle out to my car, cranking up my stereo for the drive to the restaurant where I'm meeting Rey. It's some swank Asian fusion place where it's impossible to get a table, but when I pull up and Rey takes my hand, we're shown right to the best seats in the place.

"Do you still want to kiss me?"

"I'd do more than that if I thought you'd enjoy it."

Rey chuckles. "Matty did say you had a good time."

"I really did."

"The talking?"

"Not so bad."

"And the rest?"

I swoon in my chair, and Rey laughs.

"I see. The feeling appears to be mutual. He must've called right after you left."

More butterflies. Why the fuck have I turned into a giggly adolescent? I want to roll my eyes, but I'm too damn pleased. It wouldn't be the first time someone called Rey as soon as I walked out the door, but it's the first time I'm as eager.

"When do you have time?"

"Not until July."

"Oh, kitten."

"I know. This sucks. I asked for passable. Why'd you have to find me perfection when I don't have any time to enjoy it?"

The thought of Cris giving up on me makes me queasy. I know I was so eager to be the rebound fuck, but the idea of Cris with someone else makes me feel... Is this jealousy? Is that what this is? The fury and pukey feeling and possessiveness that come over me when I think of his hands on someone else?

"Do you think he'll wait?"

"From the phone call I got last night? Yeah, he'll wait."

Relief extinguishes some, but not all, of the annoying and unfamiliar feeling. I down the remainder of my mojito to try to get rid of the rest.

I pull up my email and start sifting through my leftovers from yesterday. Jack's got a twenty-four hour rule on emails, and more than one associate's been fired for breaking it. I bang out a dozen replies, setting up meetings and conference calls and answering easy regulatory questions, and mark off a couple others to dig into when I've gotten through the rest. I dash off quick responses to let them know I'm working on it and I'll have an answer by the end of the day. Before I get the chance to start my research, there's a knock and a flustered-looking Jack—no tie, no jacket, and crazy hair—storms in.

"What are you doing for the next week?"

"I get the feeling you're going to tell me."

"You're going to Denver. Fucking Leo had a heart attack."

"Is he okay?" Leo's not my favorite, but I don't want him dead.

"Yeah, yeah, he's going to be fine, but he's not getting on a plane anytime soon." Jack paces in front of my desk and gesticulates like a raving lunatic.

"Jesus, Jack. How about you lead with that next time? You're going to give *me* a heart attack, and then where would you be?"

"Please, India, don't be ridiculous. You haven't got a heart. But you *have* got a nice rack. I like this get-up. Sexy."

"Just what I was going for." I shake my head with boredom. *Let's get this show on the road.* "So, Denver?"

"File review. You're taking Patterson, Rodriguez, Evans, and Chow."

Shit. Evans makes me want to staple my hand to the desk.

"Do I have to take Evans? You know he has a crush on me. It's pathetic."

Evans, like my trainer Adam, is a purebred puppy dog. Not a golden retriever, though—not that All-American and good-looking. Maybe some sort of spaniel? The round, adoring, melty chocolate eyes fit. *Sit, stay, stop drooling. Good Evans.*

"I'm not paying to change another plane ticket. You're taking him. I'm sure your charm in close quarters will extinguish any torch he might be carrying for you. Just don't wear that."

I heave a sigh. If Evans ever got me naked, he wouldn't know what to do with me. Fucking Boy Scout. No, not even a Boy Scout. Scouts are handy with knots.

"Fine."

"You, minion, are too saucy. You get this done, and you can have next Friday off. Does that make up for the puppy dog eyes you'll have to endure for the next seven days? Have him fetch your coffee. It won't be so bad."

Next Friday off? Two weeks is *far* better than two months. If Cris is even free. I need to call Rey, stat.

"Actual Shakespeare, Jack? Color me impressed. He'd have to get down on his knees and lick my Louboutins to make it worth my while, but next Friday off is a good start."

My retort gets me a shake of Jack's head but a short laugh to go along with it. *Rest of the office, you should* all *get down on your knees and kiss my shoes for digging Jack out of what could've been a days-long funk. A screaming, throwing-stuff, firing-people-left-and-right funk. But you'd do it badly, and that's insulting.*

Denver, huh? I can do Denver.

∿

Rey messengers me Cris's new contract while I'm at my hotel in Denver. Cris had been quick to say he's free, and I'm excited to have proof that I'll get to see him again—and so soon. It's a welcome distraction from the numbers and codes swimming in my head. I fucking hate file reviews. And Jack was wrong. Close contact with Evans doesn't seem to have doused any fire he thinks he's got burning in his loins for me; on the contrary, he's gotten worse. Now he makes me want to stick a letter opener through my eye.

I give the contract a cursory glance—I'd be surprised if anything much had changed—but when I come to the end, I frown. *Nothing* has changed. Well, the dates, but that's it. Not even the weird talking clause at the end. *What the fuck?* Cris doesn't strike me as lazy. I'm insulted he's not even bothered to review the damn thing before sending it back. I fill the tub and climb in before I punch Rey's number into my cell.

"Hey there, Rocky Mountain Highness."

"What the hell? He didn't even look at it, just sent it back."

"Not true."

"The only thing that's different are the dates."

"Yes."

Goddammit, Rey, you're annoying. I'm sure he can feel my glower from across the Rockies.

"I'm insulted, India. Did you think I wouldn't have looked at this before I sent it to you?"

"No." Rey's very thorough.

"I thought it was…unusual, so I called him. He'd like to speak with you."

"Again?"

"Apparently."

Oh, I'd like to wipe that smug look off of Rey's face. "Why?"

"Maybe he liked you."

Crap. I don't want Cris to like *me*. I want him to like Kit Bailey-Isles, submissive edition. Contracts, fake names, and the ten-foot-high barbed wire fence of anonymity Rey erects around me—that is how I roll. I don't do relationships. The damage Hunter did still smarts, and I'm not stupid enough to let that happen again.

"Did you not like him?" Rey prods.

I scowl. I did like him. Too much. And because Rey has some sort of trainer telepathy, he knows.

"I see," he says. "I suppose you could call it—"

"No!"

"That's what I thought. Matthew will see you there. Be good, be careful."

CHAPTER 10

"*K*it," he greets me, opening my door and offering me not only help down from the annoyingly high Jeep, but also a deliciously crooked smile.

"Cris."

He's even more attractive than I remembered—and that was pretty damn attractive. As my skin meets his, a thrill slips through me. He offers Matty a cursory nod and steers me to the main house with a hand at the small of my back.

"I hope you had a good trip." His voice is casual, but strained. He's nervous, too.

"I did, thank you."

Again the long flight was welcome, giving me a chance to sleep uninterrupted. Unlike when I was in Denver, with visions of Evans' hangdog face haunting me at night.

"It's a pleasant surprise, seeing you again so soon. When Mr. Walter told me July, I thought it was a nice way to give me the brush off—" I'm about to protest, but he cuts me off with a smug smile. "—but I was assured that wasn't true."

Goddammit, Rey, what did you say?

"It's just that I'm very important and extremely busy." My attempt at self-deprecation is a major fail. It's not my strong suit.

"I don't doubt it."

He shows me into the house, and it's exactly as I remembered it, including the big dining table set for two. I wonder if it's ever full. He pulls out my chair, and I sit while he heads into the kitchen, returning with plates filled with seafood paella.

I don't waste time, spearing a shrimp on my fork. So good. We eat a few bites in silence before I tease, "So, Mr. Ardmore, you wanted to speak with me?"

"I did."

"And why this time? I know it's not because you think you'll be stealing my virtue."

He snorts. Whatever he thought might be left of my virtue when I arrived last time, he took care of it.

"No. I just… I liked talking to you."

My heart thumps, and I have to work up the nerve to open my mouth. "I liked talking to you, too."

He regards me curiously. "Do you not usually speak with them?"

"No one's ever asked."

"I'd say that's a shame, but I'm glad."

"Why?" Why does Cris give a crap about whether other guys have wanted to talk to me?

"You wouldn't have gotten to me if any of them had bothered to get to know you. They'd never have let you go."

There's an explosion of warmth in my chest. Is this what it's like to have a man say he *likes* you? Not just wants to fuck you? Or that you've done good work? That he likes *you* and not the pretty little submissive you shape yourself into to have some fun or the frigid bitch you affect to get shit done? It's delicious and terrifying at the same time. I'm so flustered I can't even make a joke.

I reach for something, anything, to say before I start to blush. "How did you break your nose?"

He's surprised by the non sequitur but unlike me isn't so nonplussed he can't cover it. "Is that fair, Kit? You get to ask me personal questions, but I don't get to ask you?"

He's poking fun, a half-smile lighting up his face, but fairness is a big thing for me.

"You're right." I look down at my rapidly emptying plate. "It's not fair. I apologize."

"Hey." He uses his stern voice, and I'm feeling more like Kit than India. This is not going well. What was I thinking? How long did I think I was going to be able to pull this off? He waits for my eyes to meet his, and his face has softened. "I was teasing, Kit."

"I know."

"You've already got more dirt on me than the CIA."

"I don't."

"What do you mean? I think the only information Mr. Walter didn't ask for was my shoe size."

"And Mr. Walter's the only one who knows most of that information. Him and Mr. St. James."

His brows crease, trying to put together the scattered pieces of the Kit Bailey-Isles jigsaw puzzle. "All the more reason for us to have a conversation. You know, there's an easy way to make this fair."

"What did you have in mind?" I ask, finding my feet. I'm perfectly willing to trade sexual favors for information.

"You can ask me a question, and I get to ask you one."

That is not what I had in mind. "No."

"Two for one?"

"Two for one, and I have veto power. You don't."

"You drive a hard bargain, Ms. Isles. Are you an attorney?"

"Answer two questions and you might find out."

"Shake on it?"

I look into his slate-blue eyes. Can I do this? But he's warm and earnest, and he's ceded so much control. For people like him, that's no small thing. I put my hand in his and shake.

"You have yourself a deal, Mr. Ardmore."

He holds on too long, and it makes something pool in my belly. *A handshake? Really, India? Are you going to start going weak in the knees when you meet a client? Swoon when you seal a deal at work? For fuck's sake.* Although, when he lets go, I'm disappointed. I liked his skin on my skin.

"What would you like to know, Kit?"

This power is heady. I can ask Cris anything I'd like. How many lovers he's had, his worst fear, how much money he makes… But I don't want to abuse what he's handed me, so I reiterate, "How'd you break your nose?"

"Which time?"

Ah. I thought it'd been more than once. "Will that count as more than one question?"

"No. It's all the same, anyway. I've broken it three times, surfing. Once on a reef, once on some rocks, once on my board."

"And you still surf?" It's out of my mouth before I can help it, but he offers me an out.

"Are you sure that's how you want to use your second question?"

"Sure."

"Then, yes, I still surf. Nearly every day."

That's how he got that body. That tan. The pale scars that dot his skin. Surfing. I picture Cris on a board amongst the waves. It fits. As does the St. Michael's medal—protection against dangers at sea.

"Your St. Michael's medal isn't really doing the trick, is it?"

He blinks and fingers the disc at his throat, a compulsion. "My mom gave me this the first time I had a serious wipeout. I think it's done a yeoman's job, considering. I'm still here, only a little worse for wear. Other people haven't been so lucky."

Cris has had friends die out there, and he still goes. Does that make him dedicated to something he loves, something he couldn't live without? Or insane? I don't have time to consider because he's turning the tables.

"That's more than two. I believe it's my turn."

"It is." Nervousness claws at my stomach. But why? I've got veto power. He could ask me if I liked the paella, and I could answer no comment, although I wouldn't. It's delicious, and I'll tell him so before I turn into a pumpkin.

"So are you an attorney?"

"I have a law degree, and I've passed the bar."

He laughs, and my insides melt. "Spoken like a true lawyer."

I narrow my eyes, trying to contain my threatening grin. "I suppose so, yes."

"See, that wasn't so bad."

"No, it wasn't."

We continue our chatter over lunch, and I learn that Cris has been surfing since he was eight—competitively until he left for college—and his father taught him how to cook. I'm about to ask what his favorite dish to make is when Cris checks his watch and says it's one thirty. Oops.

Once we've completed the requisite paperwork and Matty's told me to text with major US cities, I entrust myself once again to Cris's capable hands and the games begin.

Cris is a creature of habit, though in a way that's soothing, not dull. He bathes me, and by the time he's restraining me on the table, I'm putty in his hands. After he warms me up—teasing me with bites and kisses, suckling at one breast while rolling the other nipple between talented fingers, dipping his fingers inside of me and finding me wet and wanting—he produces a riding crop.

"You've played with one of these before, pet?" He trails the keeper up my instep and over the inside of my calf to my thigh. At the gentle touch, my muscles clench from my knees all the way to my groin.

"Yes, sir."

"Did you like it?" He draws the tip farther up to my hipbone and traces a languid circle around it.

"If they wanted me to, sir." I've been both punished and rewarded with one of these devilish tools, and I wonder which Cris has in mind. I haven't misbehaved yet as far as I know, but I'm more conscious than ever of my helpless, exposed state. In addition to my arms being bound above my head, my legs are also restrained. Each ankle is bound to each thigh by cuffs and a length of chain, and my legs are spread, knees resting on rolled towels and held in place with leather straps tethering them to the outsides of the table. The bondage alone has me squirming.

"I want you to."

He drags the keeper across my pelvis to my other hipbone. The feeling it creates in my core makes me buck my hips and mewl.

"That's right, no need to be shy."

He continues his tour, looping around my navel and heading toward my breasts. He traces under them and around, making ever smaller figure eights until he's just shy of my areolas. The crop leaves my skin to return with a sharp bite to my nipple. I groan, and another blow lands in quick succession, this time to the other nipple. He's got good aim, and he's hitting me hard enough that it's at the border of pleasure and pain. The sensations are sending pulses south.

"Do you like this?"

"Yes, sir." I'm panting, and if he kept this up for long enough, I could come.

"Then let me hear you." He lands another blow, and this time I don't hold back, letting out a moan. "That's better."

His words are fanning my desire, and I'm shamelessly letting encouraging noises emanate all the way up from my core.

"Could you come from this?"

"Yes, sir."

"But you won't. Not without permission."

"No, sir."

It's getting harder to keep my word, my abdominals aching with the effort of trying to thrust my hips, restrained as I am. The blows stop, and I cry out in protest until the crop lands between my legs. The bite is pleasant and sharp against the most sensitive part of me. This, I won't be able to tolerate for long. I've closed my eyes tight with effort, and I'm straining at my bonds.

"Go ahead. Let me see what I do to you."

A few more licks land before my orgasm overtakes me, and my body tenses before it careens out of control. I'm gasping in time with the waves of release, glad to be tied down. I can't make any promises about what my body might do if I weren't. The blows have stopped, and he's holding my hipbones, providing another point of resistance for my unruly body to rage against. When my climax has burnt itself out, he strokes his thumbs across my belly. I open my eyes, and he runs his hands up my stomach, over my still-heaving chest, to cradle my head.

"Enjoy yourself?"

"Yes, sir."

"Good. Now I'd like to enjoy you."

Cris passes a thumb across my cheek, presses a kiss to the other, and then untethers me bond by bond and brings my knees together. He slides my feet off the table, leaving the backs of my knees resting against the edge. My wrists are released as well, although he doesn't take off the cuffs. He sweeps my hands to my sides and slides his hands under my back and my skull.

Of all the things Cris does to me, this is my favorite. It fills some deep need in me to feel cared for, but it's esoteric enough I don't worry he knows it. I barely help as he sits me up, meeting me eye to eye, chest to chest at the end of the table. I blink at him and raise my chin, asking, begging to be kissed, and he obliges, telling me it's okay to touch before he does.

I take full advantage of the permission I've been granted, pressing into him, sliding my hands under his open shirt, gripping the muscles of his back underneath my fingers. He returns my ardor, his hand in my hair tightening into a fist, tugging, and his hand on my back pressing me still closer. Kissing. Who would've thought?

He breaks our connection by pulling hard on a fistful of my hair, and I want to protest. But when he says, "Legs around my waist," I don't mind anymore. I hook my ankles at the base of his spine, and he releases my hair to grip my hips and slides me off the table until he's bearing my full weight. Draping my arms over his shoulders, I run my teeth over his stubbled jaw and nip at his ear before kissing my way down his neck.

He presses my back against the cross, pinning me with his hips. "Arms up."

I lean back against the wood, raising my arms to be tethered. He hooks the clasps, well-practiced, before his hands are at my neck.

"Jesus, Kit, are you ever divine."

India, I want to say, *my name is India*. What I wouldn't give for him to tell me he finds me heavenly. But that's not something I'm allowed to have—a luxury I can't afford, a gamble I'm not willing to make. I trusted someone with my heart, my secrets, my life once. I won't do it again, no matter how tempting Cris makes the prospect. I stifle the words rising in my throat with a moan before his mouth is once again on mine.

The rest of the weekend passes in a haze of pleasure. In some ways, our bodies are still getting acquainted, but in others, I feel like we're merely becoming reacquainted. I don't go in for past life stuff, but Cris's understanding of what's going to set me on fire is so intuitive I have my doubts.

This isn't normal.

On Sunday, he calls things an hour early. I'm not distraught. I know what's coming: a walk down to the cove, lazing in the hammock and wading into the warm water hand in hand. At precisely six o'clock, he sends me off with Matty, again with dinner, back to the chaos of my real life.

CHAPTER 11

The next time I get Cris's contract, I'm in Provo. When I review it, I'm more entertained than annoyed that the damn conversational clause is still there. If he wants to keep trading decadent lunches and personal information for the one-word answers I'm inclined to give, fine by me.

Instead of flying directly home when I wrap things up, I change my flights to make a stop in San Francisco, feeling the need for a tune-up from my pit crew.

Rey picks me up in the Maserati he's driving these days. I'm not sure he appreciates what a fine car it is. What he does enjoy is everyone else's attention, and we attract quite a bit of it. As we settle into the high-backed banquette in a prime corner of the nouveau French place he's brought me to, he gives me the eye.

I glare at him until our champagne cocktails arrive. "What's your damage, Walter?"

"Nothing, bluebird."

He's perusing the menu as if he hasn't already ordered our food, as if our first course won't arrive at any minute. Rey doesn't leave these kinds of thing to chance. Or to me. He knows better. I draw the tip of my finger around the rim of the flute and narrow my gaze until he looks up with a faint smile.

"I was expecting an angry phone call yesterday, that's all."

Right.

"I decided it wasn't worth getting worked up about. What the hell do I care if he wants to have a little chitchat before we fuck?"

"Chitchat?" Rey'd better knock off that smugly amused look before I knock it off for him.

I scowl as I take a deep sip. "What—you missed the India Burke shitshow?"

"No, there's plenty where that came from."

"Then what?"

Rey picks up the slim, silver dinner fork from the place setting in front of him and twirls it in his lithe fingers, back and forth like a baton. After a minute of this hypnotic party trick, his eyes meet mine.

"You should know he had a question about your stipulations for the contract."

That's not surprising. They usually do. I have some very specific requirements. The only thing that's strange is that it's taken this long for him to ask. "What about?"

The corners of Rey's mouth tug down ever-so-slightly. This is going to be bad. "He wanted to know how firm your line was on sharps."

My response is automatic. "I don't do sharps."

"I know, little one," he placates, "that's what I told him."

"If that's going to be a problem…" *Then we're going to have a problem.*

Rey's gaze skates over my alarm-widened eyes, my fingers tightened around the stem of my cocktail, my chest rising and falling too rapidly. I don't do sharps. It's non-negotiable. That's why it's under hard limits.

"It's not." Rey's easy response lets my shoulders drop a couple inches. He must've given Cris the third degree when he asked, maybe threatened him. Rey's not a pushover. If anything, he's harder to please than I am. That's why I trusted him to negotiate my first contract with Hunter and every contract I've had since. If Cris's answers satisfied him, they'd appease me, too.

"Then why are you telling me this?" As long as Rey has full knowledge, ignorance is truly my bliss.

"I didn't want you to be blindsided if he asked you about it during one of your little tête-à-têtes, that's all."

A waiter comes by and places bowls in front of us.

"Vichyssoise?" Of course it is. It's one of my favorites.

"Eat up, kitten."

I dip my spoon into the bowl, the thick potato base coating the spoon, and curse the damn talking. If this were anyone else, I wouldn't know. Rey would've either told the guy it was a no-go and to stick it somewhere else or decided it wasn't going to be an issue and sent me on my merry way. Now I need trigger warnings for my lost weekends? For fuck's sake.

I'm halfway through my plate of chicken marsala when Cris asks. Frankly, it's a relief. I've been anticipating this moment since Rey mentioned it over dinner last week. I'd been trying to decide what to do about it since then, and I still haven't made up my mind.

Cris has just finished telling me if he could go anywhere in the world, it would be County Donegal.

"Ireland?"

"Where'd you think I was going to say?"

"Maybe the Gold Coast or Jeffrey's Bay."

His face contorts in confusion before it breaks into a grin. "Been doing your homework, have you?"

My mouth drops open before I can clamp it shut. No, I have not been doing research on surfing. Because that's what I need to do with my time. More research. It was honest curiosity. I mean, there must be something about it if Cris is so into it, right? And I'll admit that there's something appealing about the artistry of it. Not to mention I'd liked picturing Cris shirtless and wet, crouched on a board, riding a curling wave. I'd thought to keep my little endeavor to myself, but now he knows. As if he needed a bigger head.

"Wait," he says before I can splutter an answer. "That's not my question. I take it back."

Slick save, but I get the feeling that was more for my benefit than for his. At least I don't have to give verbal confirmation of my mortifying extracurricular activities.

"But you're on the right track. Bundoran Beach, a few hours outside of Dublin. I've surfed all over the Pacific, but never in the Atlantic. It's a different ballgame. I guess it wouldn't hurt to get some culture while I was there, either. Never been to Europe."

I was right about the surf destination. Smugness curls in my belly. *I know you, Cris Ardmore.* The weight of satisfaction is abruptly seesawed by the way he lays a broad hand on the table, blunt fingers resting on the wood surface.

"My turn."

"Yes."

Please ask me about my preferred vacation destinations. Or, perhaps, don't. I traveled extensively through law school and up until my last year of grad school, but I haven't left the country for years. I even let my passport expire. What do I need it for? I spend any vacation time I get on this side of the divide, and I don't particularly relish telling him about my other assignations. If Cris has spent his life searching for the perfect wave, I've spent mine looking for the ideal fuck.

He takes a breath, deeper than normal, that screams, *Should I or shouldn't I?* His index finger taps the table a couple times before he's resolved.

"What's the deal with you and sharps?"

"I don't do sharps." It's my kneejerk response, and I can't stop it. Not even to replace it with a veto. I hear the word—*sharps*—and it barrels out of my mouth. Knives, needles, razors—not even that Happy Meal toy of kinksters, the Wartenberg wheel. And especially not scissors. No sharps. Ever. What do I need to do, silkscreen it on a T-shirt? I'd tattoo it on my ass, but you know… No. Fucking. Sharps.

"That's been made crystal clear. If your contract didn't spell it out in black-and-white, which it does, Mr. Walter read me the riot act the last time we talked. I know it's off-limits. It'll stay that way, I promise."

"So why are you asking?"

"Call it curiosity."

"Curiosity killed the cat." And if the scars dotting his body are any indication, I'd bet Cris doesn't have many lives to spare.

"It also got a wet dream of a woman delivered to my doorstep, so curiosity and I are on good terms at the moment. I'm still not sure you're real."

Flattery. I try to smother that increasingly familiar bloom of pleasure and weigh my options. If I veto, he'll drop it, back off and ask me something innocuous. It's what he does when he knows he's pressed too hard. An apology I'll accept. Cris isn't stupid. He's probably put two and two together, and showing him how that adds up to six isn't going to make a difference.

"You really want to know?"

"I do."

"It's not a pretty story."

"They usually aren't."

I could actually tell him some *very* pretty stories—stories that would cause his eyes to go big as saucers and make him harder than he thought humanly possible. But this one…

"Do you have any brothers or sisters?"

There's a soft shake of his head, and I expect him to give me shit for asking another question when it's my turn to answer but he doesn't. "No, I'm an only child."

I'd thought so. There are a couple of framed pictures around the main house of people who must be Cris's parents, and a few of the three of them. Still, you never know who or what's been cropped out of photographs.

"I have a sister. An older sister."

I'm sure he's perplexed as to why I'm telling him this, but he doesn't let it show. Only sits there, leaning back in his chair.

"She's never been very fond of me."

His gaze is implacable, waiting patiently for me to continue, and though I'm not thrilled, I dig in.

"When we were kids, she used to tell me all kinds of things siblings tell each other: I was adopted, she was our parents' favorite, I was an accident, they tried to give me away but no one wanted me... You know, the usual."

His brows knit and his mouth tightens as if he might argue, but how would he know?

"She also used to tell me I was a witch. Because of my eyes. Of course, I always told her I was not, in fact, a witch, but as big sisters do, she wouldn't let it go. Whenever she wanted to make me upset, she'd tease me about it. When I was six, and she was... old enough to know better, she decided to conduct her own personal witch trial and told me if I didn't pass, our parents would send me away to live with the other witches."

I feel ridiculous telling him this, but he asked for it. I didn't use my get-out-of-jail free card, didn't tell him to pass go and collect two hundred dollars, so this is how it's going to be. At least he doesn't appear to think this is funny.

"She'd done some research." A ghost of a smile lights his face. Yes, the Burkes are a whole freaking family of people obsessed with information. You'd think we would've ended up librarians. Or CIA. Maybe my sister has. I wouldn't know. "My sister had always been a straight-A student. She found some methods to determine if I was a witch, along with devising some of her own. Most of it was unpleasant but not such a big deal, and since I was the world's most stubborn kindergartner, I passed."

Yes, I had. Much to Ivy's dismay. She hadn't been expecting that. She'd probably thought telling me what she was going to do would scare me enough to "confess." I suspect that's what most children would do when faced with being pricked repeatedly with a needle, being held under water, and being buried under a pile of books.

"You noticed the scar on my back." It's not a question. I know he has. A chill passes through me as I remember how he traced it the first time we were together. An accidental brush or a palm laid flat against the mark doesn't bother me, but purposeful contact with the ruined skin presses my freak-out buttons.

"I did."

Of course he did. Most Dominants I've met have an eye for detail. If they're any good, at any rate, and Cris is very good. Not to mention a two-inch-long, jagged, cross-shaped scar on my lower left back isn't exactly subtle. It's not the brilliant red it used to be, but it stands out on my otherwise unblemished skin.

"She showed me a pair of kitchen scissors and told me if I really wasn't a witch, when she cut me, Jesus would protect me and it wouldn't hurt."

I'm laughing like I always do when I tell this story, but it's not funny. This is the part where my audience usually goes pale because they know what's coming, and Cris is no exception. The tanned skin of his face is left bloodless, and his fingers curl into a fist next to his half-full plate—which I can pretty much guarantee is going to stay that way.

"She held me down and cut me. Of course, I screamed because it hurt. And even though I told her to stop, that I'd go live with the witches to make it stop, she didn't. When she was satisfied, she let me go. She told me as long as I didn't tell our parents and did everything she said, she wouldn't tell them I was a witch and I could stay.

"Obviously, she was terrified of getting in trouble, but I didn't know that. I really, *really* did not want to go live with the witches, so even when it started to hurt pretty badly, I didn't tell anyone. It was only when I came home from school with a fever a few days later that anyone noticed something was wrong. By then, I was septic. I was in the hospital for a week. If my sister didn't care for me before, she downright loathed me afterward.

"My parents were mortified. They've always been concerned with appearances. They didn't want anyone to know. They lied to my school and told them I had appendicitis. My sister got in trouble, but they didn't take either of us to see a counselor and they refused to talk to us about it. And that, Mr. Ardmore, is why I don't do sharps."

I smile and raise my glass to him before taking several swallows. *Play it cool, Burke. Act like the mask of horror on his face isn't the mirror image of how you're feeling inside.* Why, oh, why is there no wine at lunch? Or better, gin? The burn of a strong drink sliding down my throat would be welcome. But Cris has never served me booze of any sort. Come to think of it, I've never even seen any alcohol here.

Lacking a throatful of liquid courage, I dredge up a memory I haven't needed, didn't want to think about, for a long time. But, suddenly, that voice saying those words is what I most need in the world.

Being as ignorant as Cris about my psychopath of a sister, Hunter had asked me early on if I was a witch and I'd flipped my ever-loving shit. I safe-worded on him and made a scene—not the good kind. The next time I saw him I'd given him the same explanation I just gave Cris.

Hunter had pinned me against the wall with a hand at my throat, nudged my chin up with his thumb, and pushed a thigh between my legs. He'd leaned down, his cheek a hair's breadth from mine, and when I felt his breath hot in my ear, I nearly died.

"You know when I asked you if you were a witch I was flirting with you."

"Yes, sir," I squeaked, although I hadn't until that moment.

"And anyone who asks you now that you're a lovely grown woman is doing the same."

I hesitated for a split-second, and he nudged my chin higher.

"Yes, sir."

"You've beguiled me, Kit. That's not a simple thing to do. I would imagine you've charmed more than your fair share of people before you got to me as well. So the next time someone asks you if you're a witch, you're not to be afraid, understand?

"Your sister was a brutal, nasty little wretch, and your parents were spineless dilettantes who had no business raising children. What they did to you was atrocious, but it doesn't matter anymore. The next time someone asks you if you're a witch, you'll remember it's because you've enchanted them, and they can't imagine someone with your beauty and allure isn't supernatural. Are we clear?"

"Yes, sir."

I'd spent the past twelve years building a brick wall in defense of that soft spot, but it had just been bricks until that moment. If anyone had pushed hard enough, they would've toppled, but Hunter, with his certainty and his insistence, had provided the mortar, solidifying the ramparts.

At the time I'd thought, *From now until the day I die, I won't be afraid anymore. Instead of feeling six years old, hurt, sick, and terrified, I'll hear Hunter saying in his rich, silky voice that I've beguiled him. No, I won't be afraid anymore.*

And for the most part, that's been true. It takes more than a big bad wolf to rattle my brick house. But I need him now, laid bare as I've been by Cris's inquisition.

"Kit, I—" He shaken by the impact of the blast. He was probably expecting a toy cap, and what he got was a landmine. But he's recovering from the emotional concussion, and he's gathered himself enough to offer apologies I don't want to hear.

"Told you it wasn't pretty."

"I know, but I—"

"Leave it. It was a long time ago. I'm over it." The furrow of his brow and his clenched fist tell me he doesn't buy it, not entirely, but I don't want to talk about it anymore. "I don't do sharps. End of story." I cut off his burgeoning protest with a question of my own. "What does a girl have to do to get a drink around here?"

Turns out a girl has to drive over an hour round trip to the nearest liquor store. Cris doesn't drink or keep alcohol in the house. The extent of his stash is a half-empty bottle of marsala. I might be craving a cocktail, but I'm not desperate. But it begs another question.

"Are you an alcoholic?"

It's out of my mouth before I can shut myself up. I'm not subtle, but that was a bit much, even for me.

He shakes his head, shifting the curls that fall over his forehead. "No. And I don't want to be."

Intriguing, and it makes me like him all the more. I don't think I'd have the same fortitude if I were in his position. Liquor was my father's numbing agent of choice for when he had to deal with the psychic howitzers that were my mother and sister. I chose something a little different to silence the voices, and Cris's last sentence has me wondering if he hasn't done the same thing.

"But I've got something better than a glass of pinot for taking the edge off, if that's what you're after."

"What's that?"

An easy smile spreads over his face. "Indulging in a different kind of vice?"

Yes, kink as the cure for what ails you. I'm eager to put that particular remedy into full effect, instead of rehashing more of my less-than-enchanted childhood. He's tucked my suffering in his back pocket, no doubt to be examined and worried over later. Let him, as long as I don't have to be there for it.

I raise an eyebrow. "Think that'll do the trick?"

"Only one way to find out."

As he clears our places, I dig the contracts out of my bag and start signing.

CHAPTER 12

*A*nother day, another dream about Hunter. I've been having them since Cris asked me about my aversion to sharps. It's been two months with two more visits between, and fortunately, he hasn't brought it up again. Unfortunately, it's like calling on Hunter's ghost in my time of need opened the door for other memories of him, welcome or not.

I try to stealthily stifle a yawn in my elbow while I heft the kettlebell overhead, but Adam catches me and yaps his admonishment.

"It's not naptime, Sleeping Beauty."

Goddamn goldendoodle of a morning person. He's lucky I don't heave this torture device into his model-perfect face. I get in a few more reps, but another yawn overtakes me. Fuck all am I tired, and on today of all days.

The dreams have been all over the map, ranging from the most achingly sweet memories to recollections easily categorized as nightmares. They come without warning, and the only time I can guarantee I won't have them is while I'm in Kona or when Rey sleeps in my bed. Apparently, Hunter's ghost doesn't suffer masculine competition. Other than that, there's a better than even chance Hunter will make an appearance sometime during the night.

My brain is clearly trying to tell me something: *Stay away from Cris Ardmore. He's dangerous. You've been down this road before, and you know how it ends. Do you really want to put yourself in that position again?*

My rational mind wants to fight back. Cris isn't Hunter. There's no way he's as calculating and ruthless. No one is. But the warrior princess part of me wants to batten down the hatches and not let Cris in any further. Better yet, drive him back from the borders he's encroached upon already. I get the message, Xena, and I'll be careful, but can't you let me enjoy this a little longer? I haven't had sex this good in…

Shut it down, India. You might not be able to help Hunter haunting your dreams, but you can sure as hell keep him out of your head while you're wide awake.

It's bad enough my subconscious has gone into overdrive since my last call with Rey. We'd decided after my last visit that maybe Matty didn't need to join me on my trips to see Cris anymore. I'd still check in and he'd be on stand-by to fly out if I needed him, but his physical presence and "don't fuck with me" glare were no longer required.

I'd waited with my heart in my throat to hear back from Rey. I wasn't sure if Cris would realize how major this is. I wasn't sure I wanted him to. Strike that. I *don't* want him to. But he'd said yes and offered to pick me up from the airport if I didn't want to rent a car. More than not wanting to handle an unfamiliar vehicle while effectively off-roading, I was eager to have more time with him.

What the hell, India? Why don't you just invite him over for a fucking tea party while you're at it?

Though I'd never admit it, my head's been a little fuzzy with nervous anticipation since then. Cris is distracting, and I need to shove that back in a box until this weekend. So instead, I focus on hefting the kettlebell into the air and on Adam's big hands correcting my form. His clinical touch grounds me and lets me focus on the strain of my muscles working to move and bear the weight. The sensation isn't intense enough to completely hold back the encroaching waters, but sandbags are better than nothing. They'll get me to my first cup of coffee before I drown.

My phone has been ringing off the goddamn hook. Is this what Lucy does all day? Answer my fucking phone? Lucy is in Iowa, visiting her corn-fed family on their literal dairy farm. Maybe she'll find some blond beefcake to take her for a much-needed roll in the hay and won't be so god-awful perky when she gets back. The temp who was supposed to be here never showed, and the agency didn't have anyone else. All the associates are out of town, and so for the first time in two years, I am answering my own goddamn phone.

"India Burke."

"What are you doing answering your own phone? That's a little below your pay grade, isn't it?"

"My assistant is on vacation, and my temp didn't show."

"Oh, India," Constance drawls. Southern compassion is so nice. It's almost as welcome as a SoCo cocktail. "Then I won't bother you. I just wanted to check in about next week's site visit."

"I'll send you the itinerary by close of business tomorrow. I was hoping today, but—"

"Don't trouble your pretty little head. Tomorrow's fine by me."

"Thanks, Constance. I appreciate it. Is Glory coming with you next week?"

"Yes, poor little thing could use some sun."

I love Glory. She and Constance have been together for eight years; they met in grad school. When I was back east, she was my favorite sub to hang out with. I can't count the number of evenings we sat giggling at Constance and Hunter's feet or cuddled up after they were through with us. We could talk for hours, if we were allowed. She's fun and sexy and brilliant, and I miss her.

"Tell her I can't wait to see her. I'll get Rey down to LA for dinner one night."

"Sounds perfect. I'll talk to you tomorrow. Good luck."

I take another sip of my cooled coffee before my phone rings yet again. This is turning into a lost day. I'm tempted to let it go to voicemail and deal with it later, but the specter of an enraged Jack stops me.

"India Burke."

"India?"

Fingers of unease claw at my intestines. The voice is familiar, but...

"Yes, this is India. Who is this?"

There's the briefest pause on the other end of the line. My brain makes the connection at the same time his voice comes through the line again. "It's Cris."

Hands of panic grip my throat. I can't breathe. My eyelids are fluttering like a debutante's, and I wish there were someone here to wave smelling salts under my nose because I'm about to pass out. I swallow hard to get a grip, but my heart is racing out of control.

"India?"

The sound of him saying my name brings me back. I'm overwhelmed by the incongruous sheer terror and pleasure pooling in my belly. The terror wins.

"How did you get this number?"

"India, I—"

"Stop! Stop saying my name. How do you know who I am? How did you get this number?"

"Settle down, Kit. I didn't mean to upset you."

The voice that can soothe me with a word has no power here. Not without his body to back it up.

"Answer me, Cris."

"I saw your picture in the *Times*."

Shit. I knew doing press would be the death of me, but I didn't expect it to come so soon. And in the guise of Cris of all people. God*damn* you, Brad Lennox.

"Why were you reading the *Times*?"

"It's part of my job."

Cris's job? My rage is momentarily suspended by confusion. I don't know what Cris does for a living. I've steered clear of questions about it in the hopes he'd do the same, and for the most part, he has. Until now. Now he's showing up on my metaphorical doorstep. Calling me at work. *Saying my name.* Vomit rises in my throat.

"You're in violation of our contract."

"I didn't think—"

"Fucking right you didn't think. I'm hanging up. Don't call me again."

The handset's on its way to the cradle when he begs, "Jesus, Kit, please!"

He sounds as hurt as I feel, and despite how livid I am, it tugs at some heartstring I haven't yet severed. I like Cris. If I'm brutally honest, I more than like Cris. I don't want to make him feel that way. I don't want to be the reason he sounds heartbroken and terrified. I clutch the receiver to my surging chest and wrestle it back to my ear.

"You have one minute to explain yourself. The clock starts now."

A small noise of relief rolls across the Pacific. "I'm a political cartoonist. My work's been in *The New Yorker*, *The Economist*, *Time*. You can look it up."

"No. I would've recognized your name."

"I publish under a different name. You aren't the only one

who values their privacy. Does the name Malcolm Bennett mean anything to you?"

I can't help the snort of laughter that escapes. "Yeah, it does."

He's one of my favorites. His election coverage in particular makes me cackle. It's never been clear to me what his political persuasion is, either, because he's ruthless with everyone. Yes, the name Malcolm Bennett means something to me. But when I've pictured Malcolm Bennett—and I have—the image has been of a bespectacled guy in an Oxford shirt and pocket protector. Nothing like Cris.

"That's me. Malcolm's my dad's name, Bennett's my mom's maiden name. I watch the news networks. I read the major papers. I don't usually look at the local stuff, but it was a slow news day and there you were. I knew Kit wasn't your real name, but..."

That explains how he found my photo and my name. From there, it's not hard to get my extension at work, but to *use* that information... What else could he use it for? Screw that, I *know* what he could use for, and it makes me want to feed myself through my shredder before he can. I like the life I have now. I worked hard to rebuild it out of the ashes of my old one, and I don't want to do it again. Against all instinct, I try to quash the rising panic and give him a chance.

"Why'd you call me?"

"I couldn't...not. I saw you. I wanted to hear your voice. I wanted to talk to you. I thought... I thought you'd think it was funny."

"What exactly about violating my privacy is *funny* to you?" The rage that had been smothered by a perfectly reasonable explanation reignites. Fury rips through me like wildfire.

"Absolutely nothing. Nothing about that is funny to me, and if I'd thought it through, I never would've done it. I apologize. I can't tell you how sorry I am."

His regret is doing little to soothe me. Before I can snap at him again, he says, "Please, Kit. It was stupid and impulsive. I can't stand the idea we might end this way. Please. Come this weekend like you were planning to. We'll talk—same rules as always. If you don't want to stay after that, we won't sign the contract. You'll go home. I won't bother you again. But you can't tell me you weren't looking forward to it. You were going to let me pick you up. I'll fly Matty out myself if you don't want to do that anymore, but don't toss this whole thing because I couldn't resist picking up the phone. Haven't I earned that? Another chance? I'm cashing in my royal fuck-up card. I don't expect another one. Please."

I want to go. I'd hang up and get on a plane now if I could or teleport if it had been invented. To have his hands on me... I mash my palm into my forehead. Which would be dumber? Issuing an engraved invitation to betray my trust again? Or depriving myself of this man because he made a mistake? The second man I've ever...

No, don't even go there. That would be the dumbest thing you've ever done. You like Cris. You're fond of him. He's smart and funny and thoughtful, sexy as hell, and the sex is...perfect. But the L-word? Oh, hell no. You don't L-word people.

"Okay."

"Do you want Matty to come?"

"No."

If I'm going to do this, I'm going to do it all the way. Besides, I was looking forward to Cris pulling up to the curb in his beat-up Jeep and having an extra hour with him. Not that I would've copped to that before and I certainly won't now.

"Okay. I'll see you Friday, eleven, at the airport."

"Okay."

"I really am sorry, Kit. Thank you for giving me another shot. I'll make it up to you."

I shake my head and grind the heel of my hand into my brow. "Don't make up for it. Just...just don't fuck up again."

"I won't, pet."

Please, Cris, don't. I will break into a million, tiny, fucked-up pieces, and Rey will be stuck gluing the fragments back together. Again.

"Okay," I mutter one last time, not waiting for him to say anything else. I hang up and bang my head against the desk.

CHAPTER 13

*I*t's sunny and warm as I step out the doors and scan the drive. Locating the mossy green Jeep with the mop of dark hair in the driver's seat doesn't take long. I head toward him, clutching my bag, knuckles white around the leather handles. Why did I agree to this? But when he lopes over to greet me, I remember. It's because some of the tension that's been choking me for the past several days melts when I see his face.

He stops a few feet in front of me, and before things can get super-awkward, I blurt out, "Hi."

"Thank you for coming. You look nice."

"Thanks." I find it difficult to accept compliments, even though I know the bright red sundress I changed into is more than flattering. "You don't look so bad yourself."

He doesn't. He looks delicious in a sage T-shirt, dark grey shorts, and his de rigueur flip-flops. His hair is mussed more than usual from the ride, his eyes wide with caution. He cracks a crooked grin. "Change your mind yet?"

I scowl to cover up my answering smile. "No."

"Good. Can I take your bag?"

He slings it into the back of the Jeep and opens my door,

offering me a hand up. When he turns the key in the ignition, a song I recognize comes on. "High and Dry." He pulls out into traffic, and the Jeep melts into the trickle of cars leaving the terminal.

"Radiohead's one of my favorites."

I glance sideways at him, suspicious, but he's too focused on the road, aviators glinting in the sun, to look back. When the song ends and "Daughter" comes on, I allow myself a small smile.

"Pearl Jam, too?"

"Yep."

Cris has made this mix for me. Or, at the very least, has put it in on purpose. A CD of his favorite bands: Nirvana, Red Hot Chili Peppers, Smashing Pumpkins, Stone Temple Pilots. It plays in the background as he's telling me about growing up in Kona and about his parents, Malcolm (who everyone calls Mal) and Mary. They've been happily married for forty-two years. His dad had polio as a kid and recovered, but in his mid-thirties, he started having problems with fatigue and muscle weakness and it's gotten steadily worse since then. I remember Cris telling me the first time we met that his father's not in good health. This must be what he meant.

When we get to his house, he keeps up his autobiography. He was a reckless adolescent, but when he wasn't too busy fucking around, he managed good enough grades to get him into Stanford. While he was there, he double majored in English and political science, dabbled in the art studio, and got a master's in journalism. He wanted to work for the AP in some far-flung and preferably dangerous corner of the earth, but his dad had gotten worse so he came home and never left. Small-town news didn't interest him much, but he'd worked on the Stanford paper and had done some cartoons, so he started freelancing. He landed some regular gigs, and that's what he's done ever since.

"It's nice to have flexible hours, and I can work from pretty much anywhere there's an Internet connection. The money's not great, but what do you expect for being a smart ass who draws stick figures?" He smirks and scarfs down another bite of quinoa salad.

If I ever meet Cris's dad, I'll get down on my knees and thank him for showing his son around the kitchen. Cris has never made me anything less than scrumptious.

What are you, receiving a telegram from the Mayor of Crazy Town, Burke? You're never going to meet Cris's parents.

I want to tell him not to be so self-deprecating. He's very clever, and sometimes it's only the court jester who can get away with pointing out hypocrisy and injustice without being beheaded. "Why are you telling me this?"

"I wanted to tip the scales back. I don't want you feeling bad about me knowing anything about you. When we first started playing our little game, I would've answered a dozen questions to your one. I just wanted to talk to you. You're fascinating. I knew you weren't keen on sharing, but I had no idea…

"Anyway, you can ask me anything you want this weekend, no trade necessary. I'll tell you whatever you want to know. Nothing's off-limits. I'd erase what I found from my brain if I could, but since that's not an option, this is the next best thing I could come up with. Whatever it takes to make you feel better about this, Kit, it's yours."

Whoa. "Anything?"

"Anything."

"Aren't you worried about what I could do to you? You said it yourself. I'm not the only one who values my privacy."

"No." He leans back in his chair, fingers threaded across his abdomen. He looks calm, collected. If I'd promised myself to someone like that… That's moot. It'd never happen. "You're not going to wreck me. Even though I screwed up and you've got a temper on you, you wouldn't. I get the feeling you know a little too well what that's like—"

I freeze, my body preparing for flight. I know exactly what

that's like. *Get your too-talented fingers out of my brain, Cris Ardmore.*

"—and you wouldn't do that to anybody else. No matter how pissed off you were. It's not your style."

If I don't get some relief, I'm going to suffocate from the tension constricting my lungs. Memories of my parents, of Hunter, are crashing over me, and I have to stop the flood somehow. I'm torn. Half of me wants to run all the way back to the airport, but the other half is desperate for Cris to unwind this godforsaken coil before it gets wound any tighter. "I don't want to talk anymore."

"Okay."

But I can't leave, either, so I dig the contracts out of my bag and thrust them at him with a pen. Even in my scattered state, I'm the model of efficiency.

Cris signs them after a cursory glance. "Mr. Walter is expecting a copy?"

"Yes, sir. I was going to send him pictures from my phone."

"I'll do you one better. Come, pet."

Sweet relief. *Pet.* This I can handle. There's no hesitation when he offers me his hand. I take it on reflex, and it reinforces the possibility that all will someday be right with the world. He guides me toward the door to the studio, and I'm surprised. This isn't standard operating procedure. Then he veers off toward the door that leads to his room, and I stop in my tracks. Surprised doesn't cover this.

"I have a scanner in my office."

Oh.

"And I thought you might like to see my room."

Oh. He'd said *anything*, but I haven't asked for this. I wouldn't.

"Have your other subs been in your room?"

"A few of them."

"To sleep with you?"

"No. Well, once. For…emotional reasons."

126

I frown, although I'm not sure why. Why should I care if *all* of Cris's subs had slept in his room? In his bed?

"Her sister died unexpectedly," he clarifies. "She found out in the middle of the night, and she came to me."

The picture of a teary, distraught woman being cuddled and consoled by Cris is at once heart-warming—he'd be a port in the storm, a solid lifeboat you could grieve in while the seas raged around you—and heart-rending. To be held safe in his arms while my humanity is most fully on display is something I'll never get to have, and that ugly, unfamiliar feeling rears its rangy head. Jealousy. Is this what it feels like for everyone? How do people live like this?

His thick eyebrows crease, measuring my response. "Is this okay?"

I'm about to cross a line, but it feels more like attempting to cross the Grand Canyon on a tight rope. I can step across this threshold and become something more (or less?) than a sub to Cris in recompense for him shredding my veil of anonymity. Do I want this? This…intimacy?

"Yes."

He guides me down the hallway like I'm being led to the executioner. Or maybe down the aisle. I'm not sure which prospect is more horrifying. He opens the door to a room that's larger than my room or the studio, but smaller than the main house and divided in half by wood screens.

The half closest to me has a low shelf running against one wall with a brace of monitors—TV and computer—and a desk with nothing on it in front of it. Odd.

"Doesn't look like that by the end of the day," he volunteers, "but I like to start fresh."

On the other side of his office, there's a table crowded with high-end tech: a fancy printer, the promised scanner, and some things I don't recognize. The table's surrounded by shelves full of the tools of his trade: stacks of paper, pencils, pens, inks, brushes.

And books. Always more books. What's got my attention, though, are the walls. They're covered with clippings: news stories, maps, photos, comics—a few his, most not. The thoughts and work of a lifetime accumulated on the walls of this room in the middle of paradise.

He gives me a few minutes to look around before taking my hand and steering me between the screens to where he sleeps. There's a simple, low, platform bed against one wall, covered with a navy duvet; on either side are stacks of books in place of nightstands. The rest of the room is spare, a dresser the only other furniture and a few doors cracked open to reveal a closet and a bathroom. Utilitarian but comfortable. He's spent the personal touches elsewhere, and I'm guessing doesn't spend much time in here aside from sleep.

I remember he's still holding my hand when he squeezes. "Ready?"

It's a few seconds before I gather myself and slip back into Kit's skin, which I shouldn't have shed in the first place. Whether or not we've sent the contract to Rey, I've still signed it, so a hurried "yes, sir," it is. This switching is difficult; I'm going to get whiplash. I'm relieved when Cris scans the contract and shoos me off to my room, telling me to be in the studio in twenty minutes.

He lays a towel on the center of the bed and tells me, "On your back."

I settle myself with my hips positioned over the towel and look to him for further instruction.

Instead of telling me what to do, he circles the bed, hands on his hips as he studies me. It's a leisurely inspection that makes me want to squirm. I feel my nudity keenly as he takes a few steps backward to keep me in his sights. He didn't put his shirt back on after he bathed me, and I've been lusting after, aching to touch, his perfectly tanned torso. His jeans cling to him in a way that makes me want to rip them off. It wouldn't be hard, threadbare as they are.

But I'm not allowed. I'm on display—an object to be looked at, admired. Possibly, *hopefully*, toyed with.

"Knees up and feet apart, kitten."

I do as I'm told, the soles of my feet sliding over the sheet, which is pulled tight over a surface so firm it barely qualifies as a mattress.

"Wider."

I make another adjustment, and he makes another demand, telling me to open further still and cross my wrists above my head. By the time I'm done, I'm completely exposed and struggling to keep my breath measured. He hasn't touched me, but my whole body is alive from his attention, his commands. He's staring at me from the foot of the bed, his face implacable. After observing me in silence for an incredibly long minute, a minute so long I doubt my ability to keep time, he strolls to my side and lays a hand on the inside of my thigh. The touch sends the urge to buck my hips surging through me.

He strokes me gently, his fingertips playing over the delicate flesh. When he reaches the juncture of thigh and hip, he digs in slightly, and it's as if he's awakened some secret nervous system I've never known about. The sensation travels through me, a brief but intense tweak that I'm having difficulty reading as pleasant or unpleasant. I'm nearly recovered from the shock when he slaps the inside of my other thigh.

"Look at me, pet."

My gaze skates up the trail of hair emerging from his jeans, catches on the dull glint of his medal. When I meet his eyes, I'm struck by the intensity there. His look is, for lack of a better word, penetrating. And with my legs spread wide and my vulnerable core on display, it's all I can think of. *Penetration.* I want him inside me.

"I'm going to get some cuffs. I'm only going to make one trip. Am I going to need two…" He grips my wrists in a single hand, squeezes, and my back arches in response. "Or four?"

He coasts his palms over my skin, barely grazing the outer curves of my breasts with his thumbs. His tactile tour continues over my stomach and down my legs until he reaches my ankles, squeezing. His thumbs dig into a hollow in the joints, and there it is again. That brief, extreme sensation. Fuck. If he's going to keep doing that?

"Four, please, sir."

The corner of his mouth tugs up. He thinks he's so clever, but my fondness for restraints isn't exactly a state secret. I admire the easy way he walks, his languid gait as he retrieves the cuffs and a few other things I can't quite crane my neck far enough to see. When he comes back, he lays out his trove on the small table that abuts the bed.

A few more towels, the promised cuffs, and a bottle of lube. Oh. There are a couple of possibilities given this array. Anal is my first thought, but the tenor of our session is different from your run-of-the-mill ass-fuck. Which leads me to wonder if he's going to take advantage of one of the few things left in our contract he hasn't availed himself of yet.

Cris doesn't speak as he fastens the cuffs around my wrists and affixes them to an attachment point at the head of the bed with some mouth-wateringly heavy chain. Doesn't say a word as he applies their twins to my ankles and secures them with more chain. If it didn't make my blood bolt for my pelvis, I'd laugh. The idea that he'd need to take such measures to hold down a little thing like me is preposterous, but god, I love how they look. And maybe, just maybe… If he thinks I'm that strong, maybe I *am*.

Nothing has changed, the usual fail-safes are still in place. Should anything happen, Cris could have me out of my bondage in less than a minute. But those thick links overwhelm the rational thoughts and tell me I'm his, he can do with me as he pleases, and there's not a thing I can do about it. His face is wolfish as he inspects his handiwork, theatrically tugging at the bonds as if to make sure they're true, slapping the inside of my other thigh when I just can't contain another moan.

He sits down next to me, absently rubbing his hand along my inner thigh, close, so close, to where I really want to be touched, but then he retreats, leaving me aching. "You're in luck today, pet. I'm not going to ask you to be quiet for this. In fact, you're going to talk to me through the whole thing. Can you do that?"

"Yes, sir."

As he leans down, he grips my leg so hard I squeal and raise my chin in surrender, baring my throat. He grazes his sandpaper scruff along my jaw before nipping at my ear. "You're going to talk to me. If I ask you a question, you will answer. You're going to be a good, compliant girl for me, and if you're not, the consequences will be severe. Are we understood?"

My breath gets short as my core gets tight and heavy. "Yes, sir."

He fists a hand in my hair and pins my head to the mattress, pressing a kiss to my mouth. Hot and demanding, his tongue works inside me. My mouth is full of the feel, the taste, the movement of him, in sharp contrast to the rest of me. The word echoes through the emptying chamber of my mind: *penetration*.

It only takes a minute until I'm writhing under his ministrations, careful to keep my approximate position. I take his threat of punishment very seriously, a double-edged sword of his declaration that he doesn't play games. Truthfully, I like the consistency, the steadfastness, but would it kill him to "forget" once in a while?

He palms one of my breasts and squeezes hard before closing his fingers around a nipple, rolling and tweaking until I'm moaning into his mouth. His fingers twisted in my hair hold me fast, even though my lips want to catch up with his when he leans back.

"That's better."

He disentangles himself and climbs onto the bed, settling between my widely parted thighs and staring at me long enough that I wrap my fingers around the chains pinning me to the bed. I'm relieved when he moves in closer, and places a hand on my mound, presses, and slips a finger inside me. *Yes.*

The satisfaction lasts a split-second before I want more. He teases me for a minute before obliging, slipping another finger inside of me. The rhythm of the slick movement is hypnotic, and I arch to meet him. On his next foray, he eases three fingers inside, and I inhale sharply. It doesn't hurt, not at all, but my urge has been sated. He presses down, circles his fingers, stretching me, and my suspicions are confirmed. I wanted penetration, and I'm going to get it.

He slicks my own wetness over my entrance and patiently applies pressure until I relax enough to close my eyes. With his fingers deep inside me, he leans over and uses his free hand to smooth my mussed hair away from my face.

I open my eyes to his, and he kisses me softly before trailing the tip of his craggy nose alongside mine. "There's my good girl. You're going to let me in, aren't you?"

If he'd poked and prodded at me earlier for information instead of giving everything, asking for nothing, I don't think I'd be able to give in. I'd shy away, shut it down. But he didn't, and what he's asking for now—reaching deep into my body instead of my head—*that* I can give, I want to give. When I breathe, "Yes, sir," his triumphant smile makes it all worthwhile.

He kisses me again before sitting back on his heels and grabbing the bottle. The distinctive snick of the cap as he opens it sends a breath hard and fast through my nose, and I tense as he drips the liquid over his fingers, around my opening. It's not quite cold and warms quickly from the contact with our skin, the friction of his movements.

"You've done this before?"

"Yes, sir."

"Recently?"

"No, sir."

Fisting isn't really a first date kind of thing, and though it's been in contracts of mine before, no one's made use of that particular stipulation. The last person whose hand was inside me was Hunter.

"You enjoy it?"

"I have, sir."

You'd have to be awfully familiar with the line of Cris's jaw to catch the momentary flinch, but I do. He's learned to translate my lawyer-speak, and he's read my answer correctly: I have, but I haven't always. It wasn't necessarily about my physical enjoyment so much as the expression of dominance, ownership, which I liked in and of itself. I belonged to Hunter so fully I'd accept this incursion into my body, regardless of whether it resulted in pleasure. But it could, oh, it could, and I get the feeling that both of those things are equally important to Cris.

Yes, he wants me to submit to him, and it gets him off when I do. The anticipation of invading me this way had him rubbing hard against my thigh moments earlier. But I think the idea of crushing all my defenses, including making me give in to pleasure, gives him bone-deep satisfaction.

"You're going to."

"Yes, sir."

That's when he spreads his fingers slowly, with gentle but insistent pressure, before tucking them together and adding his fourth finger. There's a stretch as my body adjusts, but it's not unpleasant, not with his deliberate handling. He adds more lube —though I'm already slick—and works at my flesh until his fingers glide easily, pressing and touching my interior walls.

Though I'm tempted to close my eyes and drop my head back, I love the look of concentration on his face. To have that much attention focused on me is both heady and disconcerting. It feels almost like devotion, and I have to weed the word from my head before it takes root. Devotion is the kind of thing reserved for partners. Partners who L-word each other. Not...whatever we are.

Cris turns his hand palm up and folds his thumb in, adding more of the viscous fluid. His eyes meet mine, and something like gravity draws me in until I don't think I'd notice if the roof blew away. He studies my face, my fingers threaded through the links above my head, my chest rising and falling with consciously even breaths.

"Okay?"

"Yes, sir."

There's a blink, a brief fan of his dark lashes over his cheeks, and then he's moving inside me again. Though he told me I'd be talking to him, he's the one keeping up a near-constant stream of chatter. Praise and reassurance in a voice that's ventured into sweet but backed by a conviction that allows me to believe him. It's all accompanied by more pressure, more spreading. But he's patient, just so fucking patient with me, not moving too fast or forcing anything I'm not ready for.

And the one time he did, he apologized and gave me more than I'd ever ask for in return. I'm comfortable with him, I trust him, and my body follows my brain, allowing him in, surrendering to his coaxing. His wrist rotates again and—

"Oh."

A tug at the corner of his mouth tells me he heard me, a repeat of the same motion tells me he liked it. He's hitting something inside that nearly topples me into ecstasy, but despite the slackening of the rules about noise, he hasn't let up on the requirements for waiting for permission to come.

He uses my reaction to push further, creating a sensual spiral inside of me. When he reaches the broadest part of his hand, he adds more lube, slicking it up to his wrist before laying his free hand on my mound and thumbing my clit. I jump at the contact, and my brain nearly short circuits. Between the feeling of fullness, surrender, and that tiny, electric touch, I'm so close.

"Are you going to come for me, pet?" His brows are raised in a cocky, satisfied smile. It's maddening. He knows damn well I'm going to, but swearing at him isn't part of the game.

"Yes, sir."

"Good. You're going to tell me when you do."

As if he wouldn't know. I'd roll my eyes, but at that moment, I'm distracted by an easy rocking motion and another glance of his thumb over my clit. I can't help the noises I'm making, nor would I want to with the intent look on his face. More pressure, more stretching, and concentrated attention on my clit tell me he's nearly there. When the heel of his hand slips inside, his fingers buried deep and grazing some magical spot, I implode. My internal muscles grip tight around his wrist, and the cuffs so carefully strapped around my wrists and ankles dig in hard enough to leave marks as I struggle against the chains that bind me.

"I—I'm coming, sir. Oh, god. Cris, I'm coming."

As soon as I've said it, I want to take it back. It's not only a breach of etiquette, a breaking of the rules he's set out for me, it's a stupid idea. This isn't Cris and India. This is Kit and her Dom, absolutely not to be confused. But it's hard to remember when a pleasure so intense I see stars is flooding my system and pretty little endorphins trip through me. It's not just the act, though that had something to do with it. It's the way he performed it and the feel—

No, India. You're not allowed to have feelings about this outside of physical bliss.

But I can only push the feelings away so far because he's still inside me, his other hand on my abdomen, warm fingers spread wide. I wonder if he can feel its twin through the layers of muscle and skin.

He leans over me to kiss and nuzzle around where his hand rests, his breath soft, his curls brushing against me. The tenderness of it slays me, and I'm glad my hands are out of play because I'd do something stupid like thread my fingers through his hair and say all the soppy things racing through my head.

It's just sex. Really goddamn good sex, but sex nonetheless. Keep your mouth shut, Burke.

"I want to feel that again," he murmurs before he bites me. I shiver at the thought, and the word drops from my mouth before I can stop it.

"Again?"

"Are you objecting?"

"No, sir."

"Good. Because when I say again, I mean it."

And before I can say, "Yes, sir," his mouth is on me and I melt. Again.

It doesn't take long for me to find another climax, not with his hand still inside me and his tongue working my clit. My orgasm isn't as powerful as the last, but fits comfortably inside the space carved out by its predecessor, like a nesting doll. After I've come down, he works his hand free, soothing me through the hardest part. When he's done, I expect him to reach for a towel, untether me, and issue more orders: *turn over* or *on your knees.*

Instead, he kneels up between my thighs so our legs cross, unzips his jeans, and takes himself in hand, bracing a hand on my knee. Watching Cris touch himself, pull with rougher strokes than I'd dare and with the hand that was just inside me… I should be piqued. Why hasn't he asked me to do this? But I'm fascinated. He's beautiful to watch, and knowing that what he's done to me, what I allowed him to do, is what's turned him on so much is a balm to the slight sting of insult.

His fingers grip my knee tighter, and his stomach muscles

contract before he spills his release over his hand, onto my stomach. It lands hot on my skin, marking me in a way that won't wash off even when the evidence is gone. He drains the last of his climax and hangs his head, shakes it, before looking up at me with a smile.

"Thought I'd give you a break. We're not done yet."

My heart beats hard, and my fingers curl around the chains that still bind me. If he's giving me a break, what's coming is going to be really, really good. "Yes, sir."

The rest of the weekend is a disconcerting mix of the same: unparalleled, uncomfortable, unfamiliar intimacy on the one hand and customary, mind-numbing, delicious sex on the other. I'd describe it as purgatory, but it's more like jarring swings between heaven and hell. Though the play is impeccable, as per usual, I'm still a bundle of exposed nerves when I go home. It's better than I expected, given the state I arrived in, but I miss the blissed-out feeling I've become accustomed to leaving with. Maybe it'll come back next time. *Next time.*

"Are you okay, Kit?"

I'm standing on the sidewalk outside of the airport with Cris, and he's taken my weekend bag out of the back of the Jeep. I drop a brusque nod and hold out my hand for it. He doesn't give it to me, but regards me with slate-blue eyes. If I have to abandon the bag, if a sacrifice play becomes necessary, I'll only lament the loss of the red sundress I arrived in. The rest of what's in there is disposable.

Cris isn't buying my nod. "Don't tell me that if it's not true. I'm not sending you home a mess."

My heart starts thudding against its cage of muscle and bone and skin, trying to escape before I can say or do something too stupid.

"I am okay. This was…stressful."

A frown darkens his face. "I'm sorry. I was trying to make things better—"

"You did. This is… It's hard. For me."

"I know. Would you tell me, sometime, why?"

My heart is playing Red Rover with my ribcage. "Sometime. Can I have my bag?"

"Yeah, Kit, of course. I'm not trying to hold you hostage."

When it's safely in my hand, I take a deep breath, pull it over my shoulder, and hesitate. I've brought something for Cris, but now it's game time and I'm unsure if I can go through with it. I look at him—his browned-from-the-sun skin, the achingly perfect amount of stubble on his cheeks, the laugh lines around his eyes and mouth. I think of everything he's given me. I told myself if I decided to come back after this weekend, I would give it to him. He's given *me* anything I've asked and a lot I didn't have to. I'd like to tell him what that meant to me—without having to actually, you know, say it.

I reach into my purse, slip out a small photograph, and thrust it at him. He takes it before I can snatch it back.

"If you're going to have a picture of me, I'd like it to be a good one. Not that grainy, unflattering newsprint thing I know you haven't thrown away." I affect prissiness so I don't choke. Or faint.

He colors. Did he think I wouldn't know he kept it? *I've met you, Cris. I've seen your sentimental streak. It's a fricking mile wide.* The photo is of me at a charity event, and I look amazing. Pictures of me are hard to come by. I avoid cameras like the plague, and this is the only one I keep in my house besides ID.

He's staring at it. He's never seen me dolled up like this and he never will, but I hope he likes it. His eyes flicker to mine. He does. I eke out a smile and turn on my heel to go.

"I like this side better."

I turn, and he's holding it up so I can see the message I wrote

138

on the back. I was hoping he wouldn't notice until I was safely in the airport or, better still, on the plane.

Cris,

    For the next time you can't not.

Below that is my personal cell number.

"Okay," I mutter as I flush and stalk off.

I picture him trying to curb his laugh so he won't make me mad, but it's clear as the water in his little cove when he calls, "Bye, Kit."

I raise a hand, not turning around, and head single-mindedly toward the door.

CHAPTER 14

I get a customary "Call me" text from Rey the next morning, but I wait until I get home from work to respond. He picks up on the first ring.

"Hello, lovah."

"What's up?"

"Your standard second-you-leave call from Cris, that's all."

He called Rey and not me? Not that I've been checking my cell to make sure I didn't miss a message or anything...

"He wanted to know if he could see you again. I'm assuming yes? When do you have time?"

"Three weeks."

"Spill."

How does Rey have a hotline into my grey matter? "I gave him my number."

Rey's eyes must be the size of dessert plates, but he manages a cool, "I see."

"Yeah."

"And you're mad he called me and not you."

"Yeah."

"You do remember the contract says he's only allowed to

contact you through me?"

"The contract he ignored?"

"For which you were going to stop seeing him?"

Dammit, Rey.

"Wouldn't you stick to the letter of the law if you were him? And don't pout those lovely lips and tell me you wouldn't have broken it in the first place. That's beside the point, you pretty little teacher's pet."

"But I gave it to him."

"Might not be enough."

Men.

"When he sends the contract, I could send it back with an amendment, make it official."

Rey may be a pain in the ass, but only because he knows me far too well.

"Okay," I grant, and we hash out the details.

"Tell me again why you can't go to Chicago?"

Jack's in full-on, flip-out mode, and this time there's nothing I can do about it. I'm going to make it worse.

"I'm overdue to go up to LA. If we don't get those vacancy numbers up, Cooper's going to have Janis's head and your balls."

This is true. I've been punting my trip because of other fires I've had to put out. It also sounds more reasonable than, "There's an imaginary line I can't cross, and Chicago's on the other side of it."

"And what about you? I know you two are like fucking Laverne and Shirley or Lucy and Ethel or whatever—"

"You're dating yourself, Jack. How old *are* you?"

He glares at me. *Oops.* But I know we're okay when he rejoins, "Brenda and Kelly? Is that any better?"

I mouth *no* as I shake my head.

"My point is you aren't going to be getting off with just a spanking, either."

Jack's choice of words is unfortunate. I can't imagine what he'd do if he knew Constance *has* taken me over her knee and I wasn't the only one getting off. I may prefer men, but my skills at pleasing a woman aren't for nothing. If Jack had a clue, Leo wouldn't be the only one recovering from a heart attack.

"You're right," I concede. Not a spanking. For breaking a promise? Maybe a whipping, but probably the cane from Constance. It's her favorite. "And you're making my argument for me. Send Julie. She's been looking bored."

"Julie's looking bored because I'm going to fire her, and today might be the day. She's not getting any new projects. You think Chow's ready?"

"Yes. She'll be fine. More than fine," I amend at Jack's glower. "Send Rodriguez to help her. They work well together."

"You want anyone else in LA?"

"You know I'm a lone wolf."

"Good. I can't afford to give you anybody, anyway. Get it done this time, India. You're not going back for a while."

I stand to head back to my office. "Aye aye, cap'n."

"Oprah and Gayle?" he calls after me.

"Better."

Cris calls me on Saturday. Seeing his number come up on my screen stems the tide of frustration over the newest vacancy numbers Janis has sent. The way things are going, I *am* going to have to lease those tenants up myself. I don't understand how we've managed to mop up so many messes, but this one is still spilled all over the floor. Call me the janitor because it's cleaning day.

But first, I am absolutely going to take this call. Even though I know it's him, I answer with a coy, "Hello?"

"Hey."

He sounds nervous. It's cute.

"What took you so long? Playing hard to get?"

"I plan to use this judiciously. I don't want my phone privileges revoked."

I snicker and cringe at the same time. "Fair enough. I was surprised you called Rey."

"I thought he'd still be brokering the contracts. Should I call you instead?"

"No, that's fine."

"Also, I didn't want…"

"For me to go postal on you for breaking our contract again?"

"I wasn't going to put it like that, but yeah."

Score yet another one for Rey. Would it kill him to be wrong every once in a while? "Now you've got yourself a permission slip."

"I do. I promise not to abuse it."

We chat on, and it's nice. It feels…normal. I haven't had a boy call me on the phone in years. It's been ten minutes when he says he'll let me go. "I hear you're very important and extremely busy."

"You heard right. I'm getting ready for another trip up to LA. Check the *Times* on Thursday."

There's a pause, and I regret it. I cover my eyes with my hand, although I don't know who I'm hiding from. There's no one else in the office, and Cris can't see me. But when he says, "Will do," with what I can tell is his crooked smile halfway across the Pacific, I feel the pleasant burn I get whenever he says anything that distills to *I like you*.

When I get up to LA, I give the cabbie the address of a building Janis has been telling me is waiting on maintenance before we can put more families in. The guy eyes me suspiciously in the rearview mirror.

"You're sure?"

"Yes."

"I wouldn't wear those pearls in that neighborhood," he advises, putting the cab into gear and locking the doors.

"I work for the housing authority." Same thing, every time.

When we pull up to the complex, I'm surprised to see cars in the parking lot. This whole building is listed as unoccupied for major repairs, but these aren't maintenance trucks. There are kids playing in the yard, music drifting from windows. I check the Post-it in my purse to make sure I haven't gotten the wrong address, but I haven't. I verify the property listings on my Blackberry to make triple-sure, but no. It's there.

Anger rips through me. *How dare you misuse public funds and keep families from getting housed?* It's followed by a pang of sheer insult. *You honestly thought you could hide this from me?* After that, I'm flooded with cold, hard satisfaction. *You're going down, Janis. Hard.*

I give the driver another address before getting on my phone.

"Jack, we've got a problem."

While we're strategizing, I go on a tour of all the buildings we've been told are vacant for repairs. Half of them are filled. There's no sign of work being done on the others. I'll have to pore over every cent on the books, but I suspect the maintenance funds are being diverted and Janis and several accomplices are collecting rent from the occupied properties under the table. Do the families living there think they're legit housing authority tenants? This is a fucking disaster. I'm pissed it's taken me so long to figure it out, but it could've taken a lot longer. Nothing in the receivership protocols indicates site visits for all properties.

After I've done my survey, I have a conference call with Cooper and Jack, and we make a plan. We'll do some more digging before we confront Janis to try to figure out how far this goes and who else might be involved. Cooper's livid, but not primarily at me. She's done the same calculus I have—it could've been worse.

A few hours later, the cab drops me off at LAHA's main offices, and I play dumb for the rest of the day. I hole up in an office left empty by one of the people who was fired when the agency first went into receivership. From there, I dive down the rabbit hole. My email outbox gets stacked with virtual reams of data, stuff I'll need to have associates scour to work out who's involved in this.

Janis, as friendly as she ever is, stops by on her way out and tells me not to burn the midnight oil. I tell her not to worry, even though I'll be here through the night and possibly the next night, too. But the only thing on fire around here is going to be her. Janis is going to be a pile of ashes by the time I leave LA. Which may be never, based on what I'm finding. For seeming so dumb, Janis and her compatriots have been clever in their cover-up— but not cleverer than me.

I work through the night, my only company some stale vending machine crackers and more phone calls with Jack and Cooper. Jack announces he'll be flying up later in the morning to deal with this. That's why his name's on the letterhead and not mine.

As the sun rises, I do a quick scrub-down with paper towels in the employee bathroom and change my clothes before making myself a cup of coffee. For the first time ever, I miss Lucy. This stuff is egregiously disgusting. I shrug it off and put on my bitch face. Today is going to be ugly.

Saturday rolls around. I'm still in LA. I've had to buy new clothes; I was expecting to stay a couple of days, but it looks like I'll be here a couple of weeks at the least. Janis has been fired, as have a dozen other people who were involved in the cover up. Some of them will be arrested for fraud. It's a nightmare through and through, and the only bright side is that Constance has flown out to manage some of this shitshow herself, including handling the press.

My phone rings in the afternoon as I'm plowing through some numbers with half a dozen associates Jack's sent up, and I excuse myself. I deserve to take five.

"Hello?"

"How are you holding up?"

Cris must've seen the coverage of this royal clusterfuck in the *Times*. And possibly called Rey. My shoulders drop three inches hearing his voice.

"Fine," I chirp, not wanting to let him know how taxing this is. I'm exhausted, and all we're turning up is more shit to hit the fan. It's going to get much worse before I see a glimmer of better.

"Okay. You can tell me if you're not."

I wish that were true, but even the fact he's offering makes me feel better.

"Tell me what to do to help, and I'll do it. We don't technically have a contract, but I'm responsible for you, Kit."

My lips part, and I have to take a few deep breaths before I can answer him. "You're doing it. Thank you."

"Can you still come on Friday?"

"Oh yes." I told Jack I'd work every minute between now and then, but if he wanted me to keep being a functional human being, he needed to give me the weekend—and he'd agreed.

"Good. I'll pick you up at eleven?"

"Ten thirty, if that's okay. I'm coming from LA."

"Even better. I'll see you then."

We say our goodbyes, and after I've pressed the end call button, I hold my phone to my chest. That two-minute conversation has fortified me to walk back into the office and give more orders. It's going to be a long six days.

CHAPTER 15

*W*ould you be offended if I didn't want to talk?"

It's ten thirty-five on Friday, and we're in Cris's car on the way out of the airport.

"Are you asking to break our contract?"

"We'll have the ride there?" Desperation makes my throat tight, and my plea comes out as a squeak.

"I'm teasing, Kit." His hand lifts from the steering wheel. I think he might put his arm around me or run a hand through my hair. Instead, he fiddles with the volume dial without actually changing the volume. He was going to touch me. I wish he had. I'm aching for his hands on me. "We'll do whatever you want."

"I need to shut my brain off. I need you to be strict with me. More than usual. Please."

Please have this in you, Cris, please. Not that he hasn't shown himself capable, but it's alternated with periods of sweetness—and sweetness leaves too much room for my mind to wander. No, sustained and harsh control will be required to wipe my mind of what's churning there. These are the only times I miss Hunter. He could keep my head in the dark for days at a time, make me forget about anything for as long as he wanted me to, for as long as I needed him to. But those weren't always the same. Not knowing the difference...that was the unfortunate thing about Hunter.

~

We race through the formalities, and ten minutes after we've arrived, I'm on my knees in the studio, waiting for Cris to join me.

When the door finally opens and he strides through, he doesn't acknowledge me. He heads over to the chest of drawers and rummages about, plucking things from the drawers and stowing them under the table. "Bathroom."

He hasn't told me to stand, so I crawl across the hardwood floor until I reach the tile, then sit back on my heels. Cris isn't big on crawling—or anything dehumanizing, really. I've always liked that about him, but to be a little less than human right now would be welcome. I don't have to be smarter than everyone else. I don't have to fix everything. I don't have to be responsible even for myself because he's going to do it for me.

As if he's read my mind, he snaps out another command. "Shower."

Still on my knees, I make my way to the other side of the door. The tile is harder on my joints than the wood, and I welcome the coarseness of the grout against my skin. This is going to hurt in a long, drawn-out way.

He washes me, more thorough than ever, and has me put my elbows and forehead to the floor as well, driving my mind into darkness with roaming, slick fingers, pressing, probing, pinching, teasing. He doesn't talk to me while he does it. I'm not a person to be chatted with; I'm an object to be prepared and then enjoyed. My elbows and knees are aching, but I don't complain. If he wants me to suffer, I'll suffer because it's not for me to say otherwise. I've handed myself over to him, and I'm his to do with as he pleases. Knowing I'm hurting, hurting for him, will please him.

By the time he's finished, I'm so wet from his attentions I don't think he'll be able to dry me off no matter how many fluffy towels he throws at the problem, but he only bothers with a cursory dry before ordering me to crawl back into the studio and stand facing the table. I've been on my hands and knees for so long that the ache has settled into an almost comfortable numbness. With the movement, the hurt comes alive again, and pain radiates up my limbs, turning into a less painful but no less intense sensation in my breasts, my pelvis. *Yes.* This is what I wanted.

He wraps cuffs around my wrists and ankles before draping a towel over the short end of the wood surface. Urging me forward until my hipbones press against the edge, he bends me over and clips my wrists to anchor points at the far side before nudging my ankles apart and tethering them to the legs of the table.

"Better, but not good enough. Head up, eyes closed."

A blindfold is slipped over my eyes, a serious one of high quality that does a thorough job of blocking my sight. When it's fastened snugly, I'm about to lay my head back down on the table when he scolds me.

"Ah, not done yet. Open your mouth."

A harsh breath escapes my lips. Cris hasn't gagged me before, though it's been greenlit in our contract since the beginning. He was saving it for a special occasion, and I'm glad. I'm no stranger to the sensation—Hunter used to gag me all the time—but not having experienced it recently gives it more weight, makes it a bigger surrender. As he presses the ball between my teeth and tightens the strap at my neck, I groan in both relief and anticipation.

His hand rests between my shoulder blades as he leans down. "Show me your safeword."

Right. Before I drift any further into no-man's land, I should remember there's an off switch. I uncurl my fingers from the palm of my hand and hit the table three times so hard it stings.

"Good girl." He withdraws once more, and I feel the absence of his touch keenly. I know better than to put my head down after I've been chastised, but I'm surprised when he slips some earbuds into my ears. Three years ago, this wouldn't have made me blink, but now the extra layer of isolation is going to be unnerving. "Head down."

It's not uncomfortable, except for the unbearable horniness. I fidget, trying to find a way to ease this ache. There's a hard smack to my ass with a paddle, a stern, "Still"—and then music floods my ears, a pressing, consuming beat.

"You can still hear me if I want you to."

I whimper in acknowledgment and sink into the fantasy world he's carefully constructed for me, where I'm not responsible for anything at all.

Cris works me over. Not light slaps—blows that land in solid thuds, not stinging and evenly paced. His hand is heavy, calling my attention. By the time he switches to the paddle, he's so thoroughly claimed my head I couldn't think of anything else if I tried.

The song loops so many times it's white noise, background for the fire being stoked on my ass. He works at me until my normally reliable timekeeping skills have been knocked askew by the sound paddling on my heated backside. His careful attentions put me under, but when he lets up for a breath, I moan around my gag.

He soothes me with a hand splayed across my lower back, assuring me he's not done yet. He strokes my warmed cheeks with his other hand, and I whimper under his attentions and squeal when he squeezes. The isolation of my senses makes every physical feeling ten times as powerful. His rough fingers start to roam, and he finds me soaking wet and slick as he strokes his fingers first inside me, then parts my folds to seek my throbbing clit. When he pinches and tugs, my whole world shrinks to a pinpoint of pleasure, and I'm about to come when there's a stinging swat to my ass. He's still got the damn paddle, and I'm not supposed to come yet.

I keen in desperation and am met with another swat of the paddle. If he thinks another impact is going to extinguish the fire he's kindled, he's wrong. He knows me, though. Knows my body. Stirring the embers is precisely what he has in mind. He walks this precipitous sensual tightrope, keeping me on the desperate edge between blows and fondling, and when he withdraws, I cry out in despair of ever being able to come. I take out my frustrations by tugging at my firmly tethered wrists.

"Settle down and be a good girl, or I swear I'll keep this up all night long."

He would, too—devious, tireless, maddening, and excruciatingly talented man. I take a deep breath and settle. I'm calling up reserves I haven't needed for a long time, and it's taking all the brainpower I have left. When I've managed to still myself into a quiet ball of barely harnessed desire, he strokes my clit and then a cool drip of something trickles down the cleft of my behind. *Please be lube. Please.*

At first, he spreads my cheeks. The idea of him watching me, studying me, drives me wild and sends my core into a clenching mass of craving. If I don't get something—*anything*—inside me soon, I'm going to die. Thankfully I feel the cool smoothness of a plug at my ass, and I relax and press back in invitation. Please. *Please.*

He works it in slowly. It's bigger than the ones he's used before—not unbearable, but substantial enough I have to concentrate to stay open and not clench in panic. I breathe deeply and remind myself he's never hurt me. When the plug slides home, I groan in relief. He presses it a few times, twists, pulls, and presses again, forcing grunts from me and whining pleas. *Jesus, Cris, please.*

His hands find my hips, digging into cheeks still smoldering and raw. He presses into me slowly, letting my body correct for the intense sensation of double penetration. Gliding in and out, he blazes a trail, and when he's thoroughly cleared it, he pumps at me hard. I'm hanging on by a thread and about to expire, permission or no.

Then there's the sweetest sound in the world, accompanied by a tweak to my over-sensitized clit: "Come for me, pet. Now."

By the time I wake up on Sunday morning, Cris has so thoroughly extinguished my anxiety that my internal spring is sagging. When I open my eyes to the familiar sight of him by my bed, I don't immediately sink into sub mode. I drop my gaze nonetheless.

"Good morning, pet."

"Good morning, sir."

"Sleep well?"

"Yes, sir, thank you."

I open my mouth to say… I don't know what. I've never asked for this before.

"Something you wanted to say?"

"Yes, sir. Would you mind…" Hard swallow, much blinking. "Would you mind if we called this a little early?"

"Is everything okay, Kit? Do you need to leave?" The concern in his voice is palpable. I picture the worry lines on his face, and it warms me.

"No, I…I'm good. Everything's fine. I thought, since we didn't get the chance on Friday, if you wanted, we could…" *Goddammit, India, spit it out.* "We could talk before I have to go."

My eyes flicker to his to see how this is being received. Relief and amusement flood his face.

"If I want?" His question comes with a smirk and a raise of his brow.

I drop my gaze again. "Yes, sir."

"But you don't care either way?"

His gentle mocking makes me want to scowl, but I can play, too, Cris. Better than you can.

"Whatever pleases you, sir."

My deadpan sass is met by silence. Is he going to take me up on my offer?

Lucky for me, Cris is more mature and much less stubborn than I am and doesn't play games, as he said. He sits on my bed and runs his hand through my hair and over my bare back, eliciting a sigh. "I'd like that. I'll see you in the main house."

He presses a kiss to my cheek before he leaves and pleasure flushes through my veins. I like when he's affectionate with India, though I don't dare show it. Save it for Kit; she's allowed to accept it unconditionally.

When I walk into the main house half an hour later in a halter top and shorts, I find Cris in his usual spot, arm slung over the back of the couch, book in hand. *Everything Is Illuminated*. I'd recommended it last time I was here. I keep a running list of books Cris should read in my head. I'm sure I forget some, but there's no way I'm writing it down.

I sit close and don't fight him when his hand slips down to rest on my shoulder. I read along with him—faster, really—until he's done with the chapter. He marks his page, shuts the book, and puts it to one side. After a beat, he inhales and strokes my shoulder with his thumb.

"I was thinking…"

My body goes rigid, my head wary. What's this?

"...if it's okay with you, that I wouldn't call you Kit anymore. When we're not playing."

My eyes widen. That's a big ask. "Why?"

"That's not... It's not you. I like your name. It feels more like you."

I pull out from under his arm and tuck my legs up as indecision worms through me. "What do I get? If I let you..."

I can't finish. *If I let you say my name, if I let you in, if I give you that power over me? What could be a good enough insurance policy against the possibility of you ripping my life apart?* He's shown his hand too early, told me anything I wanted to know, and he's got nothing left to offer.

His gaze is cool on mine. Cris is pretty good about rolling with my crazy, but this seems to be grating. It is childish, a bizarre brand of superstition, a verbal voodoo doll. How can a reasonable person offer a counter to that? Why would they *want* to? His eyes and brows drift skyward, possibly wondering the same thing.

"You could call me Crispin," he offers. "It's not the same, but no one's ever called me that before. It'd be all yours."

Always with a trick up his sleeve.

My lips part, and my breath quickens. "Crispin?"

A broad smile lights up his face. "Yeah. I like it. What do you think?"

I love it. I've loved his name since I saw it in type. Crispin— the perfect antidote to my no-*h* skepticism. Not the same, but precious. Mine alone.

More than once, I open my mouth to say yes. I must look like a fish out of water.

Cris thrusts out a hand. "I don't think I've seen you here before. Crispin."

A slow smile peels over my lips. He's the cutest. He makes things easy on me when he doesn't have to. But he wants to because he likes me. So it's with a gratitude I'll never properly be able to express that I grit my teeth, put my hand in his, and shake. Firmly. "India."

"India." My name rolls off his lips as he savors the taste of those five little letters. This time, unlike on the phone, it's far more pleasant tingle than creeping anxiety that comes over me. "Pleasure. Buy you a drink?"

My brows crease, and I laugh. "You don't drink."

"Right, I forgot. Make you an omelet?"

"Even better."

"Omelet it is."

Before he can push up from his seat, I lean over and kiss him. On the lips. I'm shocked by myself. I, *India*, haven't kissed anyone since high school. And that's what this feels like. An awkward, chaste, adorable kiss. I flush as I pull away. *What the hell?*

The look of sheer delight on Crispin's (*Crispin!*) face makes me less embarrassed, but not enough that I don't have to retreat to the bathroom to splash water on my heated face to wash the blush away.

I try to snip the ribbons of guilty pleasure wending through me as I pat my face dry, but the only thing my brain seems capable of is a singsong melody on loop: *Crispin and India, sittin' in a tree, k-i-s-s-i-n-g...*

I am in so much trouble.

When I come back out, instead of being hard at work in the kitchen, Cris—no, *Crispin*, I correct myself—is putting his cell back in his pocket and scrubbing a hand through his hair. He is not okay. Somehow, horribly, everything has changed in the time it took me to cool my burning cheeks.

"Kit—India. I'm sorry. I've got to go to Kona."

"Is everything all right?"

"Probably, but my dad's in the hospital. They're running some tests."

That doesn't sound okay to me, but I don't know anything

about the situation. If Crispin's not panicking, I'm not going to either. "Of course, you should go."

"Will you come with me?"

I choke off the "no" rising in my throat. We never go anywhere, and that's how I like it.

"To Kona?" I ask to buy myself some time.

"Yes."

"Um, sure. There must be a coffee shop near the hospital. I'll grab my Kindle, and we can go. Or should I—"

"I meant to the hospital."

"And meet your parents?"

"Yeah."

This time I can't stop it. "No."

"Why not?"

"I don't do parents." I don't do anyone. I don't do friends, and I don't do family. I didn't meet Hunter's parents nor did he meet my family. We were together from the time I was eighteen until three days before I turned twenty-five. Six years in his gracious home and behind the closed and padlocked doors of the kink community and nowhere else.

That hadn't been my idea, but I'd agreed to it because that's what Hunter had wanted and I wanted him. It didn't occur to me then, but I've wondered since if he wasn't trying to imprint his expectations without making them explicit: *If you want more of me, there are certain things you'll have to give up.*

Whatever his intentions, it wasn't always easy. Sometimes I'd wish for Hunter to be a regular boyfriend, someone who would take me to a movie, kiss me on a park bench, or be my date to my sister's wedding. It would've been nice to be able to silence my mother when she berated me for the millionth time about why—despite my looks and my money and my smarts (in that order)—I couldn't get a man to tolerate me. But for the most part, I was satisfied by what we had. Hunter had been a master of making deprivation feel like gratification.

Now Crispin wants me to meet his parents during some medical crisis? And tell them *what* about us? I don't think so.

"Please?"

"Are you asking Kit or are you asking India?"

"Does it matter?"

"Yes, it does."

If he's asking India, the answer is an unqualified no. If he's asking Kit, it'd be yes. I wouldn't be happy about it, but I'd do it. His eyes are boring into me. I want to crawl under the coffee table, but I stand my ground.

"Then never mind. Get your things. I'll have to drop you off at the airport on my way."

CHAPTER 16

*I*n the two weeks that follow, I have all kinds of time to think about my decision. Cris called Rey Sunday night to set up our next weekend, but he doesn't call me. His phone silence teaches me that I'd gotten used to talking to him every week. More than that, I'd enjoyed it, looked forward to it. I miss it more than I could've imagined.

I've never seen Crispin angry before, but that's what this is. He's ripped. At me. A feeling I'm not used to sinks my stomach after Saturday passes with no contact. I've disappointed him, let him down, and not as my Dom. I've done that before and paid the price, but how does one get punished for this? Will I even get the chance to find out? Everything's all arranged for next weekend, but maybe calling Rey was just a conditioned response. Maybe he's had a chance to reconsider.

When I get a call from Rey Thursday night, I'm almost certain that's what he'll say: *It's off.* Instead, he tells me Cris has asked if I wouldn't mind renting a car this time. That does not bode well. Not at all. I see it as a portent that he's tired of me, that this will be the brush-off. And if that's true, I don't want to face it alone, so Matty comes instead. The uncharacteristically grey skies and heavy clouds when I get off the plane don't do anything to allay my sense of dread.

It's only when Cris is helping me out of the Jeep that I realize he's not angry. He's exhausted. His broad shoulders are slumped, and there are lines on his face I haven't noticed before that aren't from smiling. He didn't call on Saturday because he didn't have the time or the energy, not because he was mad. My heart aches for him, and I want so badly to do something, anything, for him. Though it's breaking the rules, I pull the contracts from my bag, and we sign them on the porch before sending them with Matty. As he's driving away, the foreboding clouds burst, and it starts to pour.

When we walk into the house, Crispin collapses onto the couch and pats his lap. I climb onto him, rest my head on his shoulder, and slip my arms around his neck. His arms come around me, and he grips my hip with his broad hand.

"Is your dad okay?"

"Yeah, he's going to be fine. As fine as he ever is."

"I'm glad."

"Yeah. Me too."

A silence stretches out until he breaks it. "You know what I'd like?"

"Tell me."

"I'd like to take a cat to your back and then fuck you senseless."

My eyes widen. Crispin hasn't whipped me before. The price for emotional transgressions is steep. Not that I mind him taking it out on my body—it'll make me feel better, too—but Rey would want me to make sure he's under control before we start. "Are you still angry at me?"

"No, I'm not. I'm sorry I snapped at you last time. It's not for punishment. When shit like this happens...the only two things that make me feel like the world isn't coming apart at the seams are fucking and riding big surf. And unless you want me to take my board out—"

"No!" I clutch at him. Surfing during a storm seems like a terrible idea. His overtaxed St. Michael's medal doesn't seem up to the task. "No, don't. Please."

"Fuck. I didn't mean it like that. It's not a threat. I'm not issuing an ultimatum. Don't tell me yes because you're afraid of what else I might do. I won't go out, I promise." His reassurances comfort me, as do his strong arms holding me close. I loosen my hold to lean back and look in his eyes.

"I didn't. I wouldn't. It's rule number one."

"Rule number one?"

"Rey's rule number one: You never have to do anything you don't want to do. I'd say he beat it into me, but that seems in poor taste."

The corner of Crispin's mouth twitches, and some of the tension I've been holding leaves my body. *There he is.* I kiss the hint of a smile in absent relief, but he's quick to take my face in his hands and make it serious, his lips pressing into mine, his tongue working into my mouth. His hands leave my face to tug me into a straddle. We kiss this way for a minute, but I can sense his frustration in the way his fingers dig into my flesh. He needs more. Coming to his feet, he lifts me, and I wrap my legs around his torso. He starts toward the studio but stops dead in his tracks.

"Are you sure this is okay?"

"Yes."

"Do you need some time? I know it can be hard."

I shake my head no, but I appreciate the offer. I've gotten used to the buffer time our lunch dates provide. Doing without it won't be easy, but at the moment, I feel like some sort of hybrid— Kindia?—and I'll be all right. I nuzzle at him.

"I'm okay. Do whatever you need to do. I'll tell you if it's too much."

I can't imagine it would be, and Crispin will do more than a hack job patching up any physical or emotional damage he might inflict. I'll be fine.

Crispin's rough with me, but not in a way I can't handle. And he's careful to work up to it. I'm more aware than I'd like to be—still a touch India when I'd like to be all Kit. I don't sink into subspace where nothing much matters, but it's easy to bear. For him. When he's finished with the cat, he untethers me from the cross and helps me to the bed where I slither onto my stomach and rest. My mind is racing, but my body's exhausted.

He keeps a hand on me as we lay there in silence, sorting our thoughts. I hope this has made him feel better, that taking his anguish and rage out on my back in the form of angry red lashes from a whip has been the cure for what ails him. At least for a little while. I understand feeling lost and helpless. I'm glad Crispin's remedy is to control, strike, and dominate whereas mine is to yield, absorb, and submit. It's not for everyone, but it works for us.

He strokes me—my neck, my hair, my face—and I get that familiar buzz of anticipation. My body is warm, supple, willing, eager. When his thumb slips by my mouth, I lick the pad. He takes my cue, broadening his attentions. He kisses my shoulder, sinks his teeth into my earlobe. I sigh. He slides my wrists to hip-level and urges me to tuck my knees underneath my chest, careful to avoid my abraded back but also to keep some skin-to-skin contact at all times. I like this habit of his.

The metallic swishing of a spreader bar being expanded cuts the quiet. He has me lift my hips and widen my knees before he attaches my wrists and ankles to the bar. I'm spread open and vulnerable, waiting and wanting, my back stinging and raw with the evidence of his need for me. I get a rush of satisfaction as he grabs my hips. Even that minor touch is laden with want.

"Okay?"

I nod, my eyes still closed. More than okay. He kneels behind me and readjusts his grip while he admires the marks he's made, careful not to touch. He doesn't bother with fingers; I'm wet and ready. There's little resistance as he pushes in the first time before drawing back and slamming into me. The impact knocks a sound out of me, the ragged cry searing my throat. God, that feels good.

He doesn't hold back, putting the full force of his body behind his thrusts. My cheek is rubbing hard against the soft sheet with no way to brace myself. It doesn't hurt, not yet, and the feeling of being at his mercy heightens the sensations: my chest heavy against the bed, my wrists tugging against the unforgiving restraints, being penetrated over and over. When he grabs my hair, I'm done for.

"Do it, pet. Come for me now."

I shudder and buck underneath him as best I can, but the cuffs anchored to the bar hold me fast. There's no escape from my orgasm and no escape from him driving into me. He comes close behind me with an animal groan, emptying his angst and frustration into this pinpoint where he has absolute control.

When he's rubbed out every last bit of his release, he pushes back from my elevated hips and unhooks the wrist cuffs from the bar, but leaves my ankles attached. We're not done here.

~

A few hours later, my head is so scrambled I'm not sure what I'd say if someone asked me my name. At long last, he's removed the myriad restraints and toys he's made liberal use of, and we're lying on the four-poster together. He's stroking my hair, and I'm seconds from sleep.

"C'mon, mili, I'm going to put you to bed."

Mili? What's this? He's never called me that before. I hope he's not so fuck-stupid he thinks I'm someone else. That's insulting.

"On your knees, Kit."

No, he hasn't forgotten. I drag myself up while he rolls off the bed and tugs on his jeans. He stands at the side of the bed and urges me against him. "Arms around my neck."

He picks me up, and I lean heavily against him, my head resting on his shoulder while I wrap my legs around his waist. It's nice to be carried this way—no pressure on my stiff back and so close to him, his gratitude and affection for me palpable as the warmth from his sun-kissed skin.

The trip to my room seems longer than usual, and by the time he lays me in my bed, I may as well be asleep. My senses are revived when he rubs salve into my back. I whimper, but he hushes and soothes me. After the first wave of discomfort, it's not too bad. I drift off under his gentle attentions.

Hours later, I stir and something makes me blink my eyes open. I'm confused but not concerned to see Crispin sitting in the chair beside my bed. He's freshly showered and fully clothed. He hasn't been here the whole time. I'm about to speak, but he beats me to the punch.

"It's all right. I came to check on you. Go back to sleep."

This could be creepy, but it's not. It's reassuring. I blink a few times, but he doesn't move. Just sits there like it's the most natural thing in the world for him to be leaning back in his chair, watching me sleep in the middle of the night. His confidence and ease slow my brain. I close my eyes, and my head goes dark.

Come eleven, my standard wake-up time when I'm in Kona, I'm shoveling French toast with pomegranate syrup into my mouth. Hard play always leaves me starving, and Crispin's put out quite the spread this morning, knowing I'll be ravenous. It was the smell of frying bacon that roused me out of my bed at all.

He'll have to take it easy on my back for the rest of the weekend, marked and throbbing as it is, but I'm up for—no, desperate for—more. As soon as I get my fill of this French toast. And maybe some eggs. And papaya. And coffee. Definitely more coffee.

Crispin kicks back in his chair, watching me stuff myself silly. I'm sure he ate before I got up and is politely having a few bites of sweet bread so I don't feel like a total pig. I don't mind, really. He takes pleasure in my enjoyment of the food he's made; his gaze is appreciative, not incredulous or insulting, as I devour everything in my path.

Hunter used to enjoy feeding me, having me kneel beside him at the table and take morsels from his manicured hand. He'd had me do it during our first official playdate, while he and Rey negotiated the terms of our contract. It was disconcerting at first to be on my knees like some accessory or pet, but I sat back on my heels and focused on my breathing while they hashed out details of the agreement that would dictate my life for the next six years. I'd thought being fed like that would make me feel debased. That was fine. I was up for a little degradation. It would've been easy to stumble into humiliation with a single comment or off-glance. When no one blinked an eye, I'd let myself relax...and I'd felt precious, sheltered, revered.

After the meal was over and terms agreed upon, Hunter had tipped up my chin, instructing me to look at him. That's when embarrassment had flooded me because he could tell how much I'd enjoyed being at his feet.

"Such a dainty little thing with such nice manners. Did you like that, sweetheart?"

"Yes, sir."

He'd eased my mortification with a sweep of his thumb across my cheek, telling me there was no need to be ashamed. He was so pleased, and everyone there understood me. I'd been so grateful for his acceptance and indulgence. I'd soaked it up like a desperate sponge. That was the first moment I'd felt truly beholden to him.

I try to stifle the bittersweet memory in my mind while chewing yet another mouthful of my feast. I'm feeling pretty successful until Crispin interrupts my reverie.

"Who's Hunter?"

My throat goes tight, and I can't swallow the fluffy, perfectly seasoned eggs on my tongue. I cough and choke, grabbing the napkin from my lap to smother the noises—and in case I have to spit out my food because I don't know if I can force it down.

After a minute—during which Crispin becomes so alarmed he pushes out of his chair and I have to ward him off with a viciously raised finger—the panic subsides and my throat opens enough to let the forkful of food slip down. My heart is beating hard, and my breath is short.

"What do you know about Hunter?"

"Nothing." He sits back down and holds his hands above the table, open as if to ward off my attack or perhaps to show he's got nothing to hide.

You're hiding something, Crispin. You didn't get that name from me, and there's no way in hell Rey gave it to you either.

"I'm going to ask you one more time before I walk out of here. What the fuck do you know about Hunter?"

"Settle down, India. There's no need for—" I push my chair back from the table, primed to make a break for my room, and Crispin shakes his head. "Could you open up for once without me having to use a crowbar? Christ."

I wrap my arms around my waist like I've just been punched. I may as well have been. I know I'm a complete and utter head case, and I'm well aware that Crispin is far more patient with me than I deserve. Which is maybe why it hurts so much when he snaps. I'm such a disaster I've made the second-most tolerant man alive lose his cool.

My stomach churns as I review my options. I could leave as I've threatened, but I don't want to. I could give him an ultimatum—*apologize or I'm gone*—but what if he tells me to go? I'd be devastated, but I would. He doesn't owe me jack shit, never mind an apology. My heart takes a beat that feels too big, like too much blood is trying to fight its way through the valves. However cavalier my attitude, however aloof I act, I don't want to lose him.

I could tell him about Hunter… But the fear strikes hot, and I brace my hands against the table. Not an option.

I'm still sifting through the possibilities when Crispin lays a hand over mine. "Hey, I'm sorry. I'll tell you. Don't leave, please."

Despite his peace offering, my body's still pulsing with adrenaline, and the beast inside is screaming *run*. But I'm a person, not an animal. I've got a PhD in self-control, and I should use it better. If Crispin hadn't known before that Hunter's a sore spot—well, more like a gaping wound that refuses to heal—he does now. Fuck all.

His thumb strokes across my wrist where his hand's still covering mine. The weight and the motion settle the worst of my panic, and he dips his head until I look at him.

"Last night I came to check on you."

I remember. I acknowledge him with a blink, and he continues.

"When I was leaving, you said 'Hunter, please.'"

My face flames with embarrassment, and I wrench my eyes from Crispin's. How did I say it? I begged him for so many things. I've been dreaming about Hunter at home, but I thought I was safe from him here. Apparently the strange and delicious magic Crispin works on me doesn't extend that far.

My hand fists under his on the table. "What else did I say?"

"I don't know." I open my mouth to protest, but he cuts me

off. "Honest to god, I don't. I was walking through the door, and I kept going. I didn't hear anything else. I swear."

I want to pull my hand away and run to my room. Slam the door, pack up my things, and leave. Never come back. But it's not Crispin's fault Hunter still holds so much sway over me I talk to him in dreams, and I believe that he left. He knows how rabid I am about my privacy, and he's learned his lesson: there are lines he's not allowed to cross.

"I don't talk about Hunter." Even Rey broaches the topic as little as possible. I can't remember the last time I said his name out loud.

"Okay."

I thread my free arm across my stomach and hold tight, my whole body wound up taut and twitchy.

"Was he your Dom?"

I hold myself tighter, wishing I could shrivel up and disappear. If I weren't clenching my jaw so hard, my chin would be quivering.

"Was he your first?"

Crispin's prodding, gentle as it is, is not acceptable. I need to nip this in the bud, so my tone is enough to snap him like a too-curious twig. "What part of 'I don't talk about him' did you not understand?"

There's hesitation from the other side of the table. He's weighing his options as I've weighed mine, and perhaps this will be the time he decides that he's had enough, that what he gets from me isn't an even exchange for what he gives. It's not. For once, I wish that I could shut off the panic that electrifies my mental fence and drop my emotional drawbridge—because he deserves it.

But instead of a bitten-off curse and instructions to go pack my things, I get more rhythmic stroking of my skin that lets me loosen my hand under his. "Can I ask you one thing?"

I smother the kneejerk "no." I can give him one question. One tiny, vomit-inducing, rib-crushing question. I hate how small my voice sounds as I say, "Make it good because it's the only one you're going to get."

"Did he hurt you?"

My lids sink closed, and the air leaves my lungs as I roll my lips between my teeth. Did he hurt me? I define pain by how Hunter made me relate to it. He's a fucking yardstick branded into my brain. If I made a documentary about my time with Hunter, I'd call it *Dr. Strangelove or: How I Learned to Stop Worrying and Love the Whip*. And the crop. The cane. Clamps.

The first time Hunter ordered me to crawl to him, the command sent a thrill of pleasure through me and I struggled to keep my breathing measured. When I'd settled on hands and knees, I crept toward him and felt an ache, a need deep in my core. I'd done it before, for Rey, but knowing the man on the other end wasn't just my teacher, my mentor, but someone for whom my submission was a turn-on, raised that simple act to the sublime.

By the time I'd reached him, I was more aroused than I'd ever been. That's how it had been with everything. Every depraved act, every filthy word—I learned to crave, beg for, love it all. Hurt and love are so closely entwined in my head. What's the difference, really? But now's not the time to hold a seminar on the philosophy of love. A simple answer for a simple question: Did Hunter hurt me?

"Physically? No more than you do."

That's a bald-faced lie. Hunter beat the shit out of me on a regular basis and in ways Crispin wouldn't dream of, but I know what he's asking and this isn't a lie. Not really. I've answered the spirit of his question, if not the letter. Hunter followed the rules. He abided by every last word of our contract. He played safely, he respected my safewords, and he lavished me with aftercare. He was a model Dominant up until the very end. I have no physical scars from anything he did to me, as promised. As for the rest…

"Okay," Crispin says, squeezing my hand. "That's all I wanted to know."

I drag my eyes to his. I'm not expecting to get off without more of an interrogation, but his expression is earnest, if pained and discouraged. He's going to let this go. I regard him warily, waiting for him to change his mind because it's so blatantly obvious there's more to the story, but he squeezes my hand once again before he lets go and leans back in his chair.

"Are you finished with breakfast? I've got plans for you today. You're going to need your strength, so eat up."

The food on my plate holds no attraction for me anymore, though I'd been packing it away like a linebacker five minutes ago. "I'm finished."

"Good." There's a devious glint in his eye, and more of the tension leaks from my body. I know that look. I love that look. It's preceded some very good things in the past. He stands, takes up his plate and mine, and starts over to the kitchen. "I'll clean up in here. You go get ready. I'll see you in the studio in twenty minutes."

The anxiety is dissipating, and I gather up the scraps of my uncertainty. It's okay. Everything's okay. He's not thrilled, but he's going to let me have my way.

"Go on, then," he urges from where he's piling dishes in the sink.

"Yes, sir." I latch on to the familiarity of the words dropping from my lips, and it centers me, locates my body and my mind in space. I know the rules for this game. This is a part I know how to play flawlessly.

CHAPTER 17

*I*t takes me longer than I'd like to admit to realize what he's up to.

He's not touching me.

I'd been a bit smug when my standard bathing had been shorter than normal. I'd thought it was because he was so eager to start. I can't touch emotional intimacy with a ten-foot pole, but sex is my bargaining chip. My finely honed submission is what makes me worth putting up with. I thought he'd put me through my paces to reassure himself that, even if India is off-limits, Kit is open like an all-night diner, but now I'm not so sure.

He ordered me to the center of the room and wrapped cuffs around my wrists, my ankles, my thighs, above my elbows. Surrounded by the familiar trappings of bondage, out of the wreckage of this morning's emotional turmoil, I had started to salvage excitement and arousal. But instead of clipping together the cuffs, forcing me into some lovely contortion that would allow him to torture me, he'd arranged me like a paper doll: feet slightly more than shoulder-width apart, fingers splayed, palms facing forward and not touching my thighs.

"Whatever happens, you're not to move. Understood?"

I'd said, "Yes, sir," half an hour ago, and it's only now I understand his game. He's not fucking *touching* me. He drags silk over my skin again, and I shudder at the feather-light touch. Then comes the many-stranded suppleness of a deer-hide flogger, the cushiony softness of fur, the smooth wood of a well-loved paddle.

He plies me with all of it, but the pleasure I've earned from being praised for following instructions and looking so pretty as I do evaporates, replaced by an uncharacteristic flare of irritation. He's manipulating me and not in a way I care for.

"Close your eyes."

When I do, he ties the silky fabric around my head. Not the most effective blindfold—I can still distinguish between shadow and light—but it serves a purpose. I don't know what he's doing until he tugs something around my waist, then settles it down to where thigh meets torso. An audible click and a final adjustment clue me in: he's clipped an elastic band around my hips. My realization is followed by the shock of his fingers on me, finally, parting my labia and settling something over my clit.

I don't have time to enjoy his touch because, as quickly as it came, it's gone and in its place—

A sudden buzzing on my clit makes my stomach muscles contract, my fists clench, and I suck a breath through my teeth.

"Bad girl," he scolds, punctuated by the stinging thwack of what feels like a tawse on my ass. *Fuck.* The buzzing stops, and I relax, able to control my reaction better when it starts up again. "That's better, pet."

He toys with me for a while. Starting, stopping, chastising when I'm not prepared for the next spate of sensation and can't sufficiently mask my reactions—a curl of my fingers, a buck of my hips, a squeak or a sharp intake of breath. Crispin has no way of knowing because, of course, I haven't told him, but deep down I associate vibes with punishment.

Forcing orgasm after orgasm from me was Hunter's favorite

form of castigation when I'd come without permission. It was impersonal and mechanical, and I hated it. Is that what I was begging him for last night in my dreams? To stop? God knows it made me a quivering mess of pleading in reality. I dreaded it so much it took me months after things had ended with Hunter to be able to masturbate without experiencing a slash of panic when I'd come. When I just couldn't deal with the anxiety but needed the release, I'd call Rey and he'd give me the green light—sometimes teasing me first because he's annoying like that.

It's been long enough that I can take it in the spirit it's meant if it's brief and playful, but since the specter of Hunter is in my head and I already feel like I'm being reprimanded, I'm having trouble controlling myself. I dredge up all the coping mechanisms I have—a not inconsiderable list—and try to take it. I think I could if he'd just touch me, if he didn't seem so detached.

I like many, many things about Crispin, but one of the things I like best is his warmth. Not physically, though I like that, too. But underneath whatever he's doing to me, there's care, desire, a general benevolence that I've become accustomed to. No, far worse than that. Addicted to.

This act—which my body is responding to even as my mind revolts—he could be performing on anyone. He's ramped up the intensity on the vibe, and despite my best efforts, my abdomen contracts whenever he turns it on. My knees weaken and my fingertips graze my thighs whenever he stops, meaning I get a slap of the tawse on the way up and the way down. My ass and the backs of my thighs are heated and throbbing, but that's not why my eyes are watering behind the silk binding.

I need him to stop.

I could tap out, say the word. I've said it with him before when a sudden cramp in my leg left me hissing in pain—and not the good kind. He'd released me quickly, eased the spasming muscle. When it was gone and he'd looked me over, we'd started again. Crispin's not the kind of jackass who gives you a hard time when you actually use your safeword, nor is he one of those bastards who thinks safewords are for chumps. I could say it. I should say it. He'd want me to say it.

Red.

But I can't because when he'd inevitably ask me what went wrong, what would I tell him? *You know that whole intimacy thing you've been offering on tap like you've got kegs of it to spare? I've actually been sneaking sips of it when you weren't paying attention, and it's really fucking good.* If I were someone else, I'd demand a case. As things stand, I'm too chickenshit to even order a glass.

The bursts of the vibe are getting shorter and shorter as I get closer and closer to coming, and when the latest burst is over, I say, "Sir, please."

My voice comes out raw, too ugly to be called a whimper, and there's a beat before he answers me.

"Go on. You've been a good girl. You can come."

My fingernails dig into my palms as he flicks the vibrator on again. Though my body is more than willing—eager doesn't even cover it—I don't want to come this way. It's suddenly very important to me that I not. He could force me. Most of the time, I like it when he pushes me over an edge, urging me into something I wouldn't dare ask for, but this…I'll resist.

"I—"

My hands clench and open convulsively, and then it stops. I climb back onto the ledge I've been dangling over and catch my breath.

"What, pet?"

"I…"

"Tell me what you want."

I can't quite parse the tone of his disembodied voice. Do I detect a hint of mocking? Or is that a trace of pleading? Whatever it's laced with, it's an order, and Kit's required to reply. "I want you to touch me. Please, sir."

The weight of his hands on my hips forces a moan. "That's what you wanted?"

"Yes, sir."

He steers me forward, and I check the urge to put my hands out in front of me. In a few steps, the fronts of my thighs are flush with the back of the couch and his erection presses against my sore ass through the worn denim of his jeans. "I'd suggest you hold on for this."

The absence of his touch makes need claw at my insides again, but the sound of clothes hitting the floor eases the panic. He spreads me wide open and eases inside before threading his arms alongside my ribs, gripping the fronts of my shoulders tightly. Instead of bracing myself against the leather as he meant, I reach back and weave my hands through his hair, arching my back as he starts to move inside me.

He nips my arm, perhaps as an admonishment, but I tighten my hold instead of letting go and take his answering grunt as approval. The increasingly hard thrusts also smack of endorsement. The vibe is still in place, and when one of his hands leaves my shoulder, I'm not surprised when it clicks on one more time. I let myself unravel as he says, "That's right, mili. Give it up for me."

That word again. But my curiosity is smothered by the incredibly intense orgasm wreaking havoc with my body. I didn't care for the means, but the end...oh god, the end. All the agitation has been crushed under the force of my climax, and a delight I don't want to think too hard about billows through me as he clutches me tighter.

He mutters endearments and expletives into my shoulder, and I knead my fingertips into his scalp, cradling his skull as he's cradled mine so many times.

"Mine," he says, and my heart skips a beat. I lick that droplet off the tap dripping with affection, savor it on my tongue before I swallow it down to pool with the rest, hoping he won't notice.

Crispin and I come to a détente for the rest of the weekend. He's still on edge about his father and annoyed with me for being closed, inaccessible, and I'm stressed by my nocturnal confession, but we don't have a lot of time to waste. We spend most of Saturday in the studio where he wears me out. Repeatedly. On Sunday after lunch, he calls it early and brings me down to the cove. We cuddle up in the hammock, reading the same book—me on my Kindle, him in paperback. We're almost in the same place, although Crispin reads more slowly than I do.

It entertains me when I read a passage or a line I think he'll find funny and then wait for a snort or a gale of laughter minutes later. It's another secret game of intimacy I get to play. No one has to know how much I love…this. Yes, I love *this*.

CHAPTER 18

"*I* think Brad Lennox has a crush on you."

"No."

"Yeah, I do."

"He has a funny way of showing it."

We're in Crispin's Jeep, bumping over the rough roads near his house. We've been talking shop since he picked me up at the airport, trying to relocate normal after the odd way things ended the last two times and figure out where exactly all this leaves us. Or maybe that's just me.

I've been explaining to him some of the mess in LA—as best I can without giving a four-hour lecture series on public housing administration at any rate—and he asks intelligent and sophisticated questions. Crispin is not just a pretty face or, as he's said before, a smartass who draws stick figures. His understanding of government bureaucracy is impressive, but his knowledge of—and possible caveman-esque jealousy over—the man whose bylines grace every last article about LAHA in the *Times* is what's stirring something in my belly.

"I don't think so. The way to a man's heart may be through his stomach, but the way to a woman's heart is definitely through her brain." His hand leaves the steering wheel to tousle my hair.

"Which would explain why you feed me decadent and delicious things whenever I visit," I sniff, enjoying his fingers trailing through my loose curls. "Brad might do better to buy me a cookie."

"He's using his print platform to flirt with you. It's very unprofessional."

"Are you kidding me? He trashes LAHA."

"But he never trashes *you*." He points at me accusingly, his finger coming so close to my face I'm tempted to take it in my mouth.

"I wouldn't call that a love note."

"You'd set the guy on fire if he asked you out."

True. Brad's an intelligent guy, hardworking, not bad-looking, either, but he's missing that certain *je ne sais quoi*. Oh, fuck that, I know *quoi*. Man doesn't have a dominant bone in his body.

"Do you date?" Shit. I asked before thinking through how Crispin might take this. The consternation adorably crinkling his face tells me he's equally perplexed as to the best way to answer. If he says yes, will jealousy strike hot in my stomach? If he says no, will the ramparts go up? Usually I'm better about not saying stupid stuff like this, but my stomach's been all fluttery the whole way here.

Aside from steering clear of anyone with a whiff of abusiveness, I try not to think about why the men I'm with are available. It hasn't been difficult until now. Mostly, I assume they're fresh out of a break-up or not interested in long-term relationships at all, and the deal Rey offers them seems like an intriguing change of pace. Beyond that, I've never cared.

But Crispin... I can't deny the thought has occurred to me. He's not without his quirks and I suppose it's possible he's just never found the key to his lock, but I find that hard to believe. He doesn't have any super-unusual kinks, and god knows the man is patience made flesh. Not to mention he's good-looking, smart, and his cooking alone would be worth putting up with some peculiarities for. But asking is redolent of relationship talk, which is not a Pandora's Box I care to open. Crispin would dive right in and frolic like some kind of deranged porpoise.

I'm about to rescind my catch-22 because I'm now quite certain I don't want to know, but I'm interrupted by his answer.

"No."

Instead of indignation—*What are you waiting for, Crispin? For me to be a real girl? Good luck!*—the impending envy is buried by those two little letters. With a thrill of satisfaction I haven't felt for a long time, I say, "'Kay."

Then I promptly steer our talk back to the vagaries of the Code of Federal Regulations on occupancy standards, hoping to slow the rapid beat of my heart.

When Crispin and I have finished lunch, I reach into my bag for the contracts. Before I hand them over, I take a deep breath. "I wanted to apologize."

He blinks at me and hesitates. "For what?"

"For not going with you to the hospital." *For refusing you when you needed me.*

He brushes it off with a "no big thing," but I know it was. And I really am sorry. What makes it worse is that I'd do the same thing all over again and we both know it, so I'm going to make him an offer he can't refuse.

It's been on my mind since Crispin dropped me off at the airport with barely a goodbye the time before last. Introspection's not my strong suit, and if I've been stroking this thought for weeks, even after having done some penance during the visit in between, it might be a good idea for me to do something about it. And who am I kidding? Atonement through sex is easy for me.

I want to give him more than that, even if I can't hand over exactly what he wants.

Somehow Crispin's respect for my boundaries about Hunter, though it bothered him, made me more inclined to share. Like a newly sovereign nation accepting an ambassador from their former rulers. Doesn't mean I'm not going to have snipers stationed on every rooftop primed to shoot if the foray goes sour, but I'll let him in.

"I can't… I can't be with you that way. But I wanted…" *Jesus, India, fucking say it.* "I wanted to give you something else."

His expression is pure interest.

"You can ask me a question. Anything you want to know. I won't say no."

Not that I've vetoed a lot, only a few times when he'd asked too many questions about my family, but that's more than he's been allowed and I'm still being Scrooge McSlut. One question after everything he's given me isn't much, but the look on his face tells me he couldn't be happier. My brain knows I'm doing a good thing—I *should* give Crispin something in recompense for all the ridiculous crap I put him through—but my blood is shrieking through my veins, pumped by a heart that's begging, *Why did you put me on the chopping block again?*

The gears are cranking in Crispin's head, but I know what he's going to ask if he's just got the one shot, possibly ever.

"Will you tell me your story, India? Why this is so damn hard for you?"

"Did you know I was a trust fund baby?"

"Like you literally have a trust fund?"

I smile. He's usually so attentive, but he missed my use of the past tense. He'll get it soon enough. "There was an awful lot of money twiddling its interest-bearing thumbs, waiting for me to turn twenty-five. I was in my second-to-last year of grad school, and I was really looking forward to some independence."

"I'll bet." Crispin doesn't know a lot about my parents. I've been careful to keep him in the dark, but the barest scraps are enough to paint an unflattering picture of Preston and Samantha Burke.

"A few days before I was supposed to get access, my mom called. Said she and my dad wanted to take me out to dinner. I didn't think much of it. I usually saw them around my birthday. But instead of meeting at a restaurant, the car dropped me off in front of an office building. My mother had this obnoxious habit of dragging me to plastic surgeons—"

"What the hell for?"

I tap the side of my nose.

"You had a nose job?"

"No." I shake my head and laugh. No, I never did. That tiny little bump on the bridge of my nose must haunt her to this day. I hope it keeps her up at night, knowing I'm walking around the world like this, a flawed expression of her genetic code.

"I don't—"

I lay a finger over my lips, feeling them curve with amusement. He falls silent, arms crossed over his chest. "If you're going to interrupt every time someone behaves irrationally, this story is going to take all night."

His jaw clenches, and I want to pet him, protect him from the shitstorm that's looming. I forget that some people come from functional families. I bet Crispin's family was happy. He won't have the vocabulary, the capacity, to understand what happened to me, but I'll tell him, because he's asked and I've made a promise.

"Anyway, I thought she'd sprung another involuntary rhinoplasty consultation on me. It took me a while to realize I wasn't in a plastic surgeon's office but a psychiatrist's. Dr. Arnold Glazer, shrink to the rich and famous."

Crispin opens his mouth again, but I silence him with a glare.

"He told me my parents were concerned about me. They'd received some photographs that morning by messenger."

The color drains from Crispin's face and from his fingers where they're digging into his biceps. All I feel is blankness. There's no rage anymore, no terror, no autonomic reaction at all. Just the impression that I'm reciting this story as if from a script, though only one other person has heard it. Rey got every single painful detail. Crispin will get the *Reader's Digest* version.

"Dr. Glazer handed me this file—this innocuous, standard manila folder—and when I opened it, there they were. An even half-dozen."

God knows Hunter loved his symmetry. If he was going to ruin someone's life, he was going to at least do it properly, with style. And the photographs? They weren't exactly Robert Mapplethorpes, but the lighting and composition were impeccable. They could've been in some high-end, glossy, coffee table book.

"It was me, kneeling on the floor of Hunter's playroom, wearing nothing but some of the obscenely expensive lingerie he liked me in. That's not entirely true. I also had on a blindfold, my collar, and a bit gag. And some cuffs. You know, elbows bound behind my back, wrists tethered at the base of my spine and hooked to ankle cuffs."

He knows. He's had me in similar positions. And lots of others that wouldn't look out of place in the photo collection, with a few caveats. Crispin's not big on lingerie, he prefers brown leather to black, and his wood-and-light studio is more rustic than Hunter's luxe playroom with its Persian rugs and mahogany furniture.

"They weren't all that scandalous. To me. Or to you. It could've been much worse." That's what I kept trying to tell myself amidst all the rage and the panic while I tried to keep my head on straight. "But they were bad enough. My parents wanted to check me into an institution. A really swank one with an excellent reputation. I had classmates who'd ended up there for rehab, eating disorders, a half-assed suicide attempt... Rich kid problems. I tried to explain, but my mother wouldn't listen.

"She was worried whoever sent the pictures was going to go to the press. I think the humiliation would've killed her. But what she failed to see, what she always failed to see, was that it wasn't about her. They weren't meant for public consumption. You couldn't see my eyes or my scar in any of the photos—nothing that could definitively identify it as me."

No. Hunter, as ruthless as he'd been, had designed them for a very specific purpose: to force my hand. The guy may have been Machiavelli incarnate, but even the devil has a code of ethics. He wanted me destitute and dependent on him, not the laughing-stock of New York.

"I told my parents there wasn't anything wrong with me, that they weren't going to check me into an institution because of their own fucked-up worldview. That's when they threatened my trust fund. They had been holding that money over my head my whole life, and when they threatened me with it, it was usually a good indication I'd won the argument.

"They're so concerned with appearances they'd never want me out on the street—or worse, middle-class—but somehow, I didn't think they were bluffing this time.

"My mother said if I refused to enter treatment, the money would be gone. Every cent. So I said fine, I wasn't going to sell myself. My dad tried to talk me out of it, telling me I'd have nothing. When I wouldn't back down, he asked if there was anything I wanted. I asked for them to pay the rest of my tuition and give me a year's worth of my expenses. My mom said no, but my dad said yes. For the first time in my life, he stood up to her."

Too little, way too fucking late.

"I asked if they wanted anything from me, and my mother demanded I change my name. I told her I wouldn't, but I'd leave

New York, go where 'the Park Avenue Burkes' didn't mean anything. I'd go to the West Coast and never come east of the Mississippi ever again."

Crispin raises his eyebrows. No doubt it sounds like a crackpot promise. I guess it was, but at the time, it had seemed like a good idea. He also knows how seriously I take my word. I haven't breached that arbitrary border since I finished grad school. The idea of going back makes my stomach churn.

"And then I left. I slung my bag over my shoulder, walked out of there, and kept walking. And walking. And walking. I walked until my feet bled. I wasn't anywhere near home, of course, so I sat on a bench, pulled out my phone, and called Rey."

"And he came. Like he always does. He pulled up and opened the passenger-side door. When I didn't get up, he got out of the car, picked me up, put me inside, and drove me back to his apartment. Then he gave me a bath and put me to bed. When I woke up in the morning, he was holding me, and that's when I started to cry.

"I cried for hours, but he never let me go. He canceled appointments for me, but he never said anything about it. He just let me sob until I cried myself out and fell asleep again. When I woke, I told him what'd happened.

"He apologized for ever introducing me to Hunter, even though it wasn't his fault. How was he supposed to know what would happen? I heard Hunter has a twenty-four-seven, TPE slave now. I'm sure they're very happy together."

Who knows? Maybe if I'd given in and agreed on one of the many occasions he'd brought it up, *we'd* still be very happy together. We'd essentially had a Master/slave dynamic when I was on his time, if not quite a Total Power Exchange arrangement. For the most part, I enjoyed it. After all, it wasn't Hunter *wanting* a full-time slave that had been the problem. It was the thermonuclear tantrum he threw when he didn't get it.

But honestly, I don't think happily ever after was in the cards for us. I've known people who were involved in these all-encompassing, all-consuming, Master/slave relationships, and though I didn't—still don't—doubt their happiness, I did have reservations about my own capacity to be satisfied with that kind of arrangement. At least all the time. I certainly wouldn't be able to do it now.

"Anyway, I stayed with Rey for two weeks before I went back to my apartment. It was the oddest thing. I couldn't remember what I was supposed to do, aside from my schoolwork. For a while, I would find myself sitting on my couch for hours, doing nothing. I asked for more hours at my internship, started working out at the campus gym. And I read books. Lots of books. Things I'd wanted to read but never had time for."

"But you were still in school."

Oh, Crispin, you're sweet.

"It wasn't because of school. I read lots of things that weren't for my classes. They were..." I shift in my chair. "Hunter always made sure I did my homework and read whatever was popular so I could talk about it with guests."

Crispin's face has gone grey. I knew he wouldn't like that, Hunter treating me like a pet trained for the entertainment of his friends, but at the time, I didn't mind. It was another way to please him, and I desperately wanted to meet his exacting standards, make him happy, gain his elusive approval.

I don't think Crispin would blink an eye if this involved someone else. He must've seen this a thousand times, knowing the people he does. It's possible he's even done this with one or all of his other subs. But the idea of me—she of the excessive number of degrees who constantly devours and recommends books—being told what I could or could not fill my head with... I get why that would make him a little queasy. I don't think I'd be able to relinquish control of that anymore either, so it's a good thing it doesn't appeal.

But if one of the sweeter aspects of my relationship with

Hunter makes him nauseated, I'm definitely not going to mention the caning I got for my first and only B+. Hunter had been furious and lectured me for what seemed like hours—though I knew the sick feeling in my stomach from having disappointed him was stretching out the time like some vile flavor of saltwater taffy. It was probably more like fifteen minutes, maybe twenty. After that little incident, I got straight As.

I'd stop talking or give Crispin a break, but I need the momentum to keep spilling this godforsaken tale of woe. "He wanted me to keep up with current events, too. Out of spite, I stopped reading the paper, even though he didn't cancel my subscription. After about a month, I was craving some news, but I couldn't bring myself to pick up the *Times* or *The Economist*. So I bought a TV and started watching *The Daily Show*. Ever watch *The Daily Show*? Yeah. I keep meaning to sit down and write Jon Stewart a thank you note—and I will someday. The man made me laugh when I thought I'd forgotten how.

"I sleepwalked through my last year of school. I mean, I worked hard, I was top of my class, but I felt like the walking dead. I didn't talk to anyone I didn't absolutely have to. Except Rey, of course. Rey was my lifeline. I somehow managed to land my job, and I planned to move the day after commencement.

"Rey was the only one who came to my graduation. I don't think he could've been prouder. I thought I might've seen my dad at the back, but when I blinked, the guy was gone and I couldn't be sure. Rey blocked out my calendar for the week after graduation, and I was still so out of it I didn't bother to ask why. He'd been acting like my Dom for the year and a half since the fallout —without any of the fun stuff. Would you do that for someone?"

"I'd do it for you."

My lips part, and I blink at him a few times, bewildered, before I can breathe again. I frown and press my lips together, wrinkling my eyebrows before I open my mouth to say… I don't know what. What comes out is a puff of air, a tiny, forced sigh.

"You can't say shit like that to me, Crispin. Just please don't." I settle myself to look him in the eye. "You're interrupting. You're not supposed to interrupt. Don't you want to hear my story? You said you wanted to hear my story."

"I do."

"Let's get on with this train wreck, shall we?"

He nods, a short, sharp go-ahead.

"It was going to take a week for my stuff to make it to San Diego, anyway, so I did what I was told. I know it's hard to believe, but I didn't know where he was taking me until we were on the plane and the pilot mentioned St. Louis. I turned to Rey and asked why the fuck he was taking me to St. Louis.

"Rey asked me if I trusted him, and I told him I did. Farther than I could throw him. He laughed and told me not to worry my pretty little head. I could've pressed and he would've told me, but he'd steered me through the fog for a year and a half without a scratch. What was one more week?

"When we got off the plane, there was a car that took us out to these beautiful, leafy green suburbs. Right on the border of where the farms started, we pulled up to this house. No, not a house—an estate. Rey showed me in and I didn't think I was ever going to find out why we were there, but then this man came down the stairs. He was older, maybe in his early fifties. Good-looking, but not extraordinarily so. And I could tell, I could just tell...

"Rey told me his name was Elliott and that he wanted to play. I almost died. Rey had asked me a million times if I wanted to play with someone, and I'd refused. I wouldn't even consider it. It wasn't until a few weeks before graduation that I could bring myself to say 'not here' instead of 'not ever,' but I hadn't expected Rey to take that so literally. I probably should've been livid when he brought me to Elliott, and I was. A little. But not more than I wanted it."

I'd wanted it like a woman who'd been wandering the desert

craves water. Rey had steered me toward an oasis and told me to drink. He promised to stay with me, too, hold my hand so I wouldn't drown. If he'd have kept asking me, I would've kept hedging, finding other excuses, and who knows what I would've done when it all got to be too much? Maybe become an alcoholic like my dad. Or worse.

"So I did the only thing I knew with certainty. I got down on my knees. And bless his heart, Elliott walked around me, laid his hand on the top of my head, and stroked my hair. I knew I shouldn't, but when he stood beside me, I leaned into him, closed my eyes, and sighed. He called me 'precious.'

"I knew I could've walked out and Rey wouldn't have done anything but follow me, but I didn't want to." I'd wanted to drink from that spring and never stop. "Elliott kept me for a week. It was…heavenly. Now I'd find him too sweet, too gentle, almost cloying, but then, he was exactly what I needed. You know Elliott?"

"Schreiner?"

"The same."

"I do, not well. Is he still in St. Louis?"

"He is. I send him a Christmas card every year."

"I'm going to send him a case of champagne."

That makes me giggle, although I don't think he's kidding.

"That's how I started doing this. I saw Elliott a couple of times after that, to help me get on my feet, but then Rey found me someone else. And someone else after that. Whenever I'd have time, there was someone waiting for me at the end of a plane ride. They never knew my real name, and I never stayed as long as I did that first time. That's what I've done for the past two and a half years. Never east of the Mississippi."

"You didn't find anyone you wanted to be with for more than a long weekend?"

I shrug. "I saw a few of them more than once, but…no."

"And they let you go? No one ever tried to get you to stay?"

"Maybe they did. They didn't have any way to reach me. Only Rey. He keeps them away with a whip and a chair."

"More whip than chair, I suspect," Crispin observes drily.

"Say what you will about Rey, but the man knows how to wield a cat. He's none too shabby with a bullwhip, either."

"You'll never hear me say a word against Rey Walter."

I know what he's doing, softening me up with oblique compliments, but it's not going to work. "It's easier that way."

"So this is…?"

"Highly irregular. And not easy."

"You sure know how to make a guy feel special, pet."

I'm taken aback before I realize he's teasing, not mocking. I purse my lips and arch a sly brow.

"I sure do." I slink off the couch and onto my hands and knees and start over to him in a languid crawl. "I make you, in particular, feel very special. I'd like to make you feel that way now. If it would please you, sir."

He's about to protest. He has more questions for me, questions I've said I'll answer, but Crispin's a marathoner, not a sprinter. He'll take his time if he thinks it's worth it. It's one of the things I like about him.

I nuzzle his knee and blink up at him, waiting for his response.

"You'd like to please me?"

"Always, sir."

"What would please me is to have you ready and waiting in the studio in ten minutes."

"Yes, sir."

"Off with you, then."

I don't bother to respond, but rise to my feet and walk with grace toward my bedroom to prepare. On my way down the hall, I let out a sigh and realize how tense I've been. I hate talking about myself. At least I won't be saying much of anything for the next few hours.

CHAPTER 19

$\mathcal{M}$y head is busy, buzzing with too many thoughts I can't silence.

"Hey." Crispin's voice snaps me back to attention. "You're mine now, and you'd best remember it. Don't make me remind you again."

"Yes, sir."

My cheeks heat. It's embarrassing to be called out, and a phantom Rey clucks over my shoulder. He'd be so displeased. He trained me better than that.

"If you're having trouble focusing, maybe I can help you with that."

Oh, please. "Yes, sir."

He guides me by my clasped hands to a vacant corner of the studio. He's never brought me over here before, but I've stared longingly at the metal hooks and attachment points from where I've been tethered to the table or draped over his lap on the couch.

When he urges me into where the walls meet, I start to get wet. He lets go of my hands, places them at shoulder height on opposite walls, and kicks my feet apart until my stance is noticeably wide.

"Nose against the wall, bad girl."

The spring loosens as my pelvis tightens. This is the kind of discipline that gets me unbearably hot. I lean forward until my nose grazes the wall, my back bowed slightly and enough weight in my arms that I feel it, will think about it.

"You'll stay there until I come back. While I'm gone, I want you to think about all the things I'm going to do to you."

If that weren't enough to draw my attention back to the present, the warm, broad hands sliding up the insides of my thighs would be. He stops short of where I'm aching for him and backs off. I mewl in protest. That's met by a firm smack to my ass, as I knew it would be.

"If you move or make a sound, you'll be punished. Understood?"

"Yes, sir."

"You don't want to disappoint me, do you?"

"No, sir."

No, I don't. I want him to praise me, reward me with his approval. I will stand in this position until he deems me forgiven for shirking my responsibilities.

He leaves me with a brush of his hand over my ass, and I close my eyes and sigh. There are sounds in the studio as I stand against the wall: Crispin opening and closing drawers, withdrawing the tools of his trade. With every slide of the runners in the tracks, I speculate about what he's getting. Cuffs? A gag? Clamps? A paddle? My kingdom for a paddle.

His devious plot works. I get so focused on every sound he makes, every demand he might impose, that by the time he's close by, my mind is now racing with thoughts of him. He lays his hands over mine and bends down to murmur in my ear.

"Not so distracted now, are you, pet?"

"No, sir."

"Good. You can stand up straight, relax."

I ease my nose off the wall and immediately miss the sensation, but I've traded it for more contact between my body and his. A more than fair exchange. I slide my feet closer together, and he guides my hands off the walls, leaving them to rest by my sides.

"I'm going to put you through your paces soon enough. You need a break."

My eyes bug slightly. He rarely warns me about what he's going to do. This is going to be good. There are sounds and motions behind me, and I'm at a loss as to what he might be doing. Then he slips thick leather cuffs around my wrists and each ankle. Cuffs are standard; that doesn't help me narrow down the possibilities.

Next, he unclips my hair and finger-combs the locks until they spill down my back. He gathers it up, but instead of plaiting it or twisting it, he cinches some kind of tie at the base of my skull. Tightly. He divides my hair, starts to braid, and I can tell from the light tugs that whatever he used to fasten my hair is being threaded through the plait. When he finishes, he ties off and lays the result over my shoulder. I don't look down because he hasn't told me I can, but out of the corner of my eye, I can see strands of thin rope dangling down my body, a bright red that's a pretty contrast to my black hair and pale skin. In a moment of fleeting vanity, I wonder if he bought this for me.

He lays a hand against my shoulder blade and pulls back my arm, testing my range of motion. He makes an appreciative noise at how far back he can bend it. My flexible joints have been delighting bondage enthusiasts for over a decade, and now I have a pretty good idea of what I'm in for.

"No shoulder injuries?"

"No, sir."

"You'll tell me if this gets to be too much."

"Yes, sir."

There's a slight roughness to the rope that makes it impossible to ignore the drag of it over my skin. He winds it around my chest, shoulders, and arms, tying precise knots at careful intervals. You'd think his deliberate pace would bore me, but it doesn't. I love the feel of him positioning me just so, the way the rope cradles and holds me even as his hands move on to the next knot. He's giving me time to think about how vulnerable he's rendering me in this very methodical way, and it both terrifies and thrills me. The pretty fishtail of color draws my arms closer behind my back until my elbows nearly touch and my wrists are cinched together.

"Okay?"

"Yes, sir." *Oh, god, yes.*

My chest is cracked open, my heart beating like horse hooves against my sternum. Grabbing my hips, he backs me up a few paces and nudges my ankles apart with a bare foot. He attaches a spreader bar to the cuffs at my ankles, easing them still farther, and my breath quickens. He wasn't kidding about putting me through my paces. When he's satisfied, there's the familiar snick of a carabiner closing near my wrists and a tug at my hands. I get the urge to bow forward. Cris bands a warm forearm across my collarbones, gripping my shoulder with one large hand.

"You're all right. I've got you."

He pulls the rope taut with his free hand, supporting me with his arm as I fold toward the floor. My thighs feel the strain, and I give in, my head falling forward and my shoulders going loose. When Crispin's satisfied with my position, he lets go of my chest and ties the rope off. It's only then that he grasps the thin strands trailing from my hair and tugs until they're wound around a small eyebolt in the floor. I'm completely immobilized.

He won't be able to leave me like this for long—the strain on my muscles is already starting to tire me—but he doesn't need to. Every last molecule of thought is focused on the predicament he's put me in and what he might do to me. I'm hoping the answer is touch me, fucking *touch* me, and I'm not disappointed.

"You're so pretty all bound up like this, kitten."

He runs his hands from my forcibly spread ankles, up my legs, and over my hips to my stomach and my ribcage, coming to rest at my breasts where he fondles and squeezes, tweaks and pinches my nipples. I couldn't pull away even if I wanted to. With my hair bound tightly, any movement causes a yank at my scalp. Devilish man.

After a few minutes of Crispin toying with me, my breath comes short, and I'm whimpering with desire. His hands wander back to my waist before slipping to the insides of my thighs. He runs a finger along my labia and sighs.

"You're so wet. You love this, don't you? Being completely at my mercy?"

I squeak as two fingers find their way inside me, and Cris winds his arm around my hips so the thrusting motion doesn't put any more strain on my shoulders. Keeping me pinned, he drives his fingers into me over and over, occasionally slicking a thumb over my throbbing clit.

"What are you thinking about?"

His question startles me. Nothing. I'm not thinking of anything. I'm not parsing the data being flung at me. My mind isn't analyzing the flood of sensations. It's happening, and I have to accept it, like a sensual tide coming in. There's nothing for it. Who's done that for me?

"You, sir."

"Then you're going to come for me, aren't you pet? Do it now."

A few weak thrusts of my hips later, my orgasm overtakes me, and my limbs tremble and shudder in their bondage. My body feels pulled apart, the stretch and the raging against my restraints making me feel expanded and constricted all at once. His fingers dig into my hip, and I cry out, my release rolling on and on, my vision going spotty.

My muscles go limp, and the strain on my shoulders grows with the added weight. His arm stays around my hips, but the vague draw on my hair stops and my scalp is freed. Next he unclips my ankles from the spreader bar and urges my feet closer together. I should be able to take more of my own weight, but I'm wilting like an under-watered plant.

He kneels in front of me and wedges a shoulder between my chin and chest, rolling my head to the side. "You can lean on me, mili. I'm not going to let you fall."

When I give up, give in, he releases the rope holding my hands high. I sink to my knees, landing in a limp straddle over his thighs. The blood rushes out of my head into my arms, and I try to blink away the dizziness and the ache. He lifts me, one arm bearing my weight and one holding me close, and brings me to the couch, setting me down so I'm facing the back. I rest my head on the top, absorbing the heat from leather that's been warmed by the rays of sun spilling through the narrow windows.

His hands slip over my bound arms, caressing, inspecting. "Are you okay like this for a little while longer?"

I wiggle my fingers, and the tingling in them says I can take it. "A little, sir."

His voice is tight as he mutters, "I don't think this will take long."

A glow of pleasure blooms on my cheeks, and a slow smile spreads across my face. I'm not the only one affected. His concentration's been as focused on me as mine's been on him, a black hole of hedonism and desire that's sucked the air out of this room as we indulge in each other the way we like best.

There's the unmistakable sound of a fly being unzipped before he lays his hands on either side of my head. His thighs brush mine before he thrusts into me, gliding easily through my wetness. The friction is delicious. The sensation of penetration, of being possessed, is heady. It raises the possibility that he might not be the only one to find satisfaction here. When he grips my throat, hard, possibility turns into inevitability.

"Please, sir. Oh, please." My soft pleading is in no way indicative of my violent desperation. Luckily, he doesn't seem offended.

"Again, pet. Come for me again."

My climax isn't the explosive release of earlier because I've been reduced to jelly already. There's nothing left to shatter, only waves of pleasure rolling through. As my muscles contract around him, he comes with a few hard thrusts and lets go of my neck. There's a quick pat of my hair before his weight is gone.

I rest complacently against the couch back as he unties me. My head is empty of anything except his touch and the slow loosening of the rope. He takes it off, knot by knot, strand by strand, with the same concentration with which he put it on. The ties he'd laid so carefully have tightened under my weight, and now he has to work them free. The focus and the attention he lavishes on me every time he pulls the long lengths back through the knots, careful not to pull too fast and burn my skin, simultaneously delight and mortify me. But no matter how I feel about it, I have to take it. So I do, until he's removed it all and eases my arms to my sides.

He rubs the strained muscles and tells me to turn around, hefting me into his arms for the brief trip to the bed, where he lays me on my stomach and massages my limbs. His dexterous fingers dig into my sore muscles, helping blood find its way back to where it's supposed to be. I moan softly as he works me over; he strokes and soothes me, laying kisses and sweet words as he goes until I'm reduced to a puddle of worn flesh. When he's through, he says low in my ear, "Take a shower. Get dressed. I'll see you on the porch when you're ready."

I was kind of hoping for a nap, but apparently, that's not in the cards. His very well-played cards. God, he's good. It's been a while since I've been this worn out after playing. He knows how to exploit my weaknesses, and he does but not cruelly. Not in a mocking, I-told-you-so kind of way. It's more like running your fingers over a fading bruise until you're pressing really hard but it doesn't hurt anymore. What were you so afraid of in the first place? It makes me feel safe. And strong.

I make myself a cup of tea on the way back through the house, then pad barefoot out to the porch where he's waiting for me. He showered, too; his hair's still damp. He's pulled on jeans and yet another T-shirt from a surf competition. Does the man have an endless supply? He has been surfing for thirty-two years, longer than I've been alive.

I settle myself into a cushy chair and draw up my legs, resting my still-too-hot tea on my thigh.

"Did you ever talk to Hunter again?"

If I'd thought Crispin was going to ease me back into this, I was mistaken. I can't blame him for diving in, though. I might've weaseled my way out of finishing this…unpleasantness. So, though I twist my mouth up and blow a sigh out my nose, I answer.

"Yes. While I was with Rey. I called him the next afternoon. He answered the phone like nothing had happened. Called me baby. I couldn't believe it. The fucker didn't even pretend to be surprised. I swore at him, and he started tallying my punishment."

Ten strokes for asking him what the fuck he was thinking and ten more after he'd asked me if I'd care to ask him again. I had, with emphasis on the *fuck*. Hunter didn't approve of foul language. He rarely swore himself, thought it was gauche, and he wanted me to act like a lady. As I describe the call, Crispin's jaw goes rigid. He doesn't punish me for that sort of thing. I think he likes my dirty mouth.

"I asked him how he could do that to me, and he said, 'I had a problem and I solved it.'"

"What the fuck was his problem?"

Crispin's rage is bubbling out of his ears. I think if he knew where to find Hunter, Hunter would be a dead man by morning. Or at least a sorry one. The idea of the two of them facing off entertains me in a sick way. Crispin would have a couple inches and about twenty pounds on Hunter, though they're both in good shape. I'd bet on Crispin in a fight, obviously, but I'm not sure who'd win. Hunter would be cool and dispassionate, probably have some unfair advantage I can't fathom, whereas Crispin would be all fervency and bloodlust.

But Hunter wouldn't fight for me. Not anymore. I have no doubt he wouldn't have hesitated when I was his, but I'm not now. Haven't been for years, and I doubt he thinks fondly of me, if he thinks of me at all.

"His problem was that I wanted to get a job."

Crispin's rage fizzles into confusion. "A job?"

"Yeah. I was going to be finishing school in a year, and Hunter wanted to know what I planned to do after I graduated. He hadn't been thrilled when I decided to go to grad school and law school, but he hadn't tried to talk me out of it. It reflected well on him that I was so educated. But he'd had enough. He wanted me to be all his, all the time. Twenty-four-seven, TPE."

He'd asked for it before, many times, and I'd always said no. Would have continued to say no. I'd refused him other things, and he'd accepted my limits—with grace, even. No sharps, no breath play, no playing with other people if I wasn't there. I trusted him to respect my denials. I was fine with him asking as many times as he wanted to, needed to, as long as, at the end of the day, my answer was what mattered most.

"And you didn't want that."

I stare into my mug, the cooled tea the color of putty because I take it with milk. I could say no. That's what Crispin wants me to say, what he expects. He didn't phrase it as a question because he can't imagine me being anything other than what I am with him, but I wasn't always like this.

"Sometimes it seemed like a good idea. To not have anything to worry about. To have no responsibilities. To drown out the chaos in my head."

I drag my eyes up to his, fearing what I'll see. Pity or disgust are both possibilities, and I steel myself for either one. But instead I get a patient, cautious nod. "I know that's what you like about it."

Yeah, that, and the incredible amount of sensation another person can inflict on my body, whether pain or ecstasy. Preferably a mix of both. "Anyway, I said no. He offered to let me get another degree. He'd even gotten catalogues for some programs he deemed appropriate. And I still said no. I knew he was pissed, but I thought he'd get over it. Like when I got my law degree and my master's. I miscalculated."

"You didn't miscalculate. The guy's a fucking psychopath."

He puts verbal air quotes around "miscalculate." Coupled with his earnest exasperation and outrage, it warms me. I think sociopath is closer to the truth, but I won't argue semantics. "He thought he'd back me into a corner, and I'd give in."

"But you didn't."

"No, I didn't." A burst of pride and a tiny speck of regret fill my ribcage. "I told him I wanted out of our contract. He said I could have it, but he reminded me there was a clause that stipulated it had to be broken in person. So a few days later, I showed up at his house with Rey.

"Hunter had my things ready to go, boxed up by the door, but he invited us in like we were there for a cocktail party. And it made me want so badly to go back to the way things were, to pretend nothing happened and be led down the path Hunter paved for me. It was Rey who kept me anchored to reality, to do what I needed to do. If he hadn't been there..."

If Rey hadn't been there, I'd probably be with Hunter right now. On a Friday evening? Depending on the company, I'd either be on my knees at his side, being fed bites from his plate in exquisite submissive silence, or I'd be discussing the latest Dave Eggers over cocktails. A thrill of want runs through me. To be back in that house, under Hunter's iron hand, always knowing what was expected and the consequences if I didn't make the grade—it was so fucking simple.

The temptation to give in was real, despite the fact that he'd mangled my life beyond repair. Maybe *because* he had. That's what made Hunter so dangerous. And so goddamn good. "Anyway, I'm glad he was there."

"Me, too."

Crispin's soft words yank me back to the present and wedge a crowbar under the bands of metal crushing my insides, loosening it enough for me to catch a breath. *Jesus, Burke, get your shit together. This happened a lifetime ago. Read the fucking script. Make it entertainment.* I look into his earnest eyes and crack a smile.

"Hunter said he still wanted me, and when I said, 'Not in a way I'm willing to give you,' he lost it. Called me names. I think my favorite was 'obdurate cunt.' I kind of want to put that on my business cards. It's a good one, right?"

Crispin doesn't bite down on my bleak humor, but I didn't think he would. I've dragged him too far down into the muck to propel him out with a cheap trick. "After Hunter calmed down some, Rey left us alone."

"He left you alone with that—"

"I asked him to. I needed to know I could walk away myself."

And part of me—the part that hadn't had enough time or distance to disentangle myself from the treacherous web Hunter had woven—had still been loyal to him. Felt I owed him. Exhibit A: our contract. Sending those pictures had to have shredded that precious agreement, but I couldn't quite bring myself to disregard it. It had been carved into my body and mind for so long that, despite his betrayal, I couldn't completely let go of the urge to honor the rules we'd established. What was another few minutes in the scheme of six years?

"Did Hunter apologize?"

I shake my head and huff a laugh. "No. I didn't expect him to, nor did I want him to. It wouldn't have been sincere. The only thing he was sorry about was that things didn't work out the way he'd planned. The way he was so fucking sure things were going to go. So I kneeled with my head in his lap for a few more minutes and then I left. That's the last time I saw him. He never tried to contact me again. Rey still gets invites for his parties. He's gone a couple times when he's been in town."

"Are you fucking kidding me?"

"Don't be mad at Rey. I told him he should go. It's too important for his East Coast contacts to not. Hunter may be a world-class asshole, but he also knows a lot of people. He wouldn't ask Rey about me. He acts like I never existed. Really. Besides, someone needs to keep an eye out for his new girl."

Rey had agonized over that decision. His first instinct had been to burn Hunter to the ground, rat him out to everyone, get him banned from the scene, but a few things had changed his mind, the first being that I didn't want my story told. It was over, and I didn't want anyone knowing what had happened. The other thing was Rey's fear that, if Hunter had been so dangerous operating in the relative light of the community, what might he be like in darkness? I shudder to think.

I'm sure Rey made it clear to Hunter that he was effectively on probation and another incident would lead to dire consequences. If Rey was a power player when we met ten years ago, he's a force of nature now. I'm not completely familiar with his sphere of influence, nor do I want to be, but Hunter is smart enough to understand the cost should he piss Rey off again.

Crispin is still fuming about Rey despite my reassurances. He looks like he might boil over but turns it down to a simmer. I wait for him to cool a little further before I ask, "Anything else you want to know?"

I pray for him to not press me further about Hunter. I've been candid, more forthcoming than I have been with anyone else, save Rey. But it's possible I've left something important out. Something he wouldn't think to ask.

Hunter had justified his actions by claiming I wasn't fit to be out in the world by myself, that he was doing me a favor by taking the choice away from me. He'd said I was too stubborn to see the truth of it, but I needed him because, at my core, I was a terrified little girl with absolutely no common sense or survival instinct. Thinking about it sends the contents of my stomach into a riot. Not because of the fallout, though I'm still dealing with the consequences. It's really the idea that he played this game, lived this life, with someone he didn't believe could truly give consent. That's just flat-out wrong.

And that's what I'm so afraid of showing. It's not my submissiveness, necessarily, though I'd be rendered less than useless if anyone I deal with professionally ever caught a whiff of that. It was uncomfortable at first to admit how much I enjoyed being given direction, being taken care of after fighting—so fiercely— my parents' efforts to sculpt me into something they might be proud of, but I came to terms with it. It's something I like, something I need, and I have access to people who understand that.

Though I've occasionally wished to find satisfaction at the other end of the whip, I don't, and giving up my own pleasure because I don't like the form it takes seems like the very worst kind of masochism. I'm just not that big of a pain slut. It's that core of iron Hunter couldn't handle, that tiny little bit of me I had to keep to myself in order to feel safe. That piece is a lot bigger now.

I'm not sure if he felt threatened by my duality or if he was just so driven to possess every part of me that, if he couldn't conquer me, no one could have any of me at all. Like a child throwing a birthday cake on the floor because they weren't allowed to have the whole thing. Yet. I can't say for sure that, if

Hunter had given me more time, I wouldn't have agreed at some point. It's moot now.

"Did your parents give you the money?"

"Yeah. My dad had clearly handled the transfer. He was more than generous." An understatement. When I checked my bank accounts a week later, I had a million dollars. I don't know how he got it by my mother. Not my problem. "And I got a package by messenger at my internship. The title to my car, a copy of my lease, documentation for all my utilities, insurance with everything paid through graduation, a new credit card, and everything else I'd need to keep my life humming along as if nothing had changed. He sent a note, too: *You've always deserved better. I hope this will be the chance you need to find it. I love you, Rani.*"

Reason number two to never have children: so I don't disappoint them as much as my father's disappointed me.

"Why'd he call you that?"

"It means princess in Hindi."

"That's not in your contract."

Not like baby and sweetheart, no. Hunter's pet names for me weren't particularly original. "It's never been a problem. Don't call me that." I leave the "*or I will cut you*" implied.

"I wouldn't. I've got my own name for you."

"Plaything."

"You looked it up."

I blink at him. He knew I would. Milimili means *toy, favorite, beloved*, in Hawaiian. I choose to focus on the "toy," so I don't have to yell at him and tell him to stop.

"I didn't touch the money my dad gave me." Or the money Hunter had transferred into my account before I'd had the chance to close it out and open another one he couldn't access. Another cool million in blood money. I'd thought about refusing it, a final foot-stomping, and sometimes I wish I had. But I can be calculating, too. So it sits there, making more money that I hoard, except to pay for my lost weekends. Every time I board a plane or slip into a rental car, it's a metaphorical middle finger to the people who drove me to this. *How do you like me now, assholes?*

I live in a relatively cheap apartment and don't buy much—I don't have to. What I left with is more than enough to last most people a lifetime. Three lifetimes. I kept my car, a pretty shiny graduation present from my parents when I finished law school, even though it would've made more sense to sell, but I like the illusion of my old life. Or, really, the life I'd been promised, one flush with enough resources I'd never have to do anything I didn't want to do. I make pretty good bank, too, so it's less of an illusion than I'd once feared it would be, but I don't allow myself many luxuries. I don't want an illusion. I want the real thing, and I don't want anyone to be able to take that from me.

When I've finished the saga of India Kittredge Burke, Crispin takes me in his lap and holds me. He doesn't say anything, doesn't ask any more questions. He must understand now—why I am the way I am. Why I can't have a normal relationship; why I've flown all over the west looking for people to fuck, to give me what I need in small, safe doses; why the idea of intimacy scares the living crap out of me.

Because intimacy and trust equal pain. They equal hurt and having your life ripped apart. Sharing means trailing little bits of yourself into the woods, only to get to your destination and realize there's nothing left to tear off, no piece of yourself that's your own, and no trail to follow back because someone's swallowed you up. Being loved means being destroyed because you wouldn't let them have that final morsel. Ownership was carved into my body with cuts as deep, real, and painful as the scar on my back. It means broken contracts and promises, the loss of a life. My life, in particular, one I've struggled to put back together. Now he knows.

Is knowing why going to make up for the fact that it's true? It doesn't change the way I am. It doesn't resolve any of my issues. If anything, it makes them worse. I've drawn a diagram of how to fuck me over, how to twist the knife should he ever feel like shoving one in my back.

This is why I prefer to present as a submissive and nothing but a submissive. If they think I've given them my all, there's nothing left to go after, so they can't really hurt me. The bruises and the welts heal. I like to admire them in the mirror until they do. Proof that I'm resilient. But even so, there's only so much battering I can take.

This was stupid. So fucking stupid. I don't want to consider the danger I've put myself in yet again. I distract him with more sex before I'm smothered under the knowledge that I've shared my secrets and I'm going to be sorry. We never sign the contracts, and it's the first time I've fucked someone without a piece of paper since I was in high school. It feels weird but good. I'll never do it again.

When Rey calls on Monday, I ought to tell him no. No more Kona, no more Crispin. Too dangerous, I'm out. I can't do it anymore. But because I'm not very bright, the rest of my world is still turned upside down and I need Crispin's help to unwind, when Rey calls, I tell him "a month" and desperately wish it could be sooner.

CHAPTER 20

*A*fter a long, super-shitty day of unraveling more tangled webs of where the LAHA money's gone, I head to the apartment Lucy found for me in LA and take a bath. A decent bathtub was the one request I made when she was scouring Craigslist for my crash pad, and she managed not to fuck up. I've been here for two months and will probably be here for one more. I thought I couldn't loathe California more, but having to live in LA has changed my mind. I've never been so homesick for Manhattan.

I towel off, slip on a camisole and sleep shorts, and click on my Blackberry. A voicemail from Jack.

"Call me."

This does not bode well. Raging Jack I can handle. Almost-silent seething Jack is another matter. He's unpredictable when he's like this, and I hate surprises. I much prefer the devil I know. I pour myself a glass of wine, grab my omnipresent tablet, and settle myself on the dorm room couch that came as part of my "furnished" apartment.

There's half a ring before Jack is demanding, "You need to work your Cooper magic."

"Whoa, slow down. What's going on?"

"You know who Slade Lewis is?"

"Of course." Slade Lewis is the Assistant Secretary for Public Housing at HUD—i.e., Cooper's boss and the only person I've ever heard her speak of with a quaver in her voice. Slade Lewis has a reputation for being brilliant, driven, capricious, and nasty. He's also devastatingly handsome.

I've never laid eyes on him in person, but I've seen pictures. His strong jaw, hazel eyes, and dark hair greying at the temples are enough to make my little subbie heart flush. Yes, I am fully aware of who Slade Lewis is.

"He's coming, and he's on the warpath."

"Why?"

"Because shit's been hitting the fan all over the place. Philadelphia, New York, Chicago, Houston, even fucking Missoula. Can't lumberjacks build their own goddamn housing? Public housing's getting reamed in the press, and even though I don't think we could've handled this mess better, he's got to make an example out of someone and he's got his sights set on LAHA. I need you to call Cooper. Do whatever it is you do to her and direct his attention elsewhere."

"I'll call her, but I don't know—"

I'm interrupted by the click of Jack hanging up on me.

"Cooper."

It's seven o'clock EST, and I'd guess by her tone that Constance hasn't had her coffee yet.

"Constance, lovely lady," I coo. "Something you wanted to tell me?"

"I was going to call you today. I didn't think you'd be awake yet."

"I wish I weren't, but I heard Slade's on the warpath. Any way you can keep us out of the line of fire?"

"I wish I could. Honestly, I already tried, and it backfired. Don't get all freaked out, but I think he's got an interest in you personally."

"Me? Why?"

"He's been following you in the press."

Goddammit. I'm going to skin Brad Lennox alive with a pair of safety scissors and make a parasol out of his hide.

"Get him to unfollow me. You know we're doing good work here. What else does he want from us?"

"I don't know. He's playing cagey on this for reasons beyond my understanding or pay grade. I've even tried throwing Bakersfield at him in hopes it would get him off your back, but no such luck. He's gunning for you. We're coming for a site visit, with auditors. Them, you shouldn't be worried about. I've seen your books. They're spotless. I'll be there Wednesday, and Hurricane Slade makes landfall Friday morning."

Friday? No, no, no! I'm supposed to be in Kona for a much-needed break. I haven't seen Crispin for a month, and our last phone conversation was so hot I wouldn't have been surprised if the windows in my apartment had fogged up. *I already don't like you, Mr. Lewis, and fucking with my lost weekend is not the way to win a place in my heart.*

"Staying long?" I venture.

"No, we're driving out to Bakersfield for an afternoon meeting. We'll be out of your hair by eleven. Are we ruining a long weekend for you?"

"Not ruining. Delaying. Sounds like I'm going to need it even more after your visit."

"I hate to say this because you're tough as they come, but I know Slade. If he feels like raking you over the coals, you're going to burn."

This is not good, but for now, I'll keep my chin up.

"I'll see if Rey can join us for dinner Thursday. It's usually a good night for him. Is Glory coming?"

"Not this time. She's jealous I'll get to see you, but I set her up on a surprise playdate."

"Ooo, with who?"

"Ananke."

My eyes widen. "Lucky Glory." Ananke's a Domme who has a fondness for hot wax and edge play. The trifecta doesn't appeal to me and Constance isn't into the heaviest stuff. This is a nice gift to her beloved little sub, who occasionally likes her sex very, very dark.

"I think so." Constance is smug, and not-quite-jealousy tweaks my stomach. I'm not jealous of Glory playing with Ananke. I *am* envious Constance has done this for her. Has sat down and thought, *What would make my Glory happy?* That kind of relationship-y stuff usually sounds like a whole lot of work and not at all worth the trade-off—reason number thirty-two not to get married—but I can't help but wonder what Crispin would dream up for me if he had the chance.

No, stop it, India. If Crispin ever did something so sweet, you'd bite his head off.

"Why is it you only went to do a site visit after managing the authority for four months?"

I'm sweating. I don't sweat. "It's not standard procedure to—"

"You think I give a fuck about standard procedure?"

"I think you should. It's your office that wrote it, and following it is where our liability rests. If it's broken, fucking fix it. Don't blame it on me."

I've always thought hazel was a muddled color for eyes. My green one's been my favorite since I was a kid, seeming more confident of its place in the world versus the wishy-washy, can't-pick-green-or-brown of hazel. But I might have to rethink that because Slade Lewis is staring me down with indecisive eyes—but the choices are to throttle me or throw me to the ground by my hair and have his way with me. The feeling is mutual.

"India!"

Right. I might be allowed to pepper my heart-to-hearts with Jack with expletives, but it's probably a bad idea with Mr. Lewis.

"She's not wrong," Constance says in the meekest voice I've ever heard out of her mouth. "If we'd like site inspections to be part of standard receivership procedure—"

Slade holds up a hand, and Constance goes silent.

"I'm holding you responsible, Ms. Burke. You should've been more on top of this, and if your firm can't handle it, we'll find someone who can. God knows we pay you enough to do more than a half-assed job. Don't think I haven't noticed what you people wear. What is that—Prada? You're going to get us crucified."

I'm impressed he seems to know his way around haute couture, but not so well he doesn't recognize the cut of my black skirt suit as being from five years ago. And there's no way to defend myself. Poor little rich girl. My head is spinning from his dressing-down, which is twenty minutes in.

Jack clears his throat. "If Ms. Burke is your problem, I'll take her off the project."

What? Rage and embarrassment flood through me in equal measure. *He can't do that.*

"I thought you said she's the best you've got."

"She is."

"Then you've got bigger problems than this project, Mr. Valentine," Slade grinds out before turning back to me. "As have you. Your work has been sloppy, late, and some of it is downright wrong. You have a reputation, and I've been extremely disappointed to see you haven't earned it at all. Do you skate by on your looks? Because I've got to tell you, those don't impress me much either."

"Slade!" gasps Constance.

This is unbelievable. But something clicks. I know this guy. Not Slade Lewis specifically, but I know his type. Hell, I've fucked his type. Guys who get off not on embarrassing women—a little embarrassment gets me going as much as the next submissive—but *humiliating* women. That's what he's doing. Publicly. He's enjoying himself, and he's not going to stop until I'm in tears.

If I saw this scene going down at a club, I'd shrug. It's not my kink, but I'd know that both parties had consented and were having a damn good time. And if they weren't, a single word would bring the whole thing to a halt.

But this isn't a play party. There's no safeword and no dungeon monitor or solicitous host to throw him out on his ass. He's not following the rules, and it's not okay. Would it still get him off if this were negotiated and boundaries had been agreed upon?

If so…god, Slade. Let me show you a world where you could find a yin to your yang. They'd be thrilled to have you. If not, then you're just a raging asshole who should be dropped in shark-infested waters with a chum bucket for a chaser.

I don't have the capacity to dissect Slade's psychology any further because all my energy is being used to withstand his tirade. He continues to berate me, picking on every typo I've ever made, telling me Princeton called and wants their diploma back, insulting my work on unwinding this tangle of deceit—anything, everything he can think of. Constance is clued in and looks pissed. Jack seems to have no idea he's watching sex. Not the sex I'd like to have, but it's sure doing something for Slade. I'd bet money he'll excuse himself for what will be a very brief visit to a private office to "make a phone call" before he and Constance head to Bakersfield.

In the meantime, his constant barrage of insults is grinding me down. I'm guessing my resistance to what surely would've had most people in a sniveling puddle of goo on the floor is only making this more satisfying for him. India Kittredge Burke, presenting a challenge since the day I was born.

He finally gets his way when he demands, "What are you, some kind of enchantress? A goddamn witch to have all these people falling all over you like you're the Second Coming?"

I hate crying, and the fact I'm about to do it over news so old it's ancient makes me even more pissed and out of control. Even replaying Hunter's voice in my head isn't helping. At first I hear him say I've beguiled him, but it morphs into every lecture he ever gave me, every time I disappointed him.

What I'd like to do is strip off my coat, get down on my knees with my forehead to the floor, and let Slade at my ass with the black leather belt yanked from the trousers of his finely tailored suit. Who is he to berate me for my fashion choices, anyway? He's wearing fucking Burberry. But that's part of it, right? It doesn't matter how invalid his complaints. I still feel shitty and helpless, and tears are forming. I try to blink them back, but the constant criticism in front of Jack and Constance is too much. I swipe the first traitorous drop rolling down my cheek with the back of my hand.

Punish me any other way than this, you sadistic bastard.

Slade hurls a few more insults my way before declaring it's time to head to Bakersfield—but he has a call to make first.

"Is there an office I can use?"

"102." My eyes feel swollen from my efforts to resist crying, but I stare Slade down without blinking. "There's no window."

He smirks at my humorless joke and leaves. Constance goes after him, not meeting my eyes. She'll call later, but I won't get the message. My Blackberry will be sitting on my coffee table in my sorry excuse for an apartment while Crispin cleans up the mess Slade's made. Jack tries to talk to me, but I close my eyes and tighten my jaw.

"Don't worry about it. I've got a plane to catch. We'll talk Monday."

◈

When Crispin picks me up at the airport, he can tell something's not right.

"What happened, India?"

"Don't, please."

"Okay." He studies me as he closes my door. He's wary after the last time I was here, maybe trying to be respectful of the barriers I've thrown up around myself.

"You remember when I asked you to be strict with me?"

"Sure."

"You need to make that look like a nursery rhyme."

He doesn't try to talk to me for the rest of the drive but glances over periodically. I've tucked my knees up on the seat, and my arms are crossed tight over my chest. I'm trying to hold myself together until we get to his house.

I take the contracts from my bag, flip to the second-to-last page, make a change to the fourth clause on each copy, and initial by it. When I shove them across the table without saying a word, he starts to fill them out but stops when he gets to the change. Instead of reading "Pain: The submissive consents to experiencing a moderate amount of pain at the hands of the Dominant," it now says "Pain: The submissive consents to receiving a ~~moderate~~ an extreme amount of pain at the hands of the Dominant."

"India—"

"Don't, please." I drop to my knees and clutch at his jeans. "Please, Crispin. I don't ask you for much. Please."

My face is buried in the worn denim, my fingers grip the

fabric tight, and my bare knees grind into the wood floor. My hands have started shaking, and I can't make them stop. It seems like forever before Crispin is smoothing the hair on the top of my head.

"Ten minutes."

I nuzzle his thigh in gratitude before heading to my room.

Two hours later, I'm tethered blindfolded to the cross, my back stinging with raised welts from a harsh flogger, my ass and thighs reddened from a firm hand-spanking, followed by a paddling. Now Crispin is imprinting parallel lines over all that with a cane. It's not enough. He's not hitting me as hard as he can, and I'm angry.

He cracks a seventh stripe on that most diabolical of sweet spots, the sensitive crease between behind and thigh, and then the cane hits the floor. Denim-clad thighs press into my heated, raw ass, and he lays his hands over mine, untethering my wrists.

"No," I plead.

"I think you've had enough, pet." His stubble whispers against the sensitive skin behind my ear, something I usually find comforting, but it's doing nothing for me.

"No. It's not enough. More. Please. I need more."

"We're done for now. You need to rest."

My hands scramble at the wood of the cross, the loosened straps, holding myself to it even as he undoes the rest of my bondage.

"More!"

"I said no, Kit." He's broken out his best Dom voice, but it barely registers.

"What are you going to do, punish me?"

"I will when you've come to your senses, and it's not going to be in a way you'll enjoy."

I'm free, and I feel like a loaded pinball poised to career out of control. I want to slam up against things until I stop feeling anything at all, until I'm numb. I want him to hit me so hard I disappear, cease to exist. I'm still *feeling* far too much and it's his fault.

"What are you, not man enough for this, Cris? Your pretty little sub tells you that you need to hit her harder, and you can't get it up for that? What the fuck kind of Dom are you?"

I shove him in the chest as a parting shot, but he doesn't budge. He's like the goddamn Rock of Gibraltar, and his lack of reaction brings my fury to a head. I'm about to beat on his chest when he grabs my wrists in his inescapable hands.

"I'm man enough to know you've had enough. You're hurt and you're angry, and you think the way to make it go away is for me to beat the living shit out of you. I'm not going to. You've had enough."

I struggle against him, but it's useless. I don't know that I've ever been so angry. I scream at him, saying god knows what kinds of horrible things, but he keeps a hold of my wrists, letting the atom bomb that is India Burke detonate in a sparsely populated area. I'm still railing at him when his soft voice interrupts me.

"I'll make you a deal, mili."

I stop and flash my eyes to his, wary or maybe even predatory. I can't resist a bargain, and he's made some cherries in the past.

"If you take a bath and you still want more, I'll give it to you."

A dangerous offer. Warm water has a way of sapping my resolve.

"If I say no?"

"I can do this all night, and I'll put you on a plane tomorrow. Or maybe lock you in your room until your flight on Sunday. Haven't quite decided yet."

I glare at him. I'm tempted to say no to be contrary, but neither of the alternatives sound appealing in the least. He'd do it, too. Besides, the distraction of a deal has taken the wind out of the sails of my tantrum, and if I'm totally honest, my body has started to hurt. The residual sting of the flogger, the heated ache from the paddling, and the blistering pain from the cane are fresh and present now that I've reemerged from subspace.

"Fine."

"Good girl."

He loosens his grip warily, as if I'll make a run for it, but my word is good. When I take a step toward the bathroom, my legs give out, and the room spins. It's possible it would've been a good idea to eat sometime today. Luckily, Crispin is prepared, and I don't hit the floor before he scoops me up effortlessly against his chest. We don't make it to the bathroom before I start to cry.

$\mathcal{H}$e rinses me off in the shower while the bathtub fills and then slips me into the steaming water. It hurts like a bitch for the first few seconds, but after the initial sting, it's incredible. After getting me a glass of water, he undresses and slides in behind me.

"Tell me what happened."

He wraps his arms around me, and I tell him about Slade, that fucker. Though he goes tense and rigid, he doesn't say anything until I'm finished.

"Nothing he said was true."

I shrug and shake my head.

"From what you've told me about Constance and Jack, they'd never let you get away with any of that."

"No," I grant, not wanting to impugn their characters. They're two of the smartest and hardest-working people I know, and they don't pull any punches.

"So why was it so upsetting?"

"I couldn't defend myself. He was blatantly mind-fucking me, and there was nothing I could do."

"Why didn't you tell me when you got here?"

"I didn't want to rehash it. I wanted you to make it go away."

"I understand. But maybe talking about it first might have taken the edge off, and then I could give you what you need? I'm not going to hurt you. Actually…"

There's a sigh from behind me. I shift to face him, leaning up against the opposite end of the tub. "What?"

"I'm uncomfortable being so rough with you."

"Why?"

"I don't always understand what you're getting out of it."

"But you've done all this with your other subs."

He frowns but concedes. "Yes."

"So what's the problem?"

"That's all they were. I mean, I cared for them. I wanted them to be happy. I felt responsible for them. But why they were doing it wasn't that important to me because I never…"

He falters, and my heart seizes. He never *loved* them. That's what he's going to say. *Don't, Crispin. Please don't.* Love fucks everything up. It makes men think they own me down to my very core. That I'm not allowed to keep anything to myself. It means selling my soul and putting my whole self at risk. *You don't love me. Don't love me.*

But to protest would be to admit I know what he's going to say, so I shut him up the only other way I know how. I throw myself across the tub, sending waves of hot, salted water sloshing over the sides. My mouth is on his, plundering, pushing, biting his lip hard. I taste blood—not mine—and then Crispin shoves me against the far side. My challenge has been accepted. We struggle in the warm water, flailing slick limbs, pulling damp hair, digging desperate fingers into flesh.

He grabs my sore cheeks, kneading with both hands, fingering the marks he's made on me. I rake my nails down his back as I moan into his mouth. He wrenches his lips away from mine and growls, "Out."

I want to push back, but the look on his face tames me. I

climb out, naked and dripping, waiting for him. He emerges from the water and grabs my biceps, propelling me back until I hit the tiled wall hard, the cool smooth surface a shock against my skin. He pins me with his hips and kisses me again, insistent and aggressive.

He pulls away long enough to instruct, "Spread your legs," and enters me roughly. No warm-up here, just a straight-up, hard fuck against a wall. This is the *more* I needed. Not more of a beating, although that would've done eventually. This is better. He's slamming into me so hard I can't touch the ground, even up on my toes. I scale his legs with my feet, finding my way to his hips and wrapping myself around him. *Don't let go, Crispin, don't let me go.*

"Come on, India. Give this to me."

I'm startled by his use of my real name. I whine and push at him with my hands. My heart is beating hard with terror, my stomach clenching in panic, my throat closing with fear. He grabs my hair and pulls hard, forcing me to look at him.

"Goddamn it, India. Give it up. Now. Come for me."

My body is warring with my head. I'm at the edge, and it could go either way. Female desire is fickle, and one stupid word could ruin this. But I want it. I want to be India making love to Crispin, not the fuck-toy-sex-doll everyone else gets. He's the only one who's ever wanted it. Who's fought for it. For *me*.

"Yes!" As I gasp the word, an orgasm wracks my body, rolling out in waves, sending pleasure through every inch of me. Unrestrained, unadulterated pleasure. I should come as India more often. He's emptying himself inside me, and I clutch his head in my arms, holding him close as he shudders.

"India," he says with each last, uneven thrust, "India, India."

I'm yours, Crispin. I'm all yours.

After the sex, I feel better but not a hundred percent. I'm still hearing Slade's voice thudding in my head. I need to silence it before it grows any louder, otherwise all of Crispin's hard work will be for naught. I tell him so while he's holding me on the tile floor, and he's pensive for a moment.

"I'm not going to hit you anymore." He's daring me to argue, but I'm not sorry. I ache, and I'm not sure how much more I could take and still drag my ass to work on Monday. "But I think some bondage would do you a world of good."

His hand circles my wrist, and I'm instantly distracted. And horny. I love being restrained.

"Stay." He disentangles himself and comes to his feet, a column of tan, masculine flesh. I admire him from my place on the bathroom floor while he showers, his muscles moving easily under his skin. He pulls his jeans on and walks out to the studio. I curl up to await further instructions and recall the sensation of Crispin's hand around my wrist. More than the crack of the cane, it made me feel possessed by him, subject to his will. I'm meditating on it when he returns.

"India." His use of my real name snaps me back to my full faculties.

"Yeah?"

"How would you feel about moving this to your room? I'd like to keep you tied up for a good long time, but the bed in here isn't exactly made for long-term occupancy. You can say no, and I'll figure it out."

"No, that should be okay."

"Good." He's got his Dom face back on. "Get up."

An hour later, I'm propped against pillows on my comfy bed, being fed grape leaves and licking hummus from Crispin's fingers. I also happen to be blindfolded and bound to the bedframe: arms stretched along the headboard, knees spread wide and tethered to my elbows, ankles cuffed and affixed to attachment points under the mattress.

"Open," he urges and slips a bite of spanakopita into my mouth.

It is, like everything else Crispin has made for me or done to me, delicious. "Going Greek today, are we?"

"I believe I'll go Greek on you later." I almost choke on my next mouthful. "Are you finished?"

"Yes, sir." Even though I could eat half as much again, I don't want to fall into a food coma. I want to stay awake for whatever he's plotting for me.

"I'll be back in a bit. In the meantime, you'll enjoy these."

He applies some vicious clips to my nipples, and I whimper as my core clenches in wanting. I wait for him, testing my bonds periodically. Not because there's any chance of escaping—Crispin knows what he's doing—but because I can't sit still with the constant pinch on my nipples and a little hapless struggle turns me on.

I pull at my wrists again and startle when I hear Crispin's voice. "So eager to be released?"

"No, sir."

"Good. Not that it matters much. You're mine for another couple of days, and I'd forgotten how much I like having you completely at my mercy."

He unravels my bonds, starting with my ankles and ending at the blindfold, rubbing my limbs once I've been released.

"Turn around and kneel up."

I do as I've been told, and he casually clips the cuffs adorning my wrists together behind my back. I get the feeling I'll only be completely free for a few minutes at a time until I go home. Good.

He's moving things about on the bed, the only clue the soft rustle of linens. The clips are removed from my nipples, and he licks and sucks at my flesh as the blood rushes back in. I inhale sharply. He bends me at the waist over a pile of pillows until my hips are elevated; my sensitized nipples are rubbing against the sheets and my head is resting on the mattress.

"Spread your legs." He presses my bound wrists into the small of my back with one hand and drags the fingers of his other over my clit. I gasp, already throbbing. Bondage makes me disproportionately hot. I wriggle against him, trying to get more contact—it won't take much for me to get off—but instead of a glorious orgasm, I get a harsh spank.

"We're not even close. I'm going to have some fun with you before you get to have any at all."

I groan, and he threatens, "Quiet or I'll have to gag you."

He slips a finger inside of me, stroking in and out. I'm aching for more.

"Feeling a little empty, are we?"

"Yes, sir."

"We can fix that."

Lube slips down my cheeks, and Cris presses a finger into my ass.

"Relax, kitten," he chides as he works the lube into me, adding a second finger once he has enough play. I let go enough for him to prepare me, enjoying the sensation of him plumbing the most physically private part of me. His fingers leave, and then he presses a plug into me to make up for their absence.

"Better?"

"Yes, sir. Thank you, sir."

He sits me up by my shoulders and helps me off the bed, directing me to kneel up on a folded blanket on the floor. Crispin's naked, his hard body looming in front of me. I count the pale scars adorning his tanned frame while I wait for my instructions, ever-conscious of the plug buried inside me and my hands cuffed behind my back.

He cups my face and tilts my chin until I look at him.

"You're such a pretty little thing. And so talented. Do you know what would please me?"

"What, sir?"

"If you'd take me in your mouth. You'll do that, won't you?"

"Yes, sir."

"And why will you do that?"

I blink. Is this a trick question? "Because you've told me to, sir."

"And you'll do what I've ordered because you're a good girl, so eager to please, aren't you?"

"Yes, sir." Tears swim in my eyes. I know this is messed up, but Crispin's praise for my sexual prowess and my obedience pushes Slade's diatribe further from my mind. I *am* a good girl, I do like to please, and goddammit, I'm good at what I do.

I take Crispin in my mouth and work at him, stroking my tongue along his erection and pulling at the bonds on my wrists. Between the grunts and small moans of pleasure I'm eliciting from him and the tug of the restraints holding me back, I'm panting and desperate when he finds his release at the back of my throat. I finish him scrupulously, resting my head on his thigh when I'm through.

He sinks to his knees in front of me, laying kisses all over my face, my neck, and my shoulders before he takes a long stroke with his tongue from my collarbone to my ear that makes me shiver. I press myself against him shamelessly, and he takes me in his arms and hauls me onto the edge of the bed. He deposits me face up, directing me to lean back on my elbows and spread my legs with my feet braced against the frame. It's awkward in my bonds, but I forget all that when he settles himself on his knees between my thighs.

"I know you like this, but don't you come," he warns, and then he dips his head to the juncture of my thighs.

My head falls back with a groan of lust as he licks, sucks, and gently bites. If he doesn't want me to come, this is not advisable.

But he's the consummate tease, leading me up to the precipice with his ministrations only to back off when I'm about to tip into an orgasm. He edges me for half an hour, driving me insane with his mouth and fingers, mocking me gently and threatening to strap me down when I can't keep my hips still. There's no way he'll restrain me more, though, knowing how hot it makes me. I'm surprised the suggestion alone doesn't make me lose control.

He finishes his teasing, releases my wrists, and I collapse, enjoying his touch as he massages my sore arms. My whole body is alive and desperate for him, and I writhe against him when he lays the length of his body along mine. I take his curly hair in my hands and drag him toward me for a kiss, but he avoids me, clucking.

"Oh, no, I'm not through with you. You've had your Greek, and now I'd like mine."

He pulls away, stacks a few pillows in the middle of the bed, and playfully pushes me over them, binding my hands to the headboard. He pushes and tugs at the plug that's been resting devilishly inside of me all this time and commands, "Let go."

I will myself to relax enough for him to remove it, and seconds later, he presses into the empty space left in its wake. I love it when Crispin has me this way. He's skilled and considerate, making it feel incredible. He eases into me, groaning when he sinks to the hilt. He strokes in and out slowly, teasing, and I mewl.

"Not yet."

I thrust my hips against him petulantly, and he grabs them. "Is that how you want to play?"

"Yes, sir," I plead.

Before the last syllable is out of my mouth, he's thrusting hard into me. *Oh, fuck yes.* But he's still tormenting me. This is enough to make me burn for him but not get me off. He slows his pace long enough to drop the grip on my hips and slide a finger into me where he can feel himself through the thin membrane.

"Is this what you need, pet?"

"No, sir." Evil genius. He's going to tease me so hard I'll forget my name when I come.

"How about this?" He punctuates the last word with a hard tug on my hair.

"No, sir!" But I am damn close. Just, just, just... *Crispin, please.*

He slips his finger out of me, finds my clit and strokes me, and I'm close. "That's what you want, isn't it?"

"Yes, sir!" I'm dangling over the abyss with only a fingertip-hold on the edge.

"Then come for me. Show me what a good girl you are and come for me."

I hold out for him to finish his sentence, and then my body implodes. My wrists snap my bonds taut, my torso clenches convulsively, and my muscles contract around him. My climax urges his release, and his thrusts become uneven, desperate, as he spends himself inside of me. He collapses over my back, his breath coming hard before it evens out and he withdraws, leaving me briefly to clean up. When he comes back, he untethers my wrists, takes me into his arms, and pulls me close.

"That's my good girl. My good, sweet girl."

I nuzzle into him and fall asleep, all thoughts of Slade Lewis banished from my brain by the warm, glowy cloud of Crispin's praise and the strength and warmth of his body wrapped around mine.

CHAPTER 22

*C*rispin's thorough treatment gets me through the next several weeks. I barely think of Slade Lewis at all. I've been in LA for three months, but I'm confident we're nearing a tipping point that will allow me to go back to San Diego. Still, to get there I've had to buckle down and work through weekends for the past month. I've muddled my way through enough financial records to blind a lesser soul, and I've untangled the last of the money trail with the help of some forensic accountants. Janis and her compatriots managed to sack a combined 1.3 million dollars from the operating fund, and the housing authority will press charges. People will be going to jail.

We haven't fixed everything by a long shot—there's still a ton of work to do—but I don't hear another peep out of Slade Lewis. When Jack's number pops up on my Blackberry, I'm almost certain it's going to be good news.

"I need you back. Chow, Rodriguez, and Evans are coming up tomorrow morning. You'll show them what's what and then get on a plane. I just got a call from Greg Wu in Phoenix. We made the short list for the contract. If you want it, it's yours."

I'm surprised he's offered this to me in the wake of Sladegate, but it's not for HUD. Maybe this is his way of apologizing. I'll have to work non-stop for the next several weeks to keep on top of LAHA while preparing for this, which means cancelling my next trip to Kona, but for this, Crispin will understand.

"I want it."

～

It's four o'clock. Half an hour until the biggest proposal of my career. Jack and I will be talking to Greg Wu about a technical assistance gig for the City of Phoenix. It's fricking huge, and it's mine. I've been busting my ass for weeks getting prepped for it, and today's the day. I'm ready.

Rey texted me earlier:

You're going to hit it out of the court today! Call me when you're through for a virtual victory toast. ILYK

Oh, Rey and his hopelessly mixed sports metaphors. It's one of the few things that make me giggle. Crispin had sent one, too:

You'll be perfect. We'll celebrate when I see you next week. Miss you.

I'd shoved my phone deep in my purse after receiving them, knowing nothing else would show up on my cell for the rest of the day. I check it now—a tic, a formality—and I'm surprised to see half a dozen texts, three missed calls, and a voicemail from Crispin. *What the hell?*

To open or not to open? It could be important. I should call him back. But if it's important, then I shouldn't distract myself from the call I have in…twenty minutes. I don't usually get nervous about work stuff, but this has got me jittery. I need to focus. I'll check when we're through.

I take up my tablet to look over my talking points one more time when Lucy chirps through my speaker.

"Ms. Burke?"

"Yes, Lucy."

"There's a Mr. Cris Ardmore on the phone for you? He says it's important?"

What? Panic and fury flood me in equal measure as my tablet clatters to the desk.

"Put him through. Cris?"

"India—"

"Why are you calling me here?"

"I tried your cell, but you didn't pick up—"

"I'm at work. I have my big pitch in…fifteen minutes. I was going to call when it was over."

"Can you come this weekend?"

"No, I can't." I eye my watch. I'd like to go over those notes one last time…

"Please."

"I can't, and I don't have time to—"

"Please. I need you."

I roll my eyes at his melodrama. "You can need me in a week. Right now I have to—"

"My dad is sick."

"Your dad is always sick." The second the words leave my mouth, I'm flooded with regret. *Fuck.* I can't believe I've said that. I want to take it back, but—

"You can be a heartless bitch sometimes, you know that, pet?"

"Yes." Yes, I know. And so should he. I don't know why he's surprised. But even for me, that was bad. Really, really bad. So bad Crispin doesn't have anything else to say. I cut him off before he can think of something that will make me feel even worse. "I'm at work. I have to go. Don't call me here again."

There's a pause, a silence stretching out between us. "Maybe I shouldn't call you anywhere again."

My heart seizes in panic, but the rest of me is relieved —*finally, a chance to get rid of this guy*—and pissed—he's *mad at* me?

"Maybe you shouldn't. You don't get to be angry about this. You're the one who fucked up. Don't make this my fault retroactively because you don't like it when I'm mad at you. You know you're not allowed to call me here, and you need to respect my rules. I don't ask for much—"

"No, you don't. Because you don't think you deserve much."

"Would you shut up with this India-hates-herself bullshit? I happen to think I'm pretty great. I'm smoking hot, I'm smart as hell, I make good money, and I'm a damn fine lay. I like the way I live. It's worked for me for a long time. Now you've come along, and you're fucking it up. Royally."

"India…"

Rage colors my vision when he says my name. Suddenly I hate —*hate*—hearing it come out of his mouth. I knew this was a bad idea. Worse than bad. I am going to end up in pieces, and I can't afford to lose myself for another year and a half. I have shit to do. I knew letting him say my name, letting him in, was a bad idea. It's given him power over me, and all I can think of are the million ways he can hurt me.

"Oh, no. Don't you 'India' me. Privilege revoked. Don't ever call me that again. Actually, take your own advice and don't call me. We're done."

I slam the phone into the cradle on my desk and keep slamming it down, over and over. *What have I done?* I want to call him back, apologize, and ask him to forgive me. I want to yell at Lucy to get me on the next flight to Kona to be with him. How sick is Mal that Crispin would break all the rules? I should…but I can't. I have a call with Greg Wu in five minutes, and there's a five-million-dollar contract hanging in the balance. I cannot be Girl with Boyfriend Trouble. I must be India "Soulless" Burke. India "Ruthless, Driven, Take-No-Prisoners, Just-Try-to-Stab-Me-

Through-the-Heart-Crispin-Ardmore-Because-You're-Not-Going-to-Find-One" Burke.

I force myself to stop beating my phone against the desk, blink back the tears that are threatening to spill, and rest my head in my hands to give myself a little pep talk.

It's over. One less thing to worry about. It's better this way. Easier. Rey will find you someone new. Someone who's way less trouble. He's been trouble from the start, and you shouldn't have let it get this far. Look at you—you're a mess. This is what happens when you care *about people, when you have* feelings*. That stops here and now. Get your shit together, Burke, and put on your face. It's game day, and you are going to win.*

By the time I'm through, I've calmed down. Yes, this is for the best; better it happened before it got any worse.

"Lucy!"

"Yes, Ms. Burke?" Her disembodied voice wafts through the speaker. She sounds sympathetic. It makes me want to rip her throat out. Humiliation cuts through me, along with more rage at Cris. *My fucking assistant heard that, you asshole.*

"Can you do your fucking job for once and get me a goddamn cup of coffee without me having to ask?"

"Apparently not, Ms. Burke, but I'll get you one right away."

Ugh, Lucy is having feelings too? Talking with Greg and Jack will be good. They're my people; we understand each other. And it's a good thing, too, because it's go-time. I pull up my notes on my tablet and punch in the numbers for the conference call on my phone. Greg and Jack are already there. I put my feet up on my desk and take a deep breath.

"Gentlemen, let's get down to business."

Days pass in a blur. I work, I try to sleep, I work out, and that's about it. No matter what I do, I can't escape this ache. My personal cell rings, and I don't pick it up. He calls Rey, and Rey calls me.

"Cris called again."

"I'm sorry."

"Don't be sorry. It's not the first time I've screened your calls."

"I know, but they're not usually this persistent."

"No, they're not. Probably because they only wanted you for sex."

That hardly makes me feel better. I *wish* Crispin—no, privilege revoked—*Cris* only wanted me for sex. That I can do. It's all this other crap that messes everything up.

"He's worried about you."

Of course he is. When I'm the one who should be asking after him, after his dad. It's on the tip of my tongue because, surely, Rey knows. But no matter how badly I want to hear that Mal's fine and Cris's life has gone back to its regularly scheduled programming of surfing, cooking, and occasionally earning a living, I can't bring myself to ask. A clean break is what's called for here. So I break it.

"Tell him I'm fan-fucking-tastic. Tell him whatever it takes. I don't want to talk to him."

There's a pause on the other end. "Do you not?"

"Shut up, Rey. Shut the hell up. You're not making this any easier."

No, not easier at all. Just taking the heart that's been ripped out of my body and shoving it down my throat. Isn't Rey supposed to be on my side?

"Maybe it's not supposed to be easy."

"Do you want me to stop talking to you, too?" Tears are pricking at my eyes, choking me. Goddammit. He knows I would never, could never, but I hope he'll take the hint to drop it.

"No, of course not. I liked you together, that's all."

"Yeah. Me too."

My spring is left with nothing to crush because my internal

organs have been hollowed out. I feel like I'm going to die. I haven't felt this empty since I left Hunter and my parents disowned me.

This is why I didn't want to get close to anyone. Because this is how it ends: me in a crumpled, jacked-up heap of pieces Rey has to fit back together like Humpty Fucking Dumpty. I should face facts and go back to the way things were. I'm allowed to have professional success and satisfaction, a stimulating and crazy-hot sex life, and the best friend a girl could ask for. I'm just not built for love. We really can't have it all.

My ruminations are interrupted by Rey. "Hey, what are you doing Wednesday night?"

"Getting absolutely wrecked and going clubbing with you?"

"Sounds good. I'll see you at eight."

With a thunk of the lock, Rey lets himself into my apartment and sets his overnight bag down inside the door. I'm huddled on the couch, not doing anything. I've been trying to read my book, but every few pages, I come across a line that would make Cris laugh his delicious, butterfly-inducing laugh and I have to stop. I think about reading my news magazines, but if I saw one of his comics, I might die. Maybe I'll have Rey go through them for me. Let him leave kindergarten-cut, empty squares in the pages—Cris redacted.

Rey dumps himself next to me, the weight of him a familiar comfort on my couch. I lay my head in his lap and close my eyes while his fingers knead the nape of my neck.

"Still want to go?"

"Yes."

"Want to have a good cry first?"

"Yes."

I burst into tears, and Rey scoots me up until I'm sitting on his knees. He lets me exhaust my tears on his chest and doesn't offer platitudes about how it's all going to be okay. It will be, eventually, but I'm in no mood to hear it. What I am in the mood for is Rey ruffling my hair and rousing me from my heart-broken stupor.

"Picnic's waiting. Get in the shower. I'll pick you out something pretty to wear."

He tips me off his lap and smacks me affectionately on the butt as I head down the hall. Fresh out of the shower, I find clothes laid out on my bed: black leather pants, barely-there crimson halter top, and spiked heels. Excellent.

When we pull up at Picnic, a cut bouncer helps me out of my car, and Rey palms my keys to a valet. There's a line snaking halfway around the block, but we get in, no problem, with a nod from a Secret Service-looking guy with a clipboard.

"Thanks, Tony," says Rey.

We get a wink and a nod in response, and I welcome the burst of warm air that hits us as Tony holds open the door. The club is crowded for a weeknight, and clothes have already started to come off. I admire the fit bodies of men moving effortlessly to the beat, and the balls of the less-cut who are working it like they've got something to prove. There aren't many women here and even fewer men who might find me fuckable, but I like it that way. Rey's admirers drift over after we've gotten our first round, but instead of turning on the charm to get laid, he focuses their attention on me.

Soon I'm being coddled by half a dozen gay men sympathetic about my break-up. I get a lot of "oh, honeys," several brightly colored fruity cocktails, and eventually invitations to dance my cares away. On the dance floor, the pounding beats, the sweaty masculine bodies—moving skillfully, enthusiastically, but with no prurient interest against mine—and the half dozen drinks I've imbibed let me forget for a while. I'm asleep on my feet by the time Rey wrangles my drunk ass into my Mercedes. Presumably he takes me home because I wake the next morning with less of a hangover than I've earned and a note next to my bed:

ILYK. Call me.

I haul my ass to the gym, where Adam busts my chops for having been gone for so long.

"You've gone soft like a cheesecake, princess," he berates me as I do my zillionth crunch. It's true I'm a little out of shape, but no one else would notice. I'm glad Adam does and uses it as an excuse to work me like a draft horse. Another way for me to silence the longing and muffle the ache.

But as soon as Adam's no longer barking in my ear, it comes back, and every song on the radio on my sticky, sweat-drenched drive to work reminds me of what I've lost.

A few more days pass. Cris stops trying to contact me. I'm half-grateful and half-gutted. I think about calling, emailing, texting, even writing him a letter—which I think he'd like. A lot. And the waiting would be good penance for me.

I draw little stick figure Indias with speech bubbles: *I'm sorry. I miss you. I*—before I crumple them up and throw them away. I think about getting on a plane, but I don't. Instead I repeat to myself, "It's easier this way." But it doesn't feel easier. It feels like a slow, painful suicide.

I talk to Rey a lot. I think about asking him to get me someone new, but I can't afford the time away from work. Besides, Cris has me so tied up in knots, I'd feel like I was cheating on him. I've never cheated on anyone in my life, and it wouldn't count as that now. There's no contract, and no contract means no cheating. But I feel queasy when I think about being with anyone else, so work it is.

And work I do. I landed the contract with Phoenix, and it's my baby, the only kind of baby I'll ever have. Jack is going to have minimal supervision and input. I'm going to run the show. Greg Wu is going to be my new best friend for the next three years. I like him, I understand him, and though he's tough as nails and ridiculously demanding, I think he'll be happy with me. They usually are.

I set myself to developing our work plan, scheduling and assigning tasks and due dates, making notes about information I'm going to need. It's soothing to be the puppet master, to be doing something I understand, that makes sense to me, that I'm good at. I schedule a metric crapton of travel for myself. I don't care for Phoenix, but the desert won't remind me of Cris so damn much.

I'm two-thirds of the way through compiling our list of deliverables when Lucy's voice comes over the speaker.

"Ms. Burke?"

"Lucy, how many ways do I have to say I'm not to be interrupted?"

"I'm sorry. It's just that you have a phone call."

"I told you to hold all of my fucking calls. Do I need to write you a memo?"

"No, Ms. Burke. It just… It sounded important."

I close my eyes and take a deep breath. If I ripped Lucy a new one every time she deserved it, she'd be Swiss cheese.

"Who is it?"

"A Mrs. Mary Ardmore? She sounds upset."

Shit. Why the fuck is Cris's mother calling me? No scenario I come up with is good. I've never even met the woman. How does she know who I am and where to find me? Hasn't he violated my privacy and broken the rules enough? When is he going to get it through his thick skull? I don't want to talk to him. We're over, and even—no, *especially*—a phone call from his mother—*his mother!*—is not going to change that. *For fuck's sake, Cris, give it up.* This is excruciating as it is.

But I can't have her making a scene with Lucy. "Put her through."

"Yes, Ms. Burke."

I steel myself before I pick up the phone and do a fair impersonation of collected when I bring the handset to my ear. "Mrs. Ardmore, this is India Burke. What can I do for you?"

"Ms. Burke, I'm sorry to bother you—"

"It's no bother. What can I do for you?" Despite my words to the contrary, my icy and clipped tone clearly conveys this *is* a bother and she'd best get to the point. The sooner I can get Cris out of my head and move on with my life, the better.

"I'm sorry, it's only…"

Shit. Maybe I shouldn't be so mean. She does sound upset.

"Do you know my son?"

Her voice cracks, and a chill of alarm runs down my spine. "Yes… Did something happen to him? Is Cris okay?"

"No," she chokes, tears in her voice. "He's been in an accident."

Thank you for reading *Alpha in the Sheets*. I hope you enjoyed it. If you can't wait to read the second half of Cris and India's story, *Bound in the Streets* is available now! Or turn the page for an excerpt.

BOUND IN THE STREETS

I let Cris into my life and look what happened: I got attached. Now I have feelings, and feelings are the worst.

The truth is that I more than like him. I other-L-word him, which doesn't solve anything; it makes everything worse. I've loved people in the past and it got me heartbroken, betrayed, and abandoned so no thank you.

My job that I'm usually so competent at is killing me, Cris wants more, and I can't handle it all. I can give Cris grand gestures and dirty weekends, but despite everything he's given me I still can't hand over my heart. Which sucks, because I don't think he's willing to accept any substitutes. Now what the hell am I supposed to do?

I've been acting as the lady of the house for far too long, and I'm happy to be back to the role I'm supposed to play: sometime-companion, sometime-submissive. I play the companion over lunch, but I keep catching Crispin's gaze and we're both squirming in our seats. Not that there was no fooling around while I was here last, but it feels like it's been forever.

I show off my cleavage while we take our places, brushing against him whenever I get the chance. Though it's modest contact compared to our usual activities, we're so deprived this pathetic excuse for foreplay has us both on fire. While I wash up, Crispin makes his way to the sitting area and I'm disappointed. Surely if he meant to play, he'd instruct me to meet him in the studio?

When I'm finished, I kneel before him, eyes cast down, hands clasped behind my back. I wait for his acknowledgement, but nothing comes. I wonder if he's fallen asleep. It wouldn't be surprising. Despite what he'd have me believe, his recovery has been exhausting.

I wait a while longer with no movement from him before I flick my eyes up to check. I'm not met with a sleeping Crispin, easy and slack in rest. Instead, his flinty blue eyes admonish me.

"Bad girl. Are you so out of practice?"

"No, sir. I'm sorry, sir."

I've blinked my gaze back to the floor, and my heart beats faster. Perhaps we are going to play.

"It's my fault. I haven't been able to discipline you like you need. But I'm feeling better and you'd do well to be on your best behavior from here on out. Are we understood?"

"Yes, sir."

Hoping he won't notice, I squeeze my clasped hands, an escape valve for the arousal that's flooded me.

Crispin traces my collarbone, eliciting a shiver. I'm starving for his touch, aching for more than a fingertip. But he'll take his time, torture me. He grazes the notch on my sternum and continues down to the gap in my shirt. I'd worn it hoping to provoke a response, but I'm wondering if that was wise. The front is held together by only a dozen hook-and-eye closures. He crooks a finger around the first one and tugs.

"You've been teasing me since you got here, pet. These clothes..."

My skirt's not uncharacteristically short. When I'm standing. Sitting back on my heels, it's slid most of the way up my thighs and barely leaves me decent. As for the shirt, I'd debated how many hooks to leave undone, going back and forth on the top one at least four times in the mirror. He unfastens it, revealing another inch of my décolletage.

"And this mouth…" He rubs his thumb across my bottom lip, his palm cupping my chin. My body heats up, warmed and supple for him to exert his will on. "I've been thinking about your mouth all week."

The concentration with which he's regarding me is unbearably hot. Imagining that concentration on other areas makes desire spread like wildfire through my whole body. I want him with every last particle of me.

My tongue darts out to lick his thumb, and he grips my chin. I'm expecting him to scold me—that's a rookie offense—but I'm desperate for him and he is for me. He lets my illicit stroke pass without punishment. This time. But when I do it again, made bold by his neglect, he seizes the opportunity.

"So desperate for me in your mouth, are you, kitten?"

"Yes, sir." It comes out as a whimper. From these amateur touches, I'm soaked for him.

"Then open up."

His thumb pushes between my lips, and I lave him with my tongue, savoring the taste. I've missed him, missed this, and I pretend it's something else I'm fellating, knowing he's imagining the same thing.

He withdraws his thumb, and I whine in protest.

"Stand up, skirt off, and lie down on the coffee table on your back."

I strip off my skirt, not bothering to be sexy about it; it's a utility strip. While I do, he edges the table closer to where he's sitting. I hesitate because he's not told me which way to lie.

"Head at the far end."

I love that he can read my cues of confusion—and other things—and meets my needs. Or not, sadistic sonofabitch. He makes his calls using the information he's gathered, and if I'm uncomfortable, it's because I'm meant to be, not because he doesn't know any better. The thought sends desire coursing through my nerves. *The attentiveness. Dear god, the attentiveness.*

I lie down as he's instructed, knees bent to keep my feet on the smooth wood surface and eyes gazing up to the herringbone pattern of the wooden ceiling. What is he planning?

"Spread your legs, pet."

Bound in the Streets is available now!

THANK YOU!

- If you'd like to know when my next book is available, you can sign up for my new release mailing list at tamsenparker.com or follow me on social media (see the full list on my About the Author page).
- Reviews help readers discover books. I appreciate all reviews and the time it takes to share your thoughts.
- You've just read *Alpha in the Sheets*, the first book in the After Hours Series. *Bound in the Streets* is out now, along with the rest of the series. Turn the page for a full listing of my books. Thanks so much for reading, and I hope you'll keep in touch!

OTHER BOOKS BY TAMSEN

The After Hours Series

Alpha in the Sheets

Bound in the Streets

Reclaiming His Wife

For His Eyes Only

A Heart to Keep

Insidious

The Snow and Ice Games Series

Love on the Tracks

Seduction on the Slopes

On the Edge of Scandal

Fire on the Ice

On the Brink of Passion

The License to Love Series

Thrown Off Track

The Inside Track

Hot on Her Tracks (Release Date TBD)

Camp Firefly Falls

In Her Court

Love, All

Standalone Novels

School Ties

His Custody

If I Loved You Less

Short Stories and Novellas

Needs

(Originally published in the Winter Rain anthology)

Looking for a Complication

(Originally published in the For the First Time anthology)

Dedication of a Lifetime

(Originally published in the Rogue Affair anthology)

Craving Flight

Anthologies

Rogue Desire

Rogue Affair

Rogue Hearts

Best Women's Erotica of the Year Volume Four

Rogue Ever After (May 2019)

ACKNOWLEDGMENTS

The list of people I have to thank is long. I'm grateful to have so many wonderful people in my life.

My CPs and betas who have read and reread, offered advice and unflagging encouragement, and been generally awesome. I would not have survived this without AJ, Cara, Megan, Teresa, Lexi H., and Audra.

My other writer friends who have kept me sane through this whole crazy process, my small corner of the Twitterverse, my NECRWA chaptermates, and Romancelandia as a whole. I feel privileged to be a part of a community of such smart, generous, and amazing people.

My family, who have eaten far more takeout than is probably advisable and done without me on evenings and Saturdays so that I could make this happen. Especially my husband, who has been tireless in his support. If there were an award for Spouses of Romance Writers, he'd be a shoo-in.

My real-life friends, who cheered me on from the sidelines, even when they had absolutely no idea what I was talking about: RMW, MTS, AJ, LG, CB, NW, AL.

My editor, Del, who sometimes drove me crazy but in the way that editors get paid for, and my copy editor, Rebecca, who isn't afraid of the occasional semicolon. Not to mention my enthusiastic proofreader, Michele.

ABOUT THE AUTHOR

Tamsen Parker is a USA Today bestselling romance writer, with books in the erotic romance, hot contemporary, sports, and now sweet subgenres, and writes about f/f, m/f, and m/m couples falling for each other. *The Lesbian Review* named both IF I LOVED YOU LESS and FIRE ON THE ICE to their Top 15 Books of 2018, and IN HER COURT as one of the Top 10 Audiobooks of 2018. Her novella CRAVING FLIGHT was named to the Best of 2015 lists of *Heroes and Heartbreakers, Smexy Books, Romance Novel News,* and *Dear Author. Heroes and Heartbreakers* called her After Hours series "bewitching, humorous, erotically intense and emotional."

Repped by the fabulous Courtney Miller-Callihan.

facebook.com/tamsenparker

twitter.com/tamsenparker

instagram.com/authortamsenparker

bookbub.com/authors/tamsen-parker

pinterest.com/tamsenparker

Alpha in the Sheets: © 2014 by Tamsen Parker

Editing by Delphine Dryden (http://www.delphinedryden.com/)

Copy Editing by Rebecca Weston (https://www.rebeccawestonliterary.com/)

Cover Design by Lori Jackson (https://www.lorijacksondesign.com/)

❀ Created with Vellum